PENGUIN CLASSICS

THREE MEN IN A BOAT

JEROME K. JEROME was born in Walsall, Staffordshire, in 1859, and educated at Marylebone Grammar School. He left school aged fourteen to become a railway clerk, the first of a long line of jobs which included acting, teaching and journalism. He spent some time touring with various theatrical companies and lodged for a while in Tavistock Place in London with his friend George Wingrave, who later became the model for George in *Three Men in A Boat*. His first book, *On Stage and Off*, a collection of humorous pieces about the theatre, was published in 1885, and was followed in 1886 with a collection of sketches entitled *The Idle Thoughts of an Idle Fellow*. After the commercial success of this volume Jerome took up writing and journalism as a profession. He married in 1888 and settled in the following year in Chelsea Gardens in London, where he wrote his most famous work, *Three Men in a Boat*. Its sequel, *Three Men on the Bummel*, appeared in 1900 and describes a hilarious cycling tour through Germany's Black Forest.

In 1892 Jerome had, with some friends, founded *The Idler*, an illustrated monthly magazine which published humorous work by the likes of Robert Louis Stevenson and Mark Twain. When the magazine folded, Jerome turned to the theatre again and became well-known as a playwright: *The Passing of the Third Floor Back* (1908), a sentimental moral fable set in Bloomsbury, enjoyed a long and successful run in London's theatres. During the First World War he served as an ambulance driver in France. His eventful life is recorded in his autobiography *My Life and Times*, published in 1926. He died in 1927.

JEREMY LEWIS worked in publishing for much of his life after leaving Trinity College, Dublin, in 1965, and was a director of Chatto & Windus for ten years. He was Deputy Editor of the *London Magazine* from 1991 to 1994, and is now the Commissioning Editor of the *Oldie*. He has written two volumes of autobiography, *Playing for Time* and *Kindred Spirits*, and edited *The Vintage Book of Office Life*. His authorized biography of Cyril Connolly was published by

Jonathan Cape in 1997 and his biography of Tobias Smollett was published in 2003. He is currently working on a biography of Allen Lane for Penguin. The Secretary of the R. S. Surtees Society and a Fellow of the Royal Society of Literature, he is married with two daughters, and lives near Richmond Park.

JEROME K. JEROME

Three Men in a Boat

To say nothing of the Dog!

With an Introduction and Notes by
JEREMY LEWIS

PENGUIN BOOKS

PENGUIN BOOKS

Published by the Penguin Group
Penguin Books Ltd, 80 Strand, London WC2R ORL, England
Penguin Putnam Inc., 375 Hudson Street, New York, New York 10014, USA
Penguin Books Australia Ltd, 250 Camberwell Road, Camberwell, Victoria 3124, Australia
Penguin Books Canada Ltd, 10 Alcorn Avenue, Toronto, Ontario, Canada M4V 3B2
Penguin Books India (P) Ltd, 11 Community Centre, Panchsheel Park, New Delhi – 110 017, India
Penguin Books (NZ) Ltd, Cnr Rosedale and Airborne Roads, Albany, Auckland, New Zealand
Penguin Books (South Africa) (Pty) Ltd, 24 Sturdee Avenue, Rosebank 2196, South Africa

Penguin Books Ltd, Registered Offices: 80 Strand, London WC2R ORL, England

www.penguin.com

Three Men in a Boat first published 1889
Published in Penguin Books 1957
Reprinted in Penguin Classics 2004
1

Introduction and notes copyright © Jeremy Lewis, 1999, 2004
All rights reserved

The moral right of the editor has been asserted

Set in 10/12.5pt PostScript Monotype Bell
Typeset by Rowland Phototypesetting Ltd, Bury St Edmunds, Suffolk
Printed in England by Clays Ltd, St Ives plc

Contents

Introduction

'I did not intend to write a funny book, at first,'[1] Jerome K. Jerome wrote of the novel by which he is best remembered – further evidence, if such were needed, that books once embarked upon acquire a life of their own, and that famous books, like famous rivers, may well have obscure or modest origins. Just turned thirty in 1889, and beginning to make his mark as an essayist and playwright, Jerome had recently returned from his honeymoon, and was living in a top-floor flat on Chelsea Embankment, the circular drawing-room of which afforded views up and down the Thames and across to Battersea Park, and the Surrey Hills beyond. Boating on the Thames had become a popular pastime in recent years, and publishers did brisk business with guidebooks-cum-histories of the river, in which topographical details were interwoven with easily digested snippets of English history; inspired by the outlook, perhaps, Jerome planned to write just such a book, the facts and figures of which would be lightened by occasional flurries of 'humorous relief'. He decided to write these first, drawing on his own experiences of boating on the river with his friends George Wingrave and Carl Hentschel, but before long the anecdotes had elbowed aside the sober slabs of history and topography, and were threatening to take over altogether. The editor of *Home Chimes*, where Jerome's work was being serialized, had no time for the factual passages, and hurled most of them overboard; and when, the following year, *Three Men in a Boat* was published in book form, little remained of the author's original intentions. Though cold-shouldered by the critics, the book was an instant success, making Jerome a household name and casting a long shadow over his attempts, in later life, to establish himself as a serious, even portentous, writer; and the misadventures of George, Harris, J. the narrator and the dog Montmorency remain one of the best-loved books in the language, endlessly reprinted, and filmed three times.

Some ten years later, Jerome resurrected George, Harris and J. and sent them on a bicycling tour of Germany, the results of which were published as *Three Men on the Bummel* – a 'bummel' being defined, in the last paragraph of the book, as a 'journey, long or short, without an end; the only thing regulating it being the necessity of getting back within a given time to the point from which one started'.[2] As an account of Jerome's rambling, conversational technique, this could hardly be bettered; and, quite apart from their entertainment value, both novels are wonderfully redolent of the late-Victorian and Edwardian England of Mr Pooter, the ground-down hero of the Grossmiths' *The Diary of a Nobody*,[3] and W. S. Gilbert's 'The Bab Ballads'[4] and the early novels of H. G. Wells and P. G. Wodehouse's *Psmith in the City*,[5] of jocular clerks on the spree in plus-fours and fluorescent blazers, and men with heavy handlebar moustaches and mild suburban voices thoughtfully refilling their pipes before embarking on another yarn from the depths of a leather armchair.

'I did not know I was a humorist,' Jerome went on to admit – nor, indeed, had the first twenty-odd years of his life provided many occasions for mirth. His father, Jerome Clapp Jerome, was born in 1807, educated at Merchant's Taylors School, and trained as an architect. Of 'Puritan stock', he soon displayed a passion for preaching, honing his technique at the Rothwell Nonconformist Academy in Northamptonshire; though never ordained, he spent a good deal of time preaching in Congregationalist chapels, several of which he also designed. In 1838 he married the daughter of a Swansea solicitor. She had been left some money, so they moved to Appledore in Devon, where Mr Clapp – as he was known to his congregation – bought a farm and preached in the local chapel, publishing a hymn book for its special use. Misled into believing that silver could be mined on his land, he spent part of his wife's inheritance on vain attempts to bring it to the surface.

In 1855 the Jeromes moved to Walsall, in the West Midlands, where fortunes were being made from coal. Mr Jerome became a partner in an iron works instead, as well as building and designing the town's Congregational chapel. When he eventually decided to try his luck with coal, and sank two pits on Cannock Chase, his efforts were thwarted by sand and underground streams; only after he had sold out did the 'Jerome Pits' come good, but by then his wife's money had disappeared. Reduced to penury, they moved to Poplar, in the East End of London, where Mr Jerome tried, without success, to set up shop as an ironmonger. Despite the shortage of funds, Mrs Jerome worked hard to keep up appearances, employing a maid, just as the Pooters did, insisting that her two daughters wore gloves in public, and Mr Jerome his silk hat, and keeping her own lace and silk dresses for best. Young Jerome remembered that their house was the biggest in the street, replete with 'china and fine pictures and a semi-grand piano by Collard & Collard, and damask curtains in the windows'. It was, no doubt, a very English kind of 'shabby gentility'.

The fourth child of the marriage, Jerome K. Jerome was born in Walsall in 1859: the 'K' stood for Klapka, the surname of an improbable-sounding 28-year-old Hungarian general who had lodged with the family while writing his memoirs. Jerome's siblings were christened Milton Melanchton, Paulina and Blandina, and to distinguish him from his father he was referred to as 'Luther'. This seemed apposite enough since, like many young Victorians, he was brought up on Foxe's *Book of Martyrs*,[6] in which the roastings and disembowellings endured by heroic Protestant clergymen at the hands of Queen Mary and her diabolical Catholic henchmen were itemized in gruesome detail. Terrified by visions of Hell and Damnation, he came to regard organized religion with grave suspicion, and God Himself with a certain wariness.

Equally alarming was the East End itself. Populated, in part, by impoverished Russian and Polish Jews who had fled from tsarist pogroms, the haunt of Jack the Ripper and – according to Sherlock Holmes – dastardly Lascars and unreliable Chinese, the interminable terraces that stretched east for mile after mile from the City of London occupied, until the 1950s at least, a place in popular mythology similar to that now claimed by the most terrifying and run-down stretches of New York. 'There is a menace, a haunting terror, that is to be found nowhere else,' Jerome recalled. 'The awful silence of its weary streets. The ashen faces, with their lifeless eyes that rise out of the shadows and are lost. It was these surroundings in which I passed my childhood that gave me, I suppose, my melancholy, brooding disposition.' Although Jerome liked to think that he mixed with 'a bad set, which included the Wesleyan minister's two sons, also the only child of the church organist', he was persecuted by the local urchins, who let out a great cry when they saw him coming. 'It was not so much the blows as the jeers and taunts I fled from, spurted by mad terror,' he remembered in *My Life and Times*: 'My mother explained to me that it was because I was a gentleman.' Looking back on his childhood in his autobiographical novel, *Paul Kelver*, Jerome recalled 'hurrying through noisy, crowded thorough-fares, where flaring naptha lamps illumine fierce, patient, leaden-coloured faces; through dim-lit empty streets, where monstrous shadows come and go upon the close-drawn blinds; through narrow, noisesome streets, where the gutters swarm with children, and each ever-open doorway vomits riot . . .' It was a world far more akin to such grim masterpieces of late-Victorian and Edwardian social realism as Arthur Morrison's *A Child of the Jago*[7] and Robert Tressell's *The Ragged Trousered Philanthropists*[8] than to the benign escapism of *Three Men in a Boat*: it may help to explain why, though never committed to any political movement or party, Jerome instinctively sided with the underdog, and always remained uneasily aware of how thin a line separates civilized behaviour from brutality and degradation. The dead dog and the dead woman whom the three happy oarsmen encounter floating down the river shock us with their apparent incongruity, and remind us that Jerome's view of the universe was nothing like as carefree or as cheerful as his novels might have us think.

A beneficiary of W. E. Forster's 1870 Education Act, as a result of which some form of primary education was made available to all children for the first time, Jerome attended the Philological School in Lisson Grove, later upgraded to Marylebone Grammar School. During school holidays he visited the surrounding countryside, and years later he remembered the corn fields round Swiss Cottage, a stag hunt in Highgate, and cattle grazing in Walthamstow. For all the horrors of the East End, 'London was a cosier place to dwell in, when I was a young man. For one thing, it was less crowded. Life was not one everlasting scrimmage.'

Jerome was twelve when his father died, revealing on his death-bed that his thick, black pelt of hair was a wig. The family moved to Finchley, and two years later Jerome left school and became the sole bread-winner. Like many others at the time, he got a job as a clerk: the last quarter of the nineteenth century saw a phenomenal rise in the number of clerks employed in offices, most of them poor, undereducated and overworked, and he took a clerical job with the London and North-Western Railway at Euston, earning ten shillings a week. The following year his mother died, and – with his brother dead, one sister married, and the other a governess in the north of England – Jerome was alone in the world. He moved into a series of digs, in one of which a fellow lodger had hanged himself.

Even at this early age, Jerome longed to be a writer, and in *Paul Kelver* he describes how, as a boy, he once met Dickens – or someone he assumed to be Dickens – wandering about in Hackney. 'No man ever made money or fame but by writing his very best,' the Dickens figure tells him. 'If you write books thinking only of money you will be disappointed. It is easier earned in other ways.' Young Kelver forgets to ask Dickens his name. 'That makes me think of your future with hope,' the novelist tells him, no doubt recognizing a kindred spirit. 'You are an egotist, Paul; and that is the beginning of all art.' Since Dickens died in 1870, Jerome must have been very young when and if this meeting occurred: he referred to it again in his autobiography, where the great man lets fly with 'Oh, damn Mr Pickwick!'

When not consorting with important novelists, Jerome set out to master the worldly vices, among them smoking, drinking and girls: 'baccy' was to prove a lifetime's enthusiasm, but where women were concerned, 'To be on a footing of familiarity with a barmaid was the height of most young clerks' ambition.' To add variety to his life, and give himself something to write about, he involved himself with the theatre in his spare time – not something that would have pleased his Low Church parents, who regarded the theatre and its dependents with grave suspicion. He joined a repertory company, producing playbills, doing the advertising, stage-managing, and, in due course, appearing on stage himself. Eventually he gave up his job on the railways to spend nearly three years travelling round England with a touring company, leading the kind of life enjoyed by the Crummles family in Dickens's *Nicholas Nickleby* nearly half a century earlier. It was, he wrote, a 'jungle sort of existence': crooked managers made off with their wages, they slept in dressing-rooms or church porches, and he 'played every part in *Hamlet* save Ophelia'.

Back in London, Jerome lived rough for a while, moving on from one doss-house to another and enduring the same kind of poverty-stricken existence as his near-contemporary George Gissing. Still anxious to learn his trade as a writer, he bumped into an old friend who 'had fallen on evil days, and had taken to journalism'. The friend suggested that he tried his luck as a Dickensian jobbing journalist, 'penny-a-lining' from all over London and covering fêtes, fires, court cases, coroners' inquests, public meetings and even hangings ('There was a coffee shop at the Old Bailey where, for half-a-crown, they let you climb on the roof'). When penny-a-lining lost its allure, he worked for a term as a schoolmaster, teaching swimming, gymnastics and deportment, before moving on to be the secretary to a builder, and then a commission agent. He lodged for a time near the British Museum, the haunt of penniless, Gissing-like[9] Grub Street hacks, and then shared a room off the Tottenham Court Road with a bank clerk called George Wingrave. Wingrave turned out to have a shrewd business sense, and in due course helped his friend in his dealings with editors and publishers; whether – like his namesake in *Three Men in a Boat* – he found it hard to get out of bed in the morning is not recorded.

Another new friend from this period was Carl Hentschel, the 'Harris' of the novels. Polish by origin, Hentschel's father had introduced photolithography to Britain. It was a process that helped to revolutionize the Press, making it far easier and quicker to reproduce illustrations in newspapers and magazines, since the slow and laborious business of hand-engraving the blocks from which they were printed could now be done by mechanical means. Its introduction enabled newspaper editors and their proprietors to include not just line drawings and photographs, but display advertisements of the kind that horrified the more fastidious type of reader, and it coincided with vast changes in the nature and accessibility of the printed word. Whereas books, newspapers and magazines had hitherto been, to a large extent, the preserve of the educated minority, they now braced themselves for the advent of that twentieth-century phenomenon, the mass market. Although the great majority of the population still left school at fourteen, Forster's Education Act had created an immense new market of potential readers. 'Never before had there been such reading masses,' wrote H. G. Wells, while according to Bernard Shaw, 'The Education Act was producing readers who had never before bought books, nor could have read them if they had.' Many of these new readers were employed, like George or Mr Pooter, as clerks in banks, insurance offices, estate agents and the like; many of them lived in the new suburbs which – to the horror of the intelligentsia – were spreading out around London and the other great cities, addressed one another as 'Old Man', and employed a slang of their own, half-jocular and half-defiant. Uneasily aware of their lack of education, they were often eager to remedy matters through evening classes and the reading of classics in Everyman editions, and tended – if young, and of a radical persuasion – to bicycling, socialism and the wearing of knickerbockers. As Jerome would soon discover, they were looked down upon by writers and social commentators who had enjoyed the benefits of a university education, and regarded the upstart clerks and their spokesmen as bumptious philistines.

As John Carey observed in *The Intellectuals and the Masses*, 'the clerks were hardly equipped to appreciate "high" culture, which is why an alternative culture was created for them.' Alfred Harms-worth,[10] the founder of the *Daily Mail*, took full advantage of the new technologies to cater to a mass readership, while his dependence on advertising enabled him to price his papers at levels even the hard-up could afford, and at the same time undercut sober, old-fashioned rivals. New magazines and periodicals proliferated, many of them – like *Tit-Bits*, *Answers* and *Comic Cuts* – responding to the concerns of the newly literate classes with hints on etiquette, bicycling columns and snippets of self-improvement. Nor was literary fare neglected. Although *Tit-Bits* – which George Newnes[11] founded in 1881 – rejected work by Conrad and Virginia Woolf, it made a point of reprinting excerpts from classic authors; John Carey subversively suggests that 'As a means of awakening interest in books, arousing curiosity and introducing its readers to new ideas, *Tit-Bits* must compare very favourably with more acclaimed organs such as T. S. Eliot's *Criterion* and F. R. Leavis's *Scrutiny*, and its effects were infinitely more widespread.' Some of Conan Doyle's Sherlock Holmes stories first appeared in *Tit-Bits*, as well as in the *Strand Magazine*, and although the serialization of novels was a well-established Victorian tradition, the novel itself was not immune to the challenges presented by new markets and new readers. The bulky and expensive three-decker novel, beloved of the great Victorians and of Mudie's Lending Library,[12] gave way, in part, to shorter, more accessible works; the middlebrow bestseller became a staple of the publishing business, selling in huge quantities to homebound commuters from W. H. Smith's[13] railway bookstalls. Jerome was typical of this new mass readership, and in due course *Three Men in a Boat*, itself a bestseller, would be denounced by the literary establishment for its 'vulgarity' and for the 'colloquial clerks' English' in which it was written. But, as Carey points out, 'Jerome was consciously wooing a new readership: the perky clerks and shop assistants, the Mr Pollys[14] and Lupin Pooters,[15] whose stripy blazers and half-starved features still gaze triumphantly from a thousand photographs,' and although 'the genteel highbrows of the next generation – Forster, Virginia Woolf, Eliot – were to sneer at this whole breed, clerks were Jerome's class, and he liked them – especially the jaunty, stoical way they took life's knocks'. When, early in the next century, the right-wing poet T. W. H. Crosland savaged the clerking classes and all they stood for in his polemic *The Suburbans*, he noted that Wells, Shaw and Jerome, all of whom had worked as clerks, were the favourite authors of those he most despised.

But before any of this could take place, Jerome had to find his way into print. It proved a long, dispiriting business, with evenings given over to writing after a tiring day in a solicitor's office, and the amassing of a hefty wodge of rejection letters. In the end *The Lamp* accepted a story, and the author of another magazine handed a dazed Jerome five pounds in exchange for something he had written. Persistence had paid off at last, and before long Jerome was writing 'Idle Thoughts' for F. W. Robinson's *Home Chimes*, fellow-contributors to which included Mark Twain, Algernon Charles Swinburne and J. M. Barrie,[16] who was soon to become a close friend. (An affectation of idleness was to become one of Jerome's *leitmotifs*: as V. S. Pritchett remarked, hard-working and browbeaten clerks – all of whom, like George, worked on Saturdays until lunchtime, as well as long hours during the week – liked to pose as men of leisure and to 'regard idleness as a joke',[17] and J. tells us that he and his fellow-oarsmen all affect a 'general disinclination to work of any kind'.)

Published in 1885, Jerome's first book, *On the Stage – and Off*, drew on his theatrical experiences. It was followed a year later by *The Idle Thoughts of an Idle Fellow*, in which he established a recognizable and distinctive tone of voice: colloquial, discursive, both fanciful and commonsensical. Dedicated, at some length, to his pipe, it consisted of ruminative, mildly humorous essays on unalarming, everyday subjects – 'On Being Shy', 'On Being Hard-Up', 'Getting on in the World', 'Cats and Dogs' – served up with rueful, rather resigned nuggets of worldly wisdom such as might have been accompanied, if spoken, by some sagacious knocking out or tamping of the pipe. It was a genre of *belles-lettres* that lay in a direct line of descent from the essays of Addison and Charles Lamb, flourished in Edwardian England, reached its nadir in *The Times* fourth leaders, and was mercilessly ridiculed by Cyril Connolly in *Enemies of Promise*. *Idle Thoughts* was dismissed by the critics, who derided Jerome as 'Arry K. 'Arry, and an example of the 'new humorist' at his worst. 'The *Standard* spoke of me as a menace to English letters; the *Morning Post* as an example of the sad results to be expected of the over-education of the lower orders' – but it sold over 20,000 copies in Britain, and did well in America too.

Life was not all work, however, and in 1888 the 'Idle Fellow' married Georgina Stanley in St Luke's Church, Chelsea. The child of an Irish mother and a Spanish father, she had a daughter from a previous marriage. Despite his unromantic suggestion that 'Love is like the measles: we all have to go through it, and like the measles, we only take it once,' Jerome seems to have been a devoted husband. And although she remained a shadowy figure in his masculine, pipe-smoking, club-loving world, she did persuade him to give up his job in the solicitor's office to write full time. This included work for the theatre as well. Jerome was a keen theatre-goer, and in 1886 he interested the actor-manager Charles Hawtrey in his play, *Barbara*. Over the years Jerome was to enjoy some success as a playwright, above all with *The Passing of the Third Floor Back*, a portentous, quasi-religious fable featuring the Christ-like figure of the Stranger, which was immensely popular on both sides of the Atlantic. Adapted from one of his short stories, it had earlier lent its name to a collection of improving fables in which what started out as matter-of-fact, clubmanlike yarns took unexpected and usually unconvincing turns in the direction of fantasy and pious homily.

Jerome's best-known book could hardly have been more different. 'Boating up and down the Thames had been my favourite sport ever since I could afford it,' he tells us, adding that, in *Three Men in a Boat*, he 'just put down the things that happened' to the three friends while out on the river. Only Montmorency was pure invention. Carrying a hamper and 'clad in fancy "blazers"', Jerome, Hentschel and Wingrave used to meet after work on Saturday afternoons and take the train from Waterloo to Richmond, a mile or two downstream from Teddington Lock, where the Thames ceases to be tidal, and the London river gives way to a slower-moving stream intercepted by locks and weirs. 'At first,' Jerome remembered, 'we used to have the river to ourselves, but year by year it got more crowded, and Maidenhead became our starting-place.'

During the first half of the nineteenth century, the Thames was a foul and putrid river: raw sewage was dicharged into it from the towns along its banks, and according to an 'Oarsman's Guide' published in 1859, 'odours that speak aloud stalk over the face of the so-called "waters".' By then, though, things were beginning to change. Two years earlier, the Thames Conservancy Board was established, and the death in 1861 of Prince Albert from typhoid caused by the filthy drains at Windsor Castle spurred on efforts to clean up the river; and the fact that almost all the commercial traffic had been transferred from slow-moving barges to the railways left the river free for the enjoyment of fishermen, scullers and those who simply wanted to spend an afternoon or a weekend messing about in a boat. Fast and frequent trains enabled Londoners to escape to the river; most were probably daytrippers, but the fortunate few built themselves villas and bungalows in hitherto remote or secluded spots along its banks. The famous regattas, like those at Henley and Marlow, in which oarsmen from Oxford, Cambridge, London and elsewhere competed for heavy silver trophies, were already in existence, but from the 1870s the Thames acquired a new life and character as a source of pleasure and recreation. 'In its recreative character it is absolutely unique. I know of no other classic stream that is so splashed about for the mere fun of it,' Henry James observed in *English Hours*. On the slightest pretext, he went on, 'the mighty population takes to the boats. They bump each other in the narrow, charming channel, between Oxford and Richmond they make an uninterrupted procession ... If the river is the busiest suburb of London it is also by far the prettiest.' Rowing-boats, sailing boats, punts, steam-launches and even the occasional gondola jostled for place in the locks: at the height of the Season, and especially in Ascot Week, up to 800 boats per day passed through Boulter's Lock near Maidenhead, their occupants togged out in the height of fashion. By 1895 some 400 steam-launches were operating on the river; they were resented by oarsmen and fishermen for the noise they made, for the clouds of black smoke belching from their funnels and for the wash they set up, and their owners were widely regarded as pompous, self-important, overweight and overfond of the bottle.

Understandably enough, those who lived along the river did all they could to benefit from the boom. Firms like Salter Brothers in Oxford sold or hired out boats; riverside pubs and hotels did brisk business; office workers who couldn't afford a hotel or felt that a breath of fresh air would do them good, and chose instead to camp out, on land or in their boats, could buy or hire tents, hampers, bedding and the like. An Edwardian enthusiast described how shops like that visited by George, Harris J. and Montmorency (p. 114) were 'stocked with the first object of supplying boat-parties and campers with the necessaries of life'. Among these, tinned food played an important part, so much so that 'the shop-windows are almost completely furnished with supplies of tinned everything, festering in the sun'. Observant as ever, John Carey has noted how tinned food came to be symptomatic of the debasement of the masses 'because it offends against what the intellectual designates as nature: it is mechanical and soulless'. T. S. Eliot, E. M. Forster, Graham Greene and John Betjeman all wrote about tinned food with a furious disdain; Jerome, on the other hand, found it 'genial and amusing', and one of the most famous set pieces in the book revolves about an unopened and unopenable tin of pineapple chunks.

Unrepentant consumers of tinned foods, George, Harris and J. set out in search of mild adventure, very much in the spirit of Mr Pickwick and his young friends much earlier in the century. Like *The Pickwick Papers*, *Three Men in a Boat* is an innocent, inconsequential idyll, crammed with digressions and irrelevancies and authorial asides and all the other garrulous pleasantries of the picaresque novel, honed down for a more impatient generation of readers. V. S. Pritchett[17] – one of the very few critics to have written about *Three Men in a Boat* – sees Jerome as belonging, with the Grossmith brothers and his close friend W. W. Jacobs,[18] to a 'small, secure Arcadia where the comic disasters of life are the neater for being low', and his humour as 'a response of the emerging lower middle class to the inconvenience of their situation'. Well meant as this is –

Pritchett himself came from a not dissimilar background to Jerome, and writes as an admirer – it doesn't quite ring true. Jerome's Thames is, for the most part, a good deal more Arcadian than 'The Laurels', Brickfield Terrace, the Pooters' terraced house in Holloway, replete as it is with half-witted maids, irreverent errand boys, gossiping neighbours and all those other hazards that affect those who are anxious to impress but seldom succeed, and the Three Men seem far less embattled and altogether more sure of their place in the world than poor, pompous Mr Pooter, brow-beaten at work and fussily incompetent on the domestic front. Both books, Pritchett suggests, exploit 'that understatement which runs like a rheumatism through English humour', which may be true enough; but whereas *The Diary of a Nobody* is classic English social comedy, making much of class differences and the sad absurdities of social pretensions, *Three Men in a Boat* is brisker and far less agonized, and reads at times like so many 'Idle Thoughts' held together with dabs of narrative glue.

Though J. is, appropriately, a journalist, the Three Men are – like Mr Pooter's disrespectful son, Lupin – direct descendants of the perkier kind of Dickensian clerk. They live in digs with kindly but overbearing landladies; ground down at work, they prove boisterous and defiant when unleashed on the wider world. Their longing to be 'free from that fretful haste, that vehement striving, that is every day becoming more and more the bane of nineteenth-century life' has a familiar ring to it. 'At Cookham,' Pritchett sardonically observes, 'these suburbans will imagine themselves in the "wild heart of nature"', and, like many city-dwellers, they tend to romanticize and idealize country living and country folk, at least until the weather breaks. And, like most oppressed office workers, they console themselves with home-spun homilies about the vanity and transience of earthly fame and riches. 'Throw the lumber over, man!' the narrator urges his readers. 'Let your boat of life be light, packed only with what you need – a homely home and simple pleasures, one or two friends, worth the name, someone to love and someone to love you, a cat, a dog, and a pipe or two, enough to eat and enough to wear, and a little more than enough to drink . . .' They dislike the snobs who live in Maidenhead – many of them weekenders, travelling down from Paddington on the Great Western Railway – and snooty, exclusive 'riparian proprietors' who try to keep out the 'hoi-polloi' with white-painted posts and chains and 'No Trespassing' signs: the proprietors, for their part, no doubt detested these urban intruders who wandered on to their land and chopped up their trees for firewood, but their point of view remains unaired. 'Bally' counts as strong language, and when things go wrong, as they always do, those responsible are denounced as 'You cuckoo!' or 'You dunder-headed idiots!' George plays the banjo, badly ('They are all the rage this season,' he explains); much pleasure is had from joshing, facetious word-play of the kind that riled the thinking classes, so that when Harris treads on George's corns, George – mellowed by supper and a pipe and a noggin of whisky – merely murmurs 'Steady, old man, 'ware wheat!' A good deal is made of familiar problems like packing and oversleeping and unreliable weather-forecasters; as is to be expected of men on their own, they make heavy weather of sleeping arrangements, tread or sit down on astonishingly resilient pats of butter, and brew up repellent Irish stews into which every known ingredient is hurled.

As they nudge their way upstream from Kingston-on-Thames to Oxford, we're treated to a series of reminiscences and digressions, triggered off by happenings along the way, and suitably conversational in tone. J.'s pompous Uncle Podger is recalled trying to hang a picture, leaving a trail of devastation in his wake; the unavailability of hotel bedrooms in the Windsor and Datchet area is remembered in harrowing detail; in Wallingford they're subjected to a cascade of fishermen's tall stories, each more bogus than the last. Jerome makes much of the malice and vindictiveness of inanimate objects, with tow-lines, metal hoops and the tin of pineapple chunks doing their worst to frustrate his heroes. And he makes effective use of bathos, embarking on long and heartfelt passages of lush, Pre-Raphaelite prose, only to have them cut short by one of Harris's commonplace observations, or by the oarsmen ramming into a punt on which three elderly gentlemen are peacefully fishing the evening away. Harris's doomed attempts to sing extracts from

Gilbert and Sullivan before an audience of old ladies provides the book with its comic climacteric, but overall a sublime contentment reigns: 'We lit our pipes, and sat, looking out on the quiet night, and talked.'

Jerome's new publisher, Arrowsmith – whose other bestsellers included *The Diary of a Nobody* and Anthony Hope's *The Prisoner of Zenda* – was very taken with *Three Men in a Boat*: he told its author that it 'ought to do well in the holiday months', and suggested cutting up some of the longer passages in case they alarmed potential readers. The book's success on both sides of the Atlantic made Jerome's a name to conjure with, and when the proprietor of a new monthly magazine decided to pick a popular name as its editor, he chose Jerome in preference to Kipling. The first issue of *The Idler* appeared in February 1892, and included contributions from Mark Twain, Bret Harte and Oliver Wendell Holmes. Although he sometimes put in sixteen hours a day on the magazine, scrupulously sifting through the 'slush pile' in search of new authors – W. W. Jacobs among them – Jerome still maintained the pose of idleness, contributing a regular column called 'The Idlers' Club' and holding regular 'Idler at Homes' in Arundel Street off the Strand, attended by cronies like H. G. Wells, Barrie and Conan Doyle. A year later he added to his load by taking on the editorship of a weekly magazine, *Today*, serializing Robert Louis Stevenson's 'The Ebb Tide' and publishing work by Hardy, Kipling, Conan Doyle, Anthony Hope and even Aubrey Beardsley. He was a popular and convivial figure at the Fleet Street end of the London literary spectrum; overworked as he was, he still found time for bluff, all-male gatherings of writers, politicians and theatrical folk, preferring informal and often short-lived dining-clubs like the Vagabonds or the Omar Khayyam to grander, more snobbish West End clubs.

Jerome's career as an editor came to an end in 1897, when he was sued for libel over some footling matter by a Leeds company promoter. The plaintiff was awarded a farthing in damages, but both sides were ordered to pay their own costs. *The Idler* and *Today* closed down, and Jerome – who had recently become a father – was once again a freelance writer. Although he was to return to London after World War I, he decided to move to the country, and bought a house on the Thames, at Wallingford in Oxfordshire.

Although he received no royalties from the pirated American edition, earnings from *Three Men in a Boat* and his other books and plays were enough to keep the family afloat. Before long, Jerome decided to send the Three Men on their adventures again. Not surprisingly, George, Harris and J. have become stouter and more settled in the ten years since they took to the river: in Pritchett's opinion, 'they have lost the happy, impartial rudeness of unattached young men'. George weighs over twelve stone, has risen (like his original) to the rank of bank manager, and is still a bachelor. Harris and J. are respectable family men, with several children apiece and such trappings of worldly success as paddocks and cucumber frames. J. is making his way as a writer, and is bruised by snobbish and dismissive critics ('You've been reading those criticisms again,' Mrs J. tells him). Both Harris and J. enjoy playing the parts of henpecked husbands, and both are – by modern standards – unrepentantly old-fashioned in their views on marriage ('In married life,' J. explains to George, 'the man proposes, the wife submits. It is her duty; all religion teaches it'). Defiant behind their wives' backs, they long to get away with their men friends, but don't quite know how to broach the matter; when Mrs J. announces that she too would like some time to herself, J. feels quite bruised and affronted. Domestic diplomacy behind them at last, they decide to make a bicycling tour of Germany; and much of the fascination of their ensuing adventures lies in Jerome's perceptive, and disconcertingly prophetic, view of the Wilhelmine Germans as a people in whom kindliness and a passion for order are combined with passivity, a taste for brutality and authoritarian rule.

Three Men on the Bummel was published in 1900, and that same year Jerome took his family to live in Dresden. Its charms, he declared, were 'more solidly German, and more lasting' than those of Paris – yet another manifestation of the prevailing notion, inflamed by the Romantics and by philosophers like Nietszche and Herder, that German culture was somehow more profound and more rooted than the articulate but superficial Latin varieties.

Jerome's admiration for his hosts was reciprocated: a club was formed in his honour, and his new book became a set text in German schools.

Back in England, Jerome was at last taken seriously by the critics when *Paul Kelver* was published in 1902. The *Times Literary Supplement* compared it, favourably, with Olive Schreiner's *The Story of an African Farm*, and suggested that although *Three Men in a Boat* had been the literary equivalent of a millstone round its author's neck, his new novel displayed 'shrewd observations of a certain habit of mind and cast of character'. He visited St Petersburg, skied in Switzerland with Conan Doyle, and, in 1908, made his first lecture tour of America, visiting every state of the union and calling on the President, Theodore Roosevelt, who – or so it was claimed – happened to be reading one of his books at the time.

Jerome enjoyed public speaking, and was not afraid of making his views known, in person and in print. While editing *Today* he had condemned Turkish massacres of the Armenians; he campaigned on behalf of the badly-off, including his fellow-writers; a keen animal-lover, he berated the Belfast City corporation for its treatment of its tram-horses. His most dramatic outburst occurred in 1913, on his second tour of America. After one of his public readings, in Tennessee, he was moved to protest against the lynching of Negroes in the Southern states. 'The treatment of the Negro calls to Heaven for redress,' he wrote in *My Life and Times*. 'I have sat with men who, amid vile jokes and laughter, told of "Buck Niggers" being slowly roast alive; how they screamed and writhed and prayed; how their eyes rolled inwards as the flames crept upwards till nothing could be seen but two white balls . . . These burnings, these slow grillings of living men, chained down to iron bedsteads; these tearings of live, quivering flesh with red-hot pincers can only be done to glut some hideous lust for cruelty.' This is forceful writing, strongly felt, and provides further evidence of Jerome's awareness of the harsher sides of human nature. After he'd finished his tirade, he 'sat down in silence. It was quite a time before anybody moved. Then they all got up at the same moment, and moved towards the door.'

Round-faced and ruddy, with large, straight features, dark eyes and a thatch of thick white hair, Jerome in his fifties and sixties looked more like a benign English farmer than a desk-bound literary man. Conservative in dress, he continued to favour the tubular trousers, high-buttoned jackets and virulent tweeds of a late-Victorian man-about-town. On one occasion he was attacked by suffragettes who had mistaken him for Mr Asquith, the Liberal Prime Minister, and had to be escorted to safety by two policemen. He had a hatred of litter – hence, in part, his liking for Germany – and carried a sharpened stick with which to pick up rubbish; he once asked an eminent Turk what most impressed him about England, and was distressed to learn that it was the 'dirty paper' blowing about the streets. He remained a prolific writer, notching up – by the end of his life – some eighteen novels and collections of stories, twelve plays, three volumes of essays (including a second instalment of 'Idle Thoughts'), a travel book and an autobiography; his secretary remembered how 'he would walk up and down the study floor with his hands behind his back and dictate with marvellous ease page after page of pathos and humour. He would occasionally refer to his shorthand notes, and he would often rearrange the ornaments on the mantelpiece while dictating.'

When World War I broke out, Jerome found himself torn between his dislike of German militarism and his fondness for the Germans themselves. He recalled seeing German officers strutting three abreast down the street, 'insolent, conceited, overbearing, civilians compelled everywhere to cringe before them', but he hated the wave of Germanophobia that swept the country in 1914, bearing dachshunds and mild-mannered German waiters in its wake, and distrusted atrocity stories about bayonetted babies and ravished Belgian nuns. He longed to enlist, and see something of combat for himself. Too old for the British army, he wangled his way into the French ambulance service at the age of fifty-six. Helping wounded men behind the front line at Verdun, amid the rain and the rats and the rotting corpses, he was sickened by what he saw, and filled with rage against the politicians whom he held responsible. He also ran a hospital for wounded animals, among them a donkey recently awarded the Croix de Guerre. Back in England, he joined Philip Snowden, Dean Inge, E. D. Morel and John Drinkwater in campaigning for a negotiated settlement to the war.

Jerome died of a stroke in 1927, not long after being given the freedom of Walsall. The 'boat of life' had run out to sea at last, and how better to leave him than with the concluding words of *Three Men on the Bummel*, redolent as they are of Jerome the companionable, pipe-smoking amateur philosopher? Our thoughts, he wrote, 'are ever on the running of the sand. We nod and smile to many as we pass; with some we stop and talk awhile; and with a few we walk a little way. We have been much interested, and often a little tired. But on the whole we have had a pleasant time, and are sorry when 'tis over.'

Jeremy Lewis

Notes

1. Autobiographical quotations are from *My Life and Times*, published in 1926.

2. 'Bummel' is also German for a 'stroll'. As befitted Jerome's pose as an indolent man of leisure, a 'Bummler' is an 'idler' or a 'loafer'.

3. Written by George Grossmith (1847–1912) and his brother Weedon (1854–1919), who also provided the illustrations, *The Diary of a Nobody* relates the misadventures of a self-important but ineffectual clerk who is deferential in the office and regularly humiliated on the home front. Originally serialized in *Punch*, it was published in book form by Arrowsmith in 1892.

4. Comic verses written and illustrated by Jerome's friend W. S. Gilbert (1836–1911): the first volume appeared in 1869, and a second followed four years later.

5. The supreme achievement of P. G. Wodehouse (1881–1975); published in 1910, it is a masterly exposé of office life, and features the tyrannical bank manager Mr Bickersdyke.

6. John Foxe (1516–87) was a Protestant propagandist. His *Book of Martyrs*, published in 1563, left the English with an abiding suspicion of Roman Catholics and their ways.

7. Arthur Morrison (1863–1945) was a civil servant who wrote realistic novels about life in the East End slums. *A Child of the Jago* was published

in 1896: his other novels include *Tales of Mean Streets* (1894) and *The Hole in the Wall* (1902).

8. Robert Tressell was the pen-name of Robert Noonan (*c.* 1870–1911), a Liverpudlian house-painter. *The Ragged Trousered Philanthropists* was published posthumously, in 1914: it is set in Hastings, but the scenes it describes would have been all too familiar to East End dwellers.

9. Like Jerome, George Gissing (1857–1903) had experience of life at its seamiest and most destitute: in *New Grub Street* he described the existence of impoverished hack-writers, eking out a livelihood in ways familiar to the youthful Jerome.

10. Alfred Harmsworth (1865–1922) was the prototypical Press baron. He founded what was to become the Amalgamated Press in 1887: he took over the *Evening News* in 1894, and among his journalistic creations were *Answers* (1888), the *Daily Mail* (1896) and the *Daily Mirror* (1903). In due course he became Lord Northcliffe.

11. George Newnes (1851–1910) was an influential and successful newspaper and magazine proprietor. He founded *Tit-Bits* (1881) and the *Strand Magazine*, where many of the Sherlock Holmes stories first appeared in print.

12. Charles Mudie (1818–90) opened his Lending Library in Oxford Street in 1852. His name is forever associated with the long 'three-decker' novels beloved of the mid-Victorians; like W. H. Smith, he is believed to have exercised a degree of informal censorship via his disapproval of anything remotely *risqué* or immoral.

13. W. H. Smith (1825–91) opened his first railway bookstall on Euston Station in 1848: the abolition of stamp duty on newspapers in 1855 enabled him to sell cheap newspapers as well as books, and before long his shops were doing brisk business on railway stations up and down the country. Known as 'Old Morality', he shared Mudie's views about the desirability of wholesome reading; but he encouraged publishers to abandon the three-decker novel in favour of single-volume works, which took up less shelf-space and could more easily be read on trains. Later in life he took to politics, and as First Lord of the Admiralty he was mocked by W. S. Gilbert in *The Pirates of Penzance* ('Stick to your desk and never go to sea, / And you all may be rulers of the Queen's Navee': for Harris's rendition, see p. 62).

14. The embattled hero of H. G. Wells's *The History of Mr Polly* (1910): he was, in fact, a shop assistant, but has much in common with the perkier kind of late-Victorian and Edwardian clerk.

15. Mr Pooter's disrespectful son; he too works as a clerk, but unlike his

father he refuses to be got down by life or by the grandeur of those set above him.

16. J. M. Barrie (1860–1937) is best-known as the creator of Peter Pan; his other plays included *The Admirable Crichton* (1902) and *Dear Brutus* (1917).

17. See 'The Tin-Openers' in *Complete Essays* by V. S. Pritchett (Chatto & Windus, 1991).

18. W. W. Jacobs (1863–1943) was born and grew up in Wapping, and many of his short stories are set in the East End docks.

Further Reading

Carey, John   'A Victorian Clerk's Tale' in *Original Copy* (Faber, London, 1987)

Carey, John   *The Intellectuals and the Masses: Pride and Prejudice among the Literary Intelligentsia 1880–1939* (Faber, London, 1992)

Connolly, Joseph   *Jerome K. Jerome: A Critical Biography* (Orbis, London, 1982)

Jerome, Jerome K.   *Paul Kelver* (Hutchinson, London, 1902)

Jerome, Jerome K.   *My Life and Times* (Hodder & Stoughton, London, 1926)

Moss, Alfred   *Jerome K. Jerome: His Life and Work* (Selwyn & Blount, London, 1929)

Pritchett, V. S.   'The Tin-Openers' in *The Complete Essays* (Chatto & Windus, London, 1991)

Wilson, D. G.   *The Victorian Thames* (Sutton Publishing, Stroud, 1991)

THREE MEN IN A BOAT

Preface to the First Edition

The chief beauty of this book lies not so much in its literary style, or in the extent and usefulness of the information it conveys, as in its simple truthfulness. Its pages form the record of events that really happened. All that has been done is to colour them; and, for this, no extra charge has been made. George and Harris and Montmorency are not poetic ideals, but things of flesh and blood – especially George, who weighs about twelve stone. Other works may excel this in depth of thought and knowledge of human nature: other books may rival it in originality and size; but, for hopeless and incurable veracity, nothing yet discovered can surpass it. This, more than all its other charms, will, it is felt, make the volume precious in the eye of the earnest reader; and will lend additional weight to the lesson that the story teaches.

London,
August 1889

Chapter 1

There were four of us – George, and William Samuel Harris, and myself, and Montmorency. We were sitting in my room, smoking, and talking about how bad we were – bad from a medical point of view I mean, of course.

We were all feeling seedy, and we were getting quite nervous about it. Harris said he felt such extraordinary fits of giddiness come over him at times, that he hardly knew what he was doing; and then George said that *he* had fits of giddiness too, and hardly knew what *he* was doing. With me, it was my liver that was out of order. I knew it was my liver that was out of order, because I had just been reading a patent liver-pill circular, in which were detailed various symptoms by which a man could tell when his liver was out of order. I had them all.

It is a most extraordinary thing, but I never read a patent medicine advertisement without being impelled to the conclusion that I am suffering from the particular disease therein dealt with, in its most virulent form. The diagnosis seems in every case to correspond exactly with all the sensations that I have ever felt.

I remember going to the British Museum one day to read up the treatment for some slight ailment of which I had a touch – hay fever, I fancy it was. I got down the book, and read all I came to read; and then, in an unthinking moment, I idly turned the leaves, and began to indolently study diseases, generally. I forget which was the first distemper I plunged into – some fearful, devastating scourge, I know – and, before I had glanced half down the list of 'premonitory symptoms', it was borne in upon me that I had fairly got it.

I sat for a while frozen with horror; and then in the listlessness of despair, I again turned over the pages. I came to typhoid fever – read the symptoms – discovered that I had typhoid fever, must have had it for months without knowing it – wondered what else I had got; turned up St Vitus's Dance – found, as I expected, that I had that too – began to get interested in my case, and determined to sift it to the bottom, and so started alphabetically – read up ague, and learnt that I was sickening for it, and that the acute stage would commence in about another fortnight. Bright's disease, I was relieved to find, I had only in a modified form, and, so far as that was concerned, I might live for years. Cholera I had, with severe complications; and diphtheria I seemed to have been born with. I plodded conscientiously through the twenty-six letters, and the only malady I could conclude I had not got was housemaid's knee.

I felt rather hurt about this at first; it seemed somehow to be a sort of slight. Why hadn't I got housemaid's knee? Why this invidious reservation? After a while, however, less grasping feelings prevailed. I reflected that I had every other known malady in the pharmacology, and I grew less selfish, and determined to do without housemaid's knee. Gout, in its most malignant stage, it would appear, had seized me without my being aware of it; and zymosis I had evidently been suffering with from boyhood. There were no more diseases after zymosis, so I concluded there was nothing else the matter with me.

I sat and pondered. I thought what an interesting case I must be from a medical point of view, what an acquisition I should be to a class! Students would have no need 'to walk the hospitals', if they had me. I was a hospital in myself. All they need do would be to walk round me, and, after that, take their diploma.

Then I wondered how long I had to live. I tried to examine myself. I felt my pulse. I could not at first feel any pulse at all. Then, all of a sudden, it seemed to start off. I pulled out my watch and timed it. I made it a hundred and forty-seven to the minute. I tried to feel my heart. I could not feel my heart. It had stopped beating. I have since been induced to come to the opinion that it must have been there all the time, and must have been beating, but I cannot account for it. I patted myself all over my front, from what I call my waist up to my head, and I went a bit round each side, and a little way up the back. But I could not feel or hear anything. I tried to look at my tongue. I stuck it out as far as ever it would go, and I shut one eye, and tried to examine it with the other. I could only see the tip, and the only thing that I could gain from that was to feel more certain than before that I had scarlet fever.

I walked into that reading-room a happy healthy man. I crawled out a decrepit wreck.

I went to my medical man. He is an old chum of mine, and feels my pulse, and looks at my tongue, and talks about the weather, all for nothing, when I fancy I'm ill; so I thought I would do him a good turn by going to him now. 'What a doctor wants', I said, 'is practice. He shall have me. He will get more practice out of me than out of seventeen hundred of your ordinary, commonplace patients, with only one or two diseases each.' So I went straight up and saw him, and he said:

'Well, what's the matter with you?'

I said:

'I will not take up your time, dear boy, with telling you what is the matter with me. Life is brief, and you might pass away before I had finished. But I will tell you what is *not* the matter with me. I have not got housemaid's knee. Why I have not got housemaid's knee, I cannot tell you; but the fact remains that I have not got it. Everything else, however, I *have* got.'

And I told him how I came to discover it all.

Then he opened me and looked down me, and clutched hold of my wrist, and then he hit me over the chest when I wasn't expecting it – a cowardly thing to do, I call it – and immediately afterwards butted me with the side of his head. After that, he sat down and wrote out a prescription, and folded it up and gave it me, and I put it in my pocket and went out.

I did not open it. I took it to the nearest chemist's, and handed it in. The man read it, and then handed it back.

He said he didn't keep it.

I said:

'You are a chemist?'

He said:

'I am a chemist. If I was a co-operative stores and family hotel combined, I might be able to oblige you. Being only a chemist hampers me.'

I read the prescription. It ran:

> 1 lb beefsteak, with
> 1 pt bitter beer
>> every 6 hours.
> 1 ten-mile walk every morning.
> 1 bed at 11 sharp every night.

And don't stuff up your head with things you don't understand.

I followed the directions, with the happy result – speaking for myself – that my life was preserved, and is still going on.

In the present instance, going back to the liver-pill circular, I had the symptoms, beyond all mistake, the chief among them being 'a general disinclination to work of any kind'.

What I suffer in that way no tongue can tell. From my earliest infancy I have been a martyr to it. As a boy, the disease hardly ever left me for a day. They did not know, then, that it was my liver. Medical science was in a far less advanced state than now, and they used to put it down to laziness.

'Why, you skulking little devil, you,' they would say, 'get up and do something for your living, can't you?' – not knowing, of course, that I was ill.

And they didn't give me pills; they gave me clumps on the side of the head. And, strange as it may appear, those clumps on the head often cured me – for the time being. I have known one clump on the head have more effect upon my liver, and make me feel more anxious to go straight away then and there, and do what was wanted to be done, without further loss of time, than a whole box of pills does now.

You know, it often is so – those simple, old-fashioned remedies are sometimes more efficacious than all the dispensary stuff.

We sat there for half an hour, describing to each other our maladies. I explained to George and William Harris how I felt when I got up in the morning, and William Harris told us how he felt when he went to bed; and George stood on the hearth-rug, and gave us a clever and powerful piece of acting, illustrative of how he felt in the night.

George *fancies* he is ill: but there's never anything really the matter with him, you know.

At this point, Mrs Poppets knocked at the door to know if we were ready for supper. We smiled sadly at one another, and said we supposed we had better try to swallow a bit. Harris said a little something in one's stomach often kept the disease in check; and Mrs Poppets brought the tray in, and we drew up to the table, and toyed with a little steak and onions, and some rhubarb tart.

I must have been very weak at the time; because I know, after the first half-hour or so, I seemed to take no interest whatever in my food – an unusual thing for me – and I didn't want any cheese.

This duty done, we refilled our glasses, lit our pipes, and resumed the discussion upon our state of health. What it was that was actually the matter with us, we none of us could be sure of; but the unanimous opinion was that it – whatever it was – had been brought on by overwork.

'What we want is rest,' said Harris.

'Rest and a complete change,' said George. 'The overstrain upon our brains has produced a general depression throughout the system. Change of scene, and absence of the necessity for thought, will restore the mental equilibrium.'

George has a cousin who is usually described in the charge-sheet as a medical student, so that he naturally has a somewhat family-physicianary way of putting things.

I agreed with George, and suggested that we should seek out some retired and old-world spot, far from the madding crowd, and dream away a sunny week among its drowsy lanes – some half-forgotten nook, hidden away by the fairies, out of reach of the noisy world – some quaint-perched eyrie on the cliffs of Time, from whence the surging waves of the nineteenth century would sound far-off and faint.

Harris said he thought it would be humpy. He said he knew the sort of place I meant; where everybody went to bed at eight o'clock, and you couldn't get a *Referee*[1] for love or money, and had to walk ten miles to get your baccy.

'No,' said Harris, 'if you want rest and change, you can't beat a sea trip.'

I objected to the sea trip strongly. A sea trip does you good when you are going to have a couple of months of it, but, for a week, it is wicked.

You start on Monday with the idea implanted in your bosom that you are going to enjoy yourself. You wave an airy adieu to the boys on shore, light your biggest pipe, and swagger about the deck as if you were Captain Cook, Sir Francis Drake, and Christopher Columbus all rolled into one. On Tuesday, you wish you hadn't come. On Wednesday, Thursday, and Friday, you wish you were dead. On Saturday you are able to swallow a little beef tea, and to sit up on deck, and answer with a wan, sweet smile when kind-hearted people ask how you feel now. On Sunday, you begin to walk again, and take solid food. And on Monday morning, as, with your bag and umbrella in your hand, you stand by the gunwale, waiting to step ashore, you begin to thoroughly like it.

I remember my brother-in-law going for a short sea trip once for the benefit of his health. He took a return berth from London to Liverpool; and when he got to Liverpool, the only thing he was anxious about was to sell that return ticket.

It was offered round the town at a tremendous reduction, so I am told; and was eventually sold for eighteenpence to a bilious-looking youth who had just been advised by his medical men to go to the seaside, and take exercise.

'Seaside!' said my brother-in-law, pressing the ticket affectionately into his hand: 'why, you'll have enough to last you a lifetime; and as for exercise! why, you'll get more exercise, sitting down on that ship, than you would turning somersaults on dry land.'

He himself – my brother-in-law – came back by train. He said the North-Western Railway was healthy enough for him.

Another fellow I knew went for a week's voyage round the coast, and, before they started, the steward came to him to ask whether he would pay for each meal as he had it, or arrange beforehand for the whole series.

The steward recommended the latter course, as it would come so much cheaper. He said they would do him for the whole week at two-pounds-five. He said for breakfast there would be fish, followed by a grill. Lunch was at one, and consisted of four courses. Dinner at six – soup, fish, entrée, joint, poultry, salad, sweets, cheese, and dessert. And a light meat supper at ten.

My friend thought he would close on the two-pounds-five job (he is a hearty eater), and did so.

Lunch came just as they were off Sheerness. He didn't feel so hungry as he thought he should, and so contented himself with a bit of boiled beef, and some strawberries and cream. He pondered a good deal during the afternoon, and at one time it seemed to him that he had been eating nothing but boiled beef for weeks, and at other times it seemed that he must have been living on strawberries and cream for years.

Neither the beef nor the strawberries and cream seemed happy, either – seemed discontented like.

At six, they came and told him dinner was ready. The announcement aroused no enthusiasm within him, but he felt that there was some of that two-pounds-five to be worked off, and he held on to ropes and things and went down. A pleasant odour of onions and hot ham, mingled with fried fish and greens, greeted him at the bottom of the ladder; and then the steward came up with an oily smile, and said:

'What can I get you, sir?'

'Get me out of this,' was the feeble reply.

And they ran him up quick, and propped him up, over to leeward, and left him.

For the next four days he lived a simple and blameless life on thin Captain's biscuits (I mean that the biscuits were thin, not the captain) and soda-water; but, towards Saturday, he got uppish, and went in for weak tea and dry toast, and on Monday he was gorging himself on chicken broth. He left the ship on Tuesday, and as it steamed away from the landing-stage he gazed after it regretfully.

'There she goes,' he said, 'there she goes, with two pounds' worth of food on board that belongs to me, and that I haven't had.'

He said that if they had given him another day he thought he could have put it straight.

So I set my face against the sea trip. Not, as I explained, upon my own account. I was never queer. But I was afraid for George. George said he should be all right, and would rather like it, but he would advise Harris and me not to think of it, as he felt sure we should both be ill. Harris said that, to himself, it was always a mystery how people managed to get sick at sea – said he thought people must do it on purpose, from affectation – said he had often wished to be, but had never been able.

Then he told us anecdotes of how he had gone across the Channel when it was so rough that the passengers had to be tied into their berths, and he and the captain were the only two living souls on board who were not ill. Sometimes it was he and the second mate who were not ill; but it was generally he and one other man. If not he and another man, then it was he by himself.

It is a curious fact, but nobody ever is sea-sick – on land. At sea, you come across plenty of people very bad indeed, whole boat-loads of them; but I never met a man yet, on land, who had ever known at all what it was to be sea-sick. Where the thousands upon thousands of bad sailors that swarm in every ship hide themselves when they are on land is a mystery.

If most men were like a fellow I saw on the Yarmouth boat one day, I could account for the seeming enigma easily enough. It was just off Southend Pier, I recollect, and he was leaning out through one of the port-holes in a very dangerous position. I went up to him to try and save him.

'Hi! come further in,' I said, shaking him by the shoulder. 'You'll be overboard.'

'Oh my! I wish I was,' was the only answer I could get; and there I had to leave him.

Three weeks afterwards, I met him in the coffee-room of a Bath hotel, talking about his voyages, and explaining, with enthusiasm, how he loved the sea.

'Good sailor!' he replied in answer to a mild young man's envious query, 'well I did feel a little queer *once*, I confess. It was off Cape Horn. The vessel was wrecked the next morning.'

I said:

'Weren't you a little shaky by Southend Pier one day, and wanted to be thrown overboard?'

'Southend Pier!' he replied, with a puzzled expression.

'Yes; going down to Yarmouth, last Friday three weeks.'

'Oh, ah – yes,' he answered, brightening up; 'I remember now. I did have a headache that afternoon. It was the pickles, you know. They were the most disgraceful pickles I ever tasted in a respectable boat. Did *you* have any?'

For myself, I have discovered an excellent preventive against sea-sickness, in balancing myself. You stand in the centre of the deck, and, as the ship heaves and pitches, you move your body about, so as to keep it always straight. When the front of the ship rises, you lean forward, till the deck almost touches your nose; and when its back end gets up, you lean backwards. This is all very well for an hour or two; but you can't balance yourself for a week.

George said:

'Let's go up the river.'

He said we should have fresh air, exercise, and quiet; the constant change of scene would occupy our minds (including what there was of Harris's); and the hard work would give us a good appetite, and make us sleep well.

Harris said he didn't think George ought to do anything that would have a tendency to make him sleepier than he always was, as it might be dangerous. He said he didn't very well understand how George was going to sleep any more than he did now, seeing that there were only twenty-four hours in each day, summer and winter alike; but thought that if he *did* sleep any more he might just as well be dead, and so save his board and lodging.

Harris said, however, that the river would suit him to a 'T'. I don't know what a 'T' is (except a sixpenny one, which includes bread-and-butter and cake *ad lib.*, and is cheap at the price, if you haven't had any dinner). It seems to suit everybody, however, which is greatly to its credit.

It suited me to a 'T', too, and Harris and I both said it was a good idea of George's and we said it in a tone that seemed to somehow imply that we were surprised that George should have come out so sensible.

The only one who was not struck with the suggestion was Montmorency. He never did care for the river, did Montmorency.

'It's all very well for you fellows,' he says; 'you like it, but *I* don't. There's nothing for me to do. Scenery is not in my line, and I don't smoke. If I see a rat, you won't stop; and if I go to sleep, you get fooling about with the boat, and slop me overboard. If you ask me, I call the whole thing bally foolishness.'

We were three to one, however, and the motion was carried.

Chapter 2

Plans discussed – Pleasures of 'comping out', on fine nights – Ditto, wet nights – Compromise decided on – Montmorency, first impressions of – Fears lest he is too good for this world, fears subsequently dismissed as groundless – Meeting adjourns.

We pulled out the maps, and discussed plans.

We arranged to start on the following Saturday from Kingston. Harris and I would go down in the morning, and take the boat up to Chertsey, and George, who would not be able to get away from the City till the afternoon (George goes to sleep at a bank from ten to four each day, except Saturdays, when they wake him up and put him outside at two), would meet us there.

Should we 'camp out' or sleep at inns?

George and I were for camping out. We said it would be so wild and free, so patriarchal[1] like.

Slowly the golden memory of the dead sun fades from the hearts of the cold, sad clouds. Silent, like sorrowing children, the birds have ceased their song, and only the moorhen's plaintive cry and the harsh croak of the corncrake stirs the awed hush around the couch of waters, where the dying day breathes out her last.

From the dim woods on either bank, Night's ghostly army, the grey shadows, creep out with noiseless tread to chase away the lingering rearguard of the light, and pass, with noiseless, unseen feet, above the waving river-grass, and through the sighing rushes; and Night, upon her sombre throne, folds her black wings above the darkening world, and, from her phantom palace, lit by the pale stars, reigns in stillness.

Then we run our little boat into some quiet nook, and the tent is pitched, and the frugal supper cooked and eaten. Then the big pipes are filled and lighted, and the pleasant chat goes round in musical undertone; while, in the pauses of our talk, the river, playing round the boat, prattles strange old tales and secrets, sings low the old child's song that it has sung so many thousand years – will sing so many thousand years to come, before its voice grows harsh and old – a song that we, who have learnt to love its changing face, who have so often nestled on its yielding bosom, think, somehow, we understand, though we could not tell you in mere words the story that we listen to.

And we sit there, by its margin, while the moon, who loves it too, stoops down to kiss it with a sister's kiss, and throws her silver arms around it clingingly; and we watch it as it flows, ever singing, ever whispering, out to meet its king, the sea – till our voices die away in silence, and the pipes go out – till we, commonplace, everyday young men enough, feel strangely full of thoughts, half sad, half sweet, and do not care or want to speak – till we laugh, and, rising, knock the ashes from our burnt-out pipes, and say 'Good night', and, lulled by the lapping water and the rustling trees, we fall asleep beneath the great, still stars, and dream that the world is young again – young and sweet as she used to be ere the centuries of fret and care had furrowed her fair face, ere her children's sins and follies had made old her loving heart – sweet as she was in those bygone days when, a new-made mother, she nursed us, her children, upon her own deep breast – ere the wiles of painted civilization had lured us away from her fond arms, and the poisoned sneers of artificiality had made us ashamed of the simple life we led with her, and the simple, stately home where mankind was born so many thousands of years ago.

Harris said:

'How about when it rained?'

You can never rouse Harris. There is no poetry about Harris –

no wild yearning for the unattainable. Harris never 'weeps, he knows not why'. If Harris's eyes fill with tears, you can bet it is because Harris has been eating raw onions, or has put too much Worcester over his chop.

If you were to stand at night by the seashore with Harris, and say:

'Hark! Do you not hear? Is it but the mermaids singing deep below the waving waters; or sad spirits, chanting dirges for white corpses, held by seaweed?'

Harris would take you by the arm, and say:

'I know what it is, old man; you've got a chill. Now, you come along with me. I know a place round the corner here, where you can get a drop of the finest Scotch whisky you ever tasted – put you right in less than no time.'

Harris always does know a place round the corner where you can get something brilliant in the drinking line. I believe that if you met Harris up in Paradise (supposing such a thing likely), he would immediately greet you with:

'So glad you've come, old fellow; I've found a nice place round the corner here, where you can get some really first-class nectar.'

In the present instance, however, as regarded the camping out, his practical view of the matter came as a very timely hint. Camping out in rainy weather is not pleasant.

It is evening. You are wet through, and there is a good two inches of water in the boat, and all the things are damp. You find a place on the banks that is not quite so puddly as other places you have seen, and you land and lug out the tent, and two of you proceed to fix it.

It is soaked and heavy, and it flops about, and tumbles down on you, and clings round your head and makes you mad. The rain is pouring steadily down all the time. It is difficult enough to fix a tent in dry weather; in wet, the task becomes herculean. Instead of helping you, it seems to you that the other man is simply playing the fool. Just as you get your side beautifully fixed, he gives it a hoist from his end, and spoils it all.

'Here! What are you up to?' you call out.

'What are *you* up to?' he retorts. 'Leggo, can't you?'

'Don't pull it; you've got it all wrong, you stupid ass!' you shout.

'No, I haven't,' he yells back; 'let go your side!'

'I tell you you've got it all wrong!' you roar, wishing that you could get at him; and you give your ropes a lug that pulls all his pegs out.

'Ah, the bally idiot!' you hear him mutter to himself; and then comes a savage haul, and away goes your side. You lay down the mallet and start to go round and tell him what you think about the whole business, and, at the same time, he starts round in the same direction to come and explain his views to you. And you follow each other round and round, swearing at one another, until the tent tumbles down in a heap, and leaves you looking at each other across its ruins, then you both indignantly exclaim, in the same breath:

'There you are! What did I tell you?'

Meanwhile the third man, who has been baling out the boat, and who has spilled the water down his sleeve, and has been cursing away to himself steadily for the last ten minutes, wants to know what the thundering blazes you're playing at, and why the blarmed tent isn't up yet.

At last, somehow or other, it does get up, and you land the things. It is hopeless attempting to make a wood fire, so you light the methylated spirit stove, and crowd round that.

Rainwater is the chief article of diet at supper. The bread is two-thirds rainwater, the beefsteak-pie is exceedingly rich in it, and the jam, and the butter, and the salt, and the coffee have all combined with it to make soup.

After supper, you find your tobacco is damp, and you cannot smoke. Luckily you have a bottle of the stuff that cheers and inebriates, if taken in proper quantity, and this restores to you sufficient interest in life to induce you to go to bed.

There you dream that an elephant has suddenly sat down on your chest, and that the volcano has exploded and thrown you down to the bottom of the sea – the elephant still sleeping peacefully on your bosom. You wake up and grasp the idea that something terrible really has happened. Your first impression is that the end of the world has come; and then you think that this cannot be, and that it is thieves and murderers, or else fire, and this opinion you express in the usual method. No help comes, however, and all you know is that thousands of people are kicking you, and you are being smothered.

Somebody else seems in trouble, too. You can hear his faint cries coming from underneath your bed. Determining, at all events, to sell your life dearly, you struggle frantically, hitting out right and left with your arms and legs, and yelling lustily the while, and at last something gives way, and you find your head in the fresh air. Two feet off, you dimly observe a half-dressed ruffian, waiting to kill you, and you are preparing for a life-and-death struggle with him, when it begins to dawn on you that it's Jim.

'Oh, it's you, is it?' he says, recognizing you at the same moment.

'Yes,' you answer, rubbing your eyes; 'what's happened?'

'Bally tent's blown down, I think,' he says. 'Where's Bill?'

Then you both raise up your voices and shout for 'Bill!' and the ground beneath you heaves and rocks, and the muffled voice that you heard before replies from out of the ruin:

'Get off my head, can't you?'

And Bill struggles out, a muddy, trampled wreck, and in an unnecessarily aggressive mood – he being under the evident belief that the whole thing has been done on purpose.

In the morning you are all three speechless, owing to having caught severe colds in the night; you also feel very quarrelsome, and you swear at each other in hoarse whispers during the whole of breakfast time.

We therefore decided that we would sleep out on fine nights; and hotel it, and inn it, and pub it, like respectable folks, when it was wet, or when we felt inclined for a change.

Montmorency hailed this compromise with much approval. He does not revel in romantic solitude. Give him something noisy; and if a trifle low, so much the jollier. To look at Montmorency you would imagine that he was an angel sent upon the earth, for some reason withheld from mankind, in the shape of a small fox-terrier. There is a sort of Oh-what-a-wicked-world-this-is-and-how-I-wish-I-could-do-something-to-make-it-better-and-nobler expression about

Montmorency that has been known to bring the tears into the eyes of pious old ladies and gentlemen.

When first he came to live at my expense, I never thought I should be able to get him to stop long. I used to sit down and look at him, as he sat on the rug and looked up at me, and think: 'Oh, that dog will never live. He will be snatched up to the bright skies in a chariot, that is what will happen to him.'

But, when I had paid for about a dozen chickens that he had killed; and had dragged him, growling and kicking, by the scruff of his neck, out of a hundred and fourteen street fights; and had had a dead cat brought round for my inspection by an irate female, who called me a murderer; and had been summoned by the man next door but one for having a ferocious dog at large, that had kept him pinned up in his own tool-shed, afraid to venture his nose outside the door, for over two hours on a cold night; and had learned that the gardener, unknown to myself, had won thirty shillings by backing him to kill rats against time, then I began to think that maybe they'd let him remain on earth for a bit longer, after all.

To hang about a stable, and collect a gang of the most disreputable dogs to be found in the town, and lead them out to march round the slums to fight other disreputable dogs, is Montmorency's idea of 'life'; and so, as I before observed, he gave to the suggestion of inns, and pubs, and hotels his most emphatic approbation.

Having thus settled the sleeping arrangements to the satisfaction of all four of us, the only thing left to discuss was what we should take with us; and this we had begun to argue, when Harris said he'd had enough oratory for one night, and proposed that we should go out and have a smile, saying that he had found a place, round by the square, where you could really get a drop of Irish worth drinking.

George said he felt thirsty (I never knew George when he didn't); and, as I had a presentiment that a little whisky, warm, with a slice of lemon, would do my complaint good, the debate was, by common assent, adjourned to the following night; and the assembly put on its hats and went out.

Chapter 3

Arrangements settled – Harris's method of doing work – How the elderly family-man puts up a picture – George makes a sensible remark – Delights of early morning bathing – Provisions for getting upset.

So, on the following evening, we again assembled, to discuss and arrange our plans. Harris said:

'Now, the first thing to settle is what to take with us. Now, you get a bit of paper and write down, J., and you get the grocery catalogue, George, and somebody give me a bit of pencil, and then I'll make out a list.'

That's Harris all over – so ready to take the burden of everything himself, and put it on the backs of other people.

He always reminds me of my poor Uncle Podger. You never saw such a commotion up and down a house in all your life, as when my Uncle Podger undertook to do a job. A picture would have come home from the frame-maker's, and be standing in the dining-room, waiting to be put up; and Aunt Podger would ask what was to be done with it, and Uncle Podger would say:

'Oh, you leave that to *me*. Don't you, any of you, worry yourselves about that. *I'll* do all that.'

And then he would take off his coat, and begin. He would send the girl out for sixpenn'orth of nails, and then one of the boys after her to tell her what size to get; and, from that, he would gradually work down, and start the whole house.

'Now you go and get me my hammer, Will,' he would shout; 'and bring me the rule, Tom; and I shall want the step-ladder, and I had better have a kitchen chair, too; and Jim! you run round to Mr Goggles, and tell him, "Pa's kind regards and hopes his leg's better; and will he lend him his spirit-level?" And don't you go, Maria, because I shall want somebody to hold me the light; and when the girl comes back she must go out again for a bit of picture-cord; and Tom! – where's Tom? – Tom, you come here; I shall want you to hand me up the picture.'

And then he would lift up the picture, and drop it, and it would come out of the frame, and he would try to save the glass, and cut himself; and then he would spring round the room, looking for his handkerchief. He could not find his handkerchief, because it was in the pocket of the coat he had taken off, and he did not know where he had put the coat, and all the house had to leave off looking for his tools, and start looking for his coat; while he would dance round and hinder them.

'Doesn't anybody in the whole house know where my coat is? I never came across such a set in all my life – upon my word I didn't. Six of you! – and you can't find a coat that I put down not five minutes ago! Well, of all the –'

Then he'd get up, and find that he had been sitting on it, and would call out:

'Oh, you can give it up! I've found it myself now. Might just as well ask the cat to find anything as expect you people to find it.'

And when half an hour had been spent in tying up his finger, and a new glass had been got, and the tools, and the ladder, and the chair, and the candle had been brought, he would have another go, the whole family, including the girl, and the charwoman, standing round in a semi-circle, ready to help. Two people would have to hold the chair, and a third would help him up on it, and hold him there, and a fourth would hand him a nail, and a fifth would pass him up the hammer, and he would take hold of the nail, and drop it.

'There!' he would say, in an injured tone, 'now the nail's gone.'

And we would all have to go down on our knees and grovel for it, while he would stand on the chair, and grunt, and want to know if he was to be kept there all the evening.

The nail would be found at last, but by that time he would have lost the hammer.

'Where's the hammer? What did I do with the hammer? Great heavens! Seven of you, gaping round there, and you don't know what I did with the hammer!'

We would find the hammer for him, and then he would have lost sight of the mark he had made on the wall, where the nail was to go in, and each of us had to get up on the chair beside him, and see if we could find it; and we would each discover it in a different place, and he would call us all fools, one after another, and tell us to get down. And he would take the rule, and remeasure, and find that he wanted half thirty-one and three-eighths inches from the corner and would try to do it in his head, and go mad.

And we would all try to do it in our heads, and all arrive at different results, and sneer at one another. And in the general row, the original number would be forgotten, and Uncle Podger would have to measure it again.

He would use a bit of string this time, and at the critical moment, when the old fool was leaning over the chair at an angle of forty-five, and trying to reach a point three inches beyond what was possible for him to reach, the string would slip, and down he would slide on to the piano, a really fine musical effect being produced by the suddenness with which his head and body struck all the notes at the same time.

And Aunt Maria would say that she would not allow the children to stand round and hear such language.

At last, Uncle Podger would get the spot fixed again, and put the point of the nail on it with his left hand, and take the hammer in his right hand. And, with the first blow, he would smash his thumb, and drop the hammer, with a yell, on somebody's toes.

Aunt Maria would mildly observe that, next time Uncle Podger was going to hammer a nail into the wall, she hoped he'd let her know in time, so that she could make arrangements to go and spend a week with her mother while it was being done.

'Oh! you women, you make such a fuss over everything,' Uncle Podger would reply, picking himself up. 'Why, I *like* doing a little job of this sort.'

And then he would have another try, and, at the second blow, the nail would go clean through the plaster, and half the hammer after it, and Uncle Podger be precipitated against the wall with force nearly sufficient to flatten his nose.

Then we had to find the rule and the string again, and a new hole was made; and, about midnight, the picture would be up – very crooked and insecure, the wall for yards round looking as if it had been smoothed down with a rake, and everybody dead beat and wretched – except Uncle Podger.

'There you are,' he would say, stepping heavily off the chair on to the charwoman's corns, and surveying the mess he had made with evident pride. 'Why, some people would have had a man in to do a little thing like that!'

Harris will be just that sort of man when he grows up, I know, and I told him so. I said I could not permit him to take so much labour upon himself. I said:

'No, you get the paper, and the pencil, and the catalogue, and George write down, and I'll do the work.'

The first list we made out had to be discarded. It was clear that the upper reaches of the Thames would not allow of the navigation of a boat sufficiently large to take the things we had set down as indispensable; so we tore the list up, and looked at one another.

George said:

'You know we are on the wrong track altogether. We must not think of the things we could do with, but only of the things that we can't do without.'

George comes out really quite sensible at times. You'd be surprised. I call that downright wisdom, not merely as regards the present case, but with reference to our trip up the river of life generally. How many people, on that voyage, load up the boat till it is in danger of swamping with a store of foolish things which they think essential to the pleasure and comfort of the trip, but which are really only useless lumber.

How they pile the poor little craft mast-high with fine clothes and big houses; with useless servants, and a host of swell friends that do not care twopence for them, and that they do not care three ha'pence for; with expensive entertainments that nobody enjoys, with formalities and fashions, with pretence and ostentation, and with – oh, heaviest, maddest lumber of all! – the dread of what will my neighbour think, with luxuries that only cloy, with pleasures that bore, with empty show that, like the criminal's iron crown of yore, makes to bleed and swoon the aching head that wears it!

It is lumber, man – all lumber! Throw it overboard. It makes the boat so heavy to pull, you nearly faint at the oars. It makes it so cumbersome and dangerous to manage, you never know a moment's

19

freedom from anxiety and care, never gain a moment's rest for dreamy laziness – no time to watch the windy shadows skimming lightly o'er the shallows, or the glittering sunbeams flitting in and out among the ripples, or the great trees by the margin looking down at their own image, or the woods all green and golden, or the lilies white and yellow, or the sombre-waving rushes, or the sedges, or the orchis, or the blue forget-me-nots.

Throw the lumber over, man! Let your boat of life be light, packed with only what you need – a homely home and simple pleasures, one or two friends, worth the name, someone to love and someone to love you, a cat, a dog, and a pipe or two, enough to eat and enough to wear, and a little more than enough to drink; for thirst is a dangerous thing.

You will find the boat easier to pull then, and it will not be so liable to upset, and it will not matter so much if it does upset; good, plain merchandise will stand water. You will have time to think as well as to work. Time to drink in life's sunshine – time to listen to the Aeolian music that the wind of God draws from the human heart-strings around us – time to –

I beg your pardon, really. I quite forgot.

Well, we left the list to George, and he began it.

'We won't take a tent,' suggested George; 'we will have a boat with a cover. It is ever so much simpler, and more comfortable.'

It seemed a good thought, and we adopted it. I do not know whether you have ever seen the thing I mean. You fix iron hoops up over the boat, and stretch a huge canvas over them, and fasten it down all round, from stem to stern, and it converts the boat into a sort of little house, and it is beautifully cosy, though a trifle stuffy; but there, everything has its drawbacks, as the man said when his mother-in-law died, and they came down upon him for the funeral expenses.

George said that in that case we must take a rug each, a lamp, some soap, a brush and comb (between us), a toothbrush (each), a basin, some tooth-powder, some shaving tackle (sounds like a French exercise doesn't it?), and a couple of big towels for bathing. I notice that people always make gigantic arrangements for bathing when they are going anywhere near the water, but that they don't bathe much when they are there.

It is the same when you go to the seaside. I always determine – when thinking over the matter in London – that I'll get up early every morning, and go and have a dip before breakfast, and I religiously pack up a pair of drawers and a bath towel. I always get red bathing drawers. I rather fancy myself in red drawers. They suit my complexion so. But when I get to the sea I don't feel somehow that I want that early morning bathe nearly so much as I did when I was in town.

On the contrary, I feel more that I want to stop in bed till the last moment, and then come down and have my breakfast. Once or twice virtue has triumphed, and I have got out at six and half-dressed myself, and have taken my drawers and towel, and stumbled dismally off. But I haven't enjoyed it. They seem to keep a specially cutting east wind waiting for me when I go to bathe in the early morning; and they pick out all the three-cornered stones; and put them on the top, and they sharpen up the rocks and cover the points over with a bit of sand so that I can't see them, and they take the sea and put it two miles out, so that I have to huddle myself up in my arms and hop, shivering, through six inches of water. And when I do get to the sea, it is rough and quite insulting.

One huge wave catches me up and chucks me in a sitting posture as hard as ever it can, down on to a rock which has been put there for me. And, before I've said 'Oh! Ugh!' and found out what has gone, the wave comes back and carries me out to mid-ocean. I begin to strike out frantically for the shore, and wonder if I shall ever see home and friends again, and wish I'd been kinder to my little sister when a boy (when *I* was a boy, I mean). Just when I have given up all hope, a wave retires and leaves me sprawling like a star-fish on the sand, and I get up and look back and find that I've been swimming for my life in two feet of water. I hop back and dress and crawl home, where I have to pretend I liked it.

In the present instance, we all talked as if we were going to have a long swim every morning. George said it was so pleasant to wake up in the boat in the fresh morning, and plunge into the limpid river. Harris said there was nothing like a swim before breakfast to give you an appetite. He said it always gave him an appetite. George said that if it was going to make Harris eat more than Harris ordinarily ate, then he should protest against Harris having a bath at all.

He said there would be quite enough hard work in towing sufficient food for Harris up against stream, as it was.

I urged upon George, however, how much pleasanter it would be to have Harris clean and fresh about the boat, even if we did have to take a few more hundredweight of provisions; and he got to see it in my light, and withdrew his opposition to Harris's bath. Agreed, finally, that we should take *three* bath towels, so as not to keep each other waiting.

For clothes, George said two suits of flannel would be sufficient as we could wash them ourselves, in the river, when they got dirty. We asked him if he had ever tried washing flannels in the river, and he replied: 'No, not exactly himself like, but he knew some fellows who had, and it was easy enough'; and Harris and I were weak enough to fancy he knew what he was talking about, and that three respectable young men, without position or influence, and with no experience in washing, could really clean their own shirts and trousers in the River Thames with a bit of soap.

We were to learn in the days to come, when it was too late, that George was a miserable impostor, who could evidently have known nothing whatever about the matter. If you had seen these clothes after – but, as the shilling shockers[1] say, we anticipate.

George impressed upon us to take a change of underthings and plenty of socks, in case we got upset and wanted a change; also plenty of handkerchiefs, as they would do to wipe things, and a pair of leather boots as well as our boating shoes, as we should want them if we got upset.

Chapter 4

The food question – Objections to paraffin oil as an atmosphere – Advantages of cheese as a travelling companion – A married woman deserts her home – Further provisions for getting upset – I pack – Cussedness of tooth-brushes – George and Harris pack – Awful behaviour of Montmorency – We retire to rest.

Then we discussed the food question. George said:

'Begin with breakfast.' (George is so practical.) 'Now for breakfast we shall want a frying-pan' – (Harris said it was indigestible; but we merely urged him not to be an ass, and George went on) – 'a teapot and a kettle, and a methylated spirit stove.'

'No oil,' said George, with a significant look; and Harris and I agreed.

We had taken up an oil stove once, but 'never again'. It had been like living in an oil shop that week. It oozed. I never saw such a thing as paraffin oil is to ooze. We kept it in the nose of the boat, and, from there, it oozed down to the rudder, impregnating the whole boat and everything in it on its way, and it oozed over the river, and saturated the scenery and spoilt the atmosphere. Sometimes a westerly oily wind blew, and at other times an easterly oily wind, and sometimes it blew a northerly oily wind, and maybe a southerly oily wind; but whether it came from the Arctic snows, or was raised in the waste of the desert sands, it came alike to us laden with the fragrance of paraffin oil.

And that oil oozed up and ruined the sunset; and as for the moonbeams, they positively reeked of paraffin.

We tried to get away from it at Marlow. We left the boat by the bridge, and took a walk through the town to escape it, but it followed us. The whole town was full of oil. We passed through the churchyard, and it seemed as if the people had been buried in oil. The High Street stank of oil; we wondered how people could live in it. And we walked miles upon miles out Birmingham way; but it was no use, the country was steeped in oil.

At the end of that trip we met together at midnight in a lonely field, under a blasted oak, and took an awful oath (we had been swearing for a whole week about the thing in an ordinary, middle-class way, but this was a swell affair) – an awful oath never to take paraffin oil with us in a boat again – except, of course, in case of sickness.

Therefore, in the present instance, we confined ourselves to methylated spirit. Even that is bad enough. You get methylated pie and methylated cake. But methylated spirit is more wholesome when taken into the system in large quantities than paraffin oil.

For other breakfast things, George suggested eggs and bacon which were easy to cook, cold meat, tea, bread and butter, and jam. For lunch, he said, we could have biscuits, cold meat, bread and butter, and jam – but *no cheese*. Cheese, like oil, makes too much of itself. It wants the whole boat to itself. It goes through the hamper, and gives a cheesy flavour to everything else there. You can't tell whether you are eating apple pie, or German sausage, or strawberries and cream. It all seems cheese. There is too much odour about cheese.

I remember a friend of mine buying a couple of cheeses at Liverpool. Splendid cheeses they were, ripe and mellow, and with a two hundred horse-power scent about them that might have been warranted to carry three miles, and knock a man over at two hundred yards. I was in Liverpool at the time, and my friend said that if I didn't mind he would get me to take them back with me to London, as he should not be coming up for a day or two himself, and he did not think the cheeses ought to be kept much longer.

'Oh, with pleasure, dear boy,' I replied, 'with pleasure.'

I called for the cheeses, and took them away in a cab. It was a ramshackle affair, dragged along by a knock-kneed, broken-winded somnambulist, which his owner, in a moment of enthusiasm, during conversation, referred to as a horse. I put the cheeses on the top, and we started off at a shamble that would have done credit to the swiftest steam-roller ever built, and all went merry as a funeral bell, until we turned a corner. There, the wind carried a whiff from the cheeses full on our steed. It woke him up, and, with a snort of terror, he dashed off at three miles an hour. The wind still blew in his direction, and before we reached the end of the street he was laying himself out at the rate of nearly four miles an hour, leaving the cripples and stout old ladies simply nowhere.

It took two porters as well as the driver to hold him in at the station; and I do not think they would have done it, even then, had not one of the men had the presence of mind to put a handkerchief over his nose, and to light a bit of brown paper.

I took my ticket, and marched proudly up the platform, with my cheeses, the people falling back respectfully on either side. The train was crowded, and I had to get into a carriage where there were already seven other people. One crusty old gentleman objected, but I got in, notwithstanding; and, putting my cheeses upon the rack, squeezed down with a pleasant smile, and said it was a warm day. A few moments passed, and then the old gentleman began to fidget.

'Very close in here,' he said.

'Quite oppressive,' said the man next to him.

And then they both began sniffing, and, at the third sniff, they caught it right on the chest, and rose up without another word and went out. And then a stout lady got up, and said it was disgraceful that a respectable married woman should be harried about in this way, and gathered up a bag and eight parcels and went. The remaining four passengers sat on for a while, until a solemn-looking man in the corner who, from his dress and general appearance, seemed to belong to the undertaker class, said it put him in mind of a dead baby; and the other three passengers tried to get out of the door at the same time, and hurt themselves.

I smiled at the black gentleman, and said I thought we were going to have the carriage to ourselves; and he laughed pleasantly and said that some people made such a fuss over a little thing. But even he grew strangely depressed after we had started, and so, when we reached Crewe, I asked him to come and have a drink. He accepted, and we forced our way into the buffet, where we yelled, and stamped, and waved our umbrellas for a quarter of an hour; and then a young lady came and asked us if we wanted anything.

'What's yours?' I said, turning to my friend.

'I'll have half-a-crown's worth[1] of brandy, neat, if you please, miss,' he responded.

And he went off quietly after he had drunk it and got into another carriage, which I thought mean.

From Crewe I had the compartment to myself, though the train was crowded. As we drew up at the different stations, the people, seeing my empty carriage, would rush for it. 'Here y' are, Maria; come along, plenty of room.' 'All right, Tom; we'll get in here,' they would shout. And they would run along, carrying heavy bags, and fight round the door to get in first. And one would open the door and mount the steps and stagger back into the arms of the man behind him; and they would all come and have a sniff, and then drop off and squeeze into other carriages, or pay the difference and go first.

From Euston I took the cheeses down to my friend's house. When his wife came into the room, she smelt round for an instant. Then she said:

'What is it? Tell me the worst.'

I said:

'It's cheeses. Tom bought them in Liverpool, and asked me to bring them up with me.'

And I added that I hoped she understood that it had nothing to do with me; and she said that she was sure of that, but that she would speak to Tom about it when he came back.

My friend was detained in Liverpool longer than he expected; and three days later, as he hadn't returned home, his wife called on me. She said:

'What did Tom say about those cheeses?'

I replied that he had directed they were to be kept in a moist place, and that nobody was to touch them.

She said:

'Nobody's likely to touch them. Had he smelt them?'

I thought he had, and added that he seemed greatly attached to them.

'You think he would be upset,' she queried, 'if I gave a man a sovereign² to take them away and bury them?'

I answered that I thought he would never smile again.

An idea struck her. She said:

'Do you mind keeping them for him? Let me send them round to you.'

'Madam,' I replied, 'for myself I like the smell of cheese, and the journey the other day with them from Liverpool I shall ever look back upon as a happy ending to a pleasant holiday. But, in this world, we must consider others. The lady under whose roof I have the honour of residing is a widow, and, for all I know, possibly an orphan too. She has a strong, I may say an eloquent, objection to being what she terms "put upon". The presence of your husband's cheese in her house she would, I instinctively feel, regard as a "put upon"; and it shall never be said that I put upon the widow and the orphan.'

'Very well, then,' said my friend's wife, rising, 'all I have to say is, that I shall take the children and go to an hotel until those cheeses are eaten. I decline to live any longer in the same house with them.'

She kept her word, leaving the place in charge of the charwoman, who, when asked if she could stand the smell, replied: 'What smell?' and who, when taken close to the cheese and told to sniff hard, said she could detect a faint odour of melons. It was argued from this that little injury could result to the woman from the atmosphere, and she was left.

The hotel bill came to fifteen guineas;[3] and my friend, after reckoning everything up, found that the cheeses had cost him eight-and-sixpence[4] a pound. He said he dearly loved a bit of cheese, but it was beyond his means; so he determined to get rid of them. He threw them into the canal; but had to fish them out again, as the bargemen complained. They said it made them feel quite faint. And, after that, he took them one dark night and left them in the parish mortuary. But the coroner discovered them, and made a fearful fuss.

He said it was a plot to deprive him of his living by waking up the corpses.

My friend got rid of them, at last, by taking them down to a seaside town, and burying them on the beach. It gained the place quite a reputation. Visitors said they had never noticed before how strong the air was, and weak-chested and consumptive people used to throng there for years afterwards.

Fond as I am of cheese, therefore, I hold that George was right in declining to take any.

'We shan't want any tea,' said George (Harris's face fell at this);

27

'but we'll have a good round, square, slap-up meal at seven – dinner, tea, and supper combined.'

Harris grew more cheerful. George suggested meat and fruit pies, cold meat, tomatoes, fruit, and green stuff. For drink, we took some wonderful sticky concoction of Harris's, which you mixed with water and called lemonade, plenty of tea, and a bottle of whisky, in case, as George said, we got upset.

It seemed to me that George harped too much on the getting-upset idea. It seemed to me the wrong spirit to go about the trip in.

But I'm glad we took the whisky.

We didn't take beer or wine. They are a mistake up the river. They make you feel sleepy and heavy. A glass in the evening when you are doing a mooch round the town and looking at the girls is all right enough; but don't drink when the sun is blazing down on your head, and you've got hard work to do.

We made a list of the things to be taken, and a pretty lengthy one it was before we parted that evening. The next day, which was Friday, we got them all together, and met in the evening to pack. We got a big Gladstone[5] for the clothes, and a couple of hampers for the victuals and the cooking utensils. We moved the table up against the window, piled everything in a heap in the middle of the floor, and sat round and looked at it.

I said I'd pack.

I rather pride myself on my packing. Packing is one of those many things that I feel I know more about than any other person living. (It surprises me myself, sometimes, how many of these subjects there are.) I impressed the fact upon George and Harris and told them that they had better leave the whole matter entirely to me. They fell into the suggestion with a readiness that had something uncanny about it. George put on a pipe and spread himself over the easy-chair, and Harris cocked his legs on the table and lit a cigar.

This was hardly what I intended. What I had meant, of course, was, that I should boss the job, and that Harris and George should potter about under my directions, I pushing them aside every now and then with, 'Oh, you –!' 'Here, let me do it.' 'There you are, simple enough!' – really teaching them, as you might say. Their taking it in the way they did irritated me. There is nothing does irritate me more than seeing other people sitting about doing nothing when I'm working.

I lived with a man once who used to make me mad that way. He would loll on the sofa and watch me doing things by the hour together, following me round the room with his eyes, wherever I went. He said it did him real good to look on at me messing about. He said it made him feel that life was not an idle dream to be gaped and yawned through, but a noble task, full of duty and stern work. He said he often wondered now how he could have gone on before he met me, never having anybody to look at while they worked.

Now, I'm not like that. I can't sit still and see another man slaving and working. I want to get up and superintend, and walk round with my hands in my pockets, and tell him what to do. It is my energetic nature. I can't help it.

However, I did not say anything, but started the packing. It seemed a longer job than I had thought it was going to be; but I got the bag finished at last, and I sat on it and strapped it.

'Ain't you going to put the boots in?' said Harris.

And I looked round, and found I had forgotten them. That's just like Harris. He couldn't have said a word until I'd got the bag shut and strapped, of course. And George laughed – one of those irritating, senseless, chuckle-headed, crack-jawed laughs of his. They do make me so wild.

I opened the bag and packed the boots in; and then, just as I was going to close it, a horrible idea occurred to me. Had I packed my tooth-brush? I don't know how it is, but I never do know whether I've packed my tooth-brush.

My tooth-brush is a thing that haunts me when I'm travelling, and makes my life a misery. I dream that I haven't packed it, and wake up in a cold perspiration, and get out of bed and hunt for it. And, in the morning, I pack it before I have used it, and have to unpack again to get it, and it is always the last thing I turn out of the bag; and then I repack and forget it, and have to rush upstairs for it at the last moment and carry it to the railway station wrapped up in my pocket-handkerchief.

Of course I had to turn every mortal thing out now, and, of course, I could not find it. I rummaged the things up into much the same state that they must have been before the world was created, and when chaos reigned. Of course, I found George's and Harris's eighteen times over, but I couldn't find my own. I put the things back one by one, and held everything up and shook it. Then I found it inside a boot. I repacked once more.

When I had finished, George asked if the soap was in. I said I didn't care a hang whether the soap was in or whether it wasn't; and I slammed the bag to and strapped it, and found that I had packed my tobacco pouch in it, and had to reopen it. It got shut up finally at 10.5 p.m., and then there remained the hampers to do. Harris said that we should be wanting to start in less than twelve hours' time and thought that he and George had better do the rest; and I agreed and sat down, and they had a go.

They began in a light-hearted spirit, evidently intending to show me how to do it. I made no comment; I only waited. When George is hanged Harris will be the worst packer in this world; and I looked at the piles of plates and cups, and kettles, and bottles, and jars, and pies, and stoves, and cakes, and tomatoes, etc., and felt that the thing would soon become exciting.

It did. They started with breaking a cup. That was the first thing they did. They did that just to show you what they *could* do, and to get you interested.

Then Harris packed the strawberry jam on top of a tomato and squashed it, and they had to pick out the tomato with a teaspoon.

And then it was George's turn, and he trod on the butter. I didn't say anything, but I came over and sat on the edge of the table and watched them. It irritated them more than anything I could have said. I felt that. It made them nervous and excited, and they stepped on things, and put things behind them, and then couldn't find them when they wanted them; and they packed the pies at the bottom, and put heavy things on top, and smashed the pies in.

They upset salt over everything, and as for the butter! I never saw two men do more with one-and-twopence worth of butter in my whole life than they did. After George had got it off his slipper, they tried to put it in the kettle. It wouldn't go in, and what *was* in wouldn't come out. They did scrape it out at last, and put it down on a chair, and Harris sat on it, and it stuck to him, and they went looking for it all over the room.

'I'll take my oath I put it down on that chair,' said George, staring at the empty seat.

'I saw you do it myself, not a minute ago,' said Harris.

Then they started round the room again looking for it; and then they met again in the centre and stared at one another.

'Most extraordinary thing I ever heard of,' said George. 'So mysterious!' said Harris.

Then George got round at the back of Harris and saw it.

'Why, here it is all the time,' he exclaimed, indignantly.

'Where?' cried Harris, spinning round.

'Stand still, can't you?' roared George, flying after him.

And they got it off, and packed it in the teapot.

Montmorency was in it all, of course. Montmorency's ambition in life is to get in the way and be sworn at. If he can squirm in anywhere where he particularly is not wanted, and be a perfect nuisance, and make people mad, and have things thrown at his head, then he feels his day has not been wasted.

To get somebody to stumble over him, and curse him steadily for an hour, is his highest aim and object; and, when he has succeeded in accomplishing this, his conceit becomes quite unbearable.

He came and sat down on things, just when they were wanted to be packed; and he laboured under the fixed belief that, whenever Harris or George reached out their hand for anything, it was his cold damp nose that they wanted. He put his leg into the jam, and he worried the teaspoons, and he pretended that the lemons were rats, and got into the hamper and killed three of them before Harris could land him with the frying-pan.

Harris said I encouraged him. I didn't encourage him. A dog like that don't want any encouragement. It's the natural, original sin that is born in him that makes him do things like that.

The packing was done at 12.50; and Harris sat on the big hamper, and said he hoped nothing would be found broken. George said that

THREE MEN IN A BOAT

if anything was broken it *was* broken, which reflection seemed to comfort him. He also said he was ready for bed. We were all ready for bed. Harris was to sleep with us that night, and we went upstairs.

We tossed for bed, and Harris had to sleep with me. He said:

'Do you prefer the inside or the outside, J.?'

I said I generally preferred to sleep *inside* a bed.

Harris said it was old.

George said:

'What time shall I wake you fellows?'

Harris said:

'Seven.'

I said:

'No – six,' because I wanted to write some letters.

Harris and I had a bit of a row over it, but at last split the difference, and said half past six.

'Wake us at 6.30, George,' we said.

George made no answer, and we found, on going over, that he had been asleep for some time; so we placed the bath where he could tumble into it on getting out in the morning, and went to bed ourselves.

Chapter 5

Mrs P. arouses us – George, the sluggard – The 'weather forecast' swindle –
Our luggage – Depravity of the small boy – The people gather around us –
We drive off in great style, and arrive at Waterloo – Innocence of South
Western Officials concerning such worldly things as trains – We are afloat,
afloat in an open boat.

It was Mrs Poppets that woke me up next morning.

She said:

'Do you know that it's nearly nine o'clock, sir?'

'Nine o' what?' I cried, starting up.

'Nine o'clock,' she replied, through the keyhole. 'I thought you was a-oversleeping yourselves.'

I woke Harris, and told him. He said:

'I thought you wanted me to get up at six?'

'So I did,' I answered. 'Why didn't you wake me?' he retorted. 'Now we shan't get on the water till after twelve. I wonder you take the trouble to get up at all.'

'Um,' I replied, 'lucky for you that I do. If I hadn't woke you, you'd have lain there for the whole fortnight.'

We snarled at one another in this strain for the next few minutes, when we were interrupted by a defiant snore from George. It reminded us, for the first time since our being called, of his existence. There he lay – the man who had wanted to know what time he should wake us – on his back, with his mouth wide open, and his knees stuck up.

I don't know why it should be, I am sure, but the sight of another man asleep in bed when I am up maddens me. It seems to me so shocking to see the precious hours of a man's life – the priceless moments that will never come back to him again – being wasted in mere brutish sleep.

There was George, throwing away in hideous sloth the inestimable gift of time; his valuable life, every second of which he would have to account for hereafter, passing away from him, unused. He might have been up stuffing himself with eggs and bacon, irritating the dog, or flirting with the slavey, instead of sprawling there, sunk in soul-clogging oblivion.

It was a terrible thought. Harris and I appeared to be struck by it at the same instant. We determined to save him, and, in this noble resolve, our own dispute was forgotten. We flew across and slung the clothes off him, and Harris landed him one with a slipper, and I shouted in his ear, and he awoke.

'Wassermarrer?' he observed, sitting up.

'Get up, you fat-headed chunk!' roared Harris. 'It's quarter to ten.'

'What!' he shrieked, jumping out of bed into the bath; '– Who the thunder put this thing here?'

We told him he must have been a fool not to see the bath.

We finished dressing, and, when it came to the extras, we remembered that we had packed the tooth-brushes and the brush and comb (that tooth-brush of mine will be the death of me, I know), and we had to go downstairs, and fish them out of the bag. And when we had done that, George wanted the shaving tackle. We told him that he would have to go without shaving that morning, as we weren't going to unpack that bag again for him, nor for anyone like him.

He said:

'Don't be absurd. How can I go into the City like this?'

It was certainly rather tough on the City, but what cared we for human suffering? As Harris said, in his common, vulgar way, the City would have to lump it.

We went downstairs to breakfast. Montmorency had invited two other dogs to come and see him off, and they were whiling away the time by fighting on the doorstep. We calmed them with an umbrella, and sat down to chops and cold beef.

Harris said:

'The great thing is to make a good breakfast,' and he started with a couple of chops, saying that he would take these while they were hot, as the beef could wait.

George got hold of the paper, and read us out the boating fatalities, and the weather forecast, which latter prophesied 'rain, cold, wet to fine' (whatever more than usually ghastly thing in weather that may be), 'occasional local thunderstorms, east wind, with general depression over the Midland Counties (London and Channel). Bar. falling.'

I do think that of all the silly, irritating tomfoolishness by which we are plagued, this 'weather-forecast' fraud is about the most aggravating. It 'forecasts' precisely what happened yesterday or the day before, and precisely the opposite of what is going to happen today.

I remember a holiday of mine being completely ruined one late autumn by our paying attention to the weather report of the local newspaper. 'Heavy showers, with thunderstorms, may be expected today', it would say on Monday, and so we would give up our picnic, and stop indoors all day, waiting for the rain. And people would pass the house, going off in wagonettes and coaches as jolly and merry as could be, the sun shining out, and not a cloud to be seen.

'Ah!' we said, as we stood looking out at them through the window, 'won't they come home soaked!'

And we chuckled to think how wet they were going to get, and came back and stirred the fire, and got our books, and arranged our specimens of seaweed and cockleshells. By twelve o'clock with the sun pouring into the room, the heat became quite oppressive, and we wondered when those heavy showers and occasional thunderstorms were going to begin.

'Ah! They'll come in the afternoon, you'll find,' we said to each other. 'Oh, *won't* those people get wet. What a lark!'

At one o'clock the landlady would come in to ask if we weren't going out, as it seemed such a lovely day.

'No, no,' we replied, with a knowing chuckle, 'not we. *We* don't mean to get wet – no, no.'

And when the afternoon was nearly gone, and still there was no sign of rain, we tried to cheer ourselves up with the idea that it would come down all at once, just as people had started for home, and were out of the reach of any shelter, and that they would thus get more drenched than ever. But not a drop ever fell, and it finished a grand day, and a lovely night after it.

The next morning we would read that it was going to be a 'warm, fine to set-fair day; much heat'; and we would dress ourselves in flimsy things, and go out, and, half an hour after we had started, it would commence to rain hard, and a bitterly cold wind would spring up, and both would keep on steadily for the whole day, and we would come home with colds and rheumatism all over us, and go to bed.

The weather is a thing that is beyond me altogether. I never can understand it. The barometer is useless; it is as misleading as the newspaper forecast.

There was one hanging up in a hotel at Oxford at which I was staying last spring, and, when I got there, it was pointing to 'set fair'. It was simply pouring with rain outside, and had been all day; and I couldn't quite make matters out. I tapped the barometer, and it jumped up and pointed to 'very dry'. The Boots[1] stopped as he was passing and said he expected it meant tomorrow. I fancied that maybe it was thinking of the week before last, but Boots said, No, he thought not.

I tapped it again the next morning, and it went up still higher, and the rain came down faster than ever. On Wednesday I went and hit it again, and the pointer went round towards 'set fair', 'very dry', and 'much heat', until it was stopped by the peg, and couldn't go any further. It tried its best, but the instrument was built so that it couldn't prophesy fine weather any harder than it did without breaking itself. It evidently wanted to go on, and prognosticate drought, and water famine, and sunstroke, and simooms, and such things, but the peg prevented it, and it had to be content with pointing to the mere commonplace 'very dry'.

Meanwhile, the rain came down in a steady torrent, and the lower part of the town was under water, owing to the river having overflowed.

Boots said it was evident that we were going to have a prolonged spell of grand weather *some time*, and read out a poem which was printed over the top of the oracle, about

Long foretold, long past;
Short notice, soon past.

The fine weather never came that summer. I expect that machine must have been referring to the following spring.

Then there are those new style of barometers, the long straight ones. I never can make head or tail of those. There is one side for 10 a.m. yesterday, and one side for 10 a.m. today; but you can't always get there as early as ten, you know. It rises or falls for rain and fine, with much or less wind, and one end is 'Nly' and the other 'Ely' (what's Ely got to do with it?), and if you tap it, it doesn't tell you anything. And you've got to correct it to sea-level and reduce it to Fahrenheit, and even then I don't know the answer.

But who wants to be foretold the weather? It is bad enough when it comes, without our having the misery of knowing about it beforehand. The prophet we like is the old man who, on the particularly gloomy-looking morning of some day when we particularly want it to be fine, looks round the horizon with a particularly knowing eye, and says:

'Oh, no, sir, I think it will clear up all right. It will break all right enough, sir.'

'Ah, he knows,' we say, as we wish him good-morning, and start off; 'wonderful how these old fellows can tell!'

And we feel an affection for that man which is not at all lessened by the circumstance of its *not* clearing up, but continuing to rain steadily all day.

'Ah, well,' we feel, 'he did his best.'

For the man that prophesies us bad weather, on the contrary, we entertain only bitter and revengeful thoughts.

'Going to clear up, d'ye think?' we shout, cheerily, as we pass.

'Well, no, sir; I'm afraid it's settled down for the day,' he replies, shaking his head.

'Stupid old fool!' we mutter, 'what's *he* know about it?' And, if his portent proves correct, we come back feeling still more angry against him, and with a vague notion that, somehow or other, he has had something to do with it.

It was too bright and sunny on this especial morning for George's blood-curdling readings about 'Bar. falling', 'atmospheric disturbance, passing in an oblique line over Southern Europe', and 'pressure increasing', to very much upset us; and so, finding that he could not make us wretched, and was only wasting his time, he sneaked the cigarette that I had carefully rolled up for myself, and went.

Then Harris and I, having finished up the few things left on the table, carted out our luggage on to the doorstep, and waited for a cab.

There seemed a good deal of luggage, when we put it all together. There was the Gladstone and the small hand-bag, and the two hampers, and a large roll of rugs, and some four or five overcoats and mackintoshes, and a few umbrellas, and then there was a melon by itself in a bag, because it was too bulky to go in anywhere, and a couple of pounds of grapes in another bag, and a Japanese paper umbrella, and a frying pan, which, being too long to pack, we had wrapped round with brown paper.

It did look a lot, and Harris and I began to feel rather ashamed of it, though why we should be, I can't see. No cab came by, but the street boys did, and got interested in the show, apparently, and stopped.

Biggs's boy was the first to come round. Biggs is our greengrocer, and his chief talent lies in securing the services of the most abandoned

37

and unprincipled errand-boys that civilization has as yet produced. If anything more than usually villainous in the boy-line crops up in our neighbourhood, we know that it is Biggs's latest. I was told that, at the time of the Great Coram Street murder,[2] it was promptly concluded by our street that Biggs's boy (for that period) was at the bottom of it, and had he not been able, in reply to the severe cross-examination to which he was subjected by No. 19, when he called there for orders the morning after the crime (assisted by No. 21, who happened to be on the step at the time), to prove a complete alibi, it would have gone hard with him. I didn't know Biggs's boy at that time, but, from what I have seen of them since, I should not have attached much importance to that alibi myself.

Biggs's boy, as I have said, came round the corner. He was evidently in a great hurry when he first dawned upon the vision, but, on catching sight of Harris and me, and Montmorency, and the things, he eased up and stared. Harris and I frowned at him. This might have wounded a more sensitive nature, but Biggs's boys are not, as a rule, touchy. He came to a dead stop, a yard from our step, and, leaning up against the railing, and selecting a straw to chew, fixed us with his eye. He evidently meant to see this thing out.

In another moment, the grocer's boy passed on the opposite side of the street. Biggs's boy hailed him:

'Hi! ground floor o' 42's a-moving.'

The grocer's boy came across, and took up a position on the other side of the step. Then the young gentleman from the boot-shop stopped, and joined Biggs's boy; while the empty-can superintendent from 'The Blue Posts' took up an independent position on the kerb.

'They ain't a-going to starve, are they?' said the gentleman from the boot-shop.

'Ah! you'd want to take a thing or two with *you*,' retorted 'The Blue Posts', 'if you was a-going to cross the Atlantic in a small boat.'

'They ain't a-going to cross the Atlantic,' struck in Biggs's boy; 'they're a-going to find Stanley.'[3]

By this time, quite a small crowd had collected, and people were asking each other what was the matter. One party (the young and giddy portion of the crowd) held that it was a wedding, and pointed out Harris as the bridegroom; while the elder and more thoughtful among the populace inclined to the idea that it was a funeral, and that I was probably the corpse's brother.

At last, an empty cab turned up (it is a street where, as a rule, and when they are not wanted, empty cabs pass at the rate of three a minute, and hang about, and get in your way), and packing ourselves and our belongings into it, and shooting out a couple of Montmorency's friends, who had evidently sworn never to forsake him, we drove away amidst the cheers of the crowd, Biggs's boy shying a carrot after us for luck.

We got to Waterloo at eleven, and asked where the eleven-five started from. Of course nobody knew; nobody at Waterloo ever does know where a train is going to start from, or where a train when it does start is going to, or anything about it. The porter who took our things thought it would go from number two platform, while another porter, with whom he discussed the question, had heard a rumour that it would go from number one. The stationmaster, on the other hand, was convinced it would start from the local.

To put an end to the matter we went upstairs and asked the traffic superintendent, and he told us that he had just met a man who said he had seen it at number three platform. We went to number three platform, but the authorities there said that they rather thought that train was the Southampton express, or else the Windsor loop. But they were sure it wasn't the Kingston train, though why they were sure it wasn't they couldn't say.

Then our porter said he thought that it must be it on the high-level platform; said he thought he knew the train. So we went to the high-level platform and saw the engine-driver, and asked him if he was going to Kingston. He said he couldn't say for certain of course, but that he rather thought he was. Anyhow, if he wasn't the 11.5 for Kingston, he said he was pretty confident he was the 9.32 for Virginia Water, or the 10 a.m. express for the Isle of Wight, or somewhere in that direction, and we should all know when we got there. We slipped half-a-crown into his hand, and begged him to be the 11.5 for Kingston.

'Nobody will ever know, on this line,' we said, 'what you are, or where you're going. You know the way, you slip off quietly and go to Kingston.'

'Well, I don't know, gents,' replied the noble fellow, 'but I suppose *some* train's got to go to Kingston; and I'll do it. Gimme the half-crown.'

Thus we got to Kingston by the London and South-Western Railway.

We learnt afterwards that the train we had come by was really the Exeter mail, and that they had spent hours at Waterloo looking for it, and nobody knew what had become of it.

Our boat was waiting for us at Kingston just below the bridge, and to it we wended our way, and round it we stored our luggage, and into it we stepped.

'Are you all right, sir?' said the man.

'Right it is,' we answered; and with Harris at the sculls and I at the tiller-lines, and Montmorency, unhappy and deeply suspicious, in the prow, out we shot on to the waters which, for a fortnight, were to be our home.

Chapter 6

Kingston – Instructive remarks on early English history – Instructive observations on carved oak and life in general – Sad case of Stivvings, junior – Musings on antiquity – I forget that I am steering – Interesting result – Hampton Court Maze – Harris as a guide.

It was a glorious morning, late spring or early summer, as you care to take it, when the dainty sheen of grass and leaf is blushing to a deeper green; and the year seems like a fair young maid, trembling with strange, wakening pulses on the brink of womanhood.

The quaint back-streets of Kingston, where they came down to the water's edge, looked quite picturesque in the flashing sunlight, the glinting river with its drifting barges, the wooded towpath, the trim-kept villas on the other side, Harris, in a red and orange blazer, grunting away at the sculls, the distant glimpses of the grey old palace of the Tudors, all made a sunny picture, so bright but calm, so full of life, and yet so peaceful, that, early in the day though it was, I felt myself being dreamily lulled off into a musing fit.

I mused on Kingston, or 'Kyningestun', as it was once called in the days when Saxon 'kinges' were crowned there.[1] Great Caesar crossed the river there, and the Roman legions camped upon its sloping uplands. Caesar, like, in later years, Elizabeth, seems to have stopped everywhere: only he was more respectable than good Queen Bess; he didn't put up at the public-houses.

She was nuts on public-houses, was England's Virgin Queen. There's scarcely a pub of any attractions within ten miles of London that she does not seem to have looked in at, or stopped at, or slept at, some time or other. I wonder now, supposing Harris, say, turned over a new leaf, and became a great and good man, and got to be Prime Minister, and died, if they would put up signs over the public-houses that he had patronized: 'Harris had a glass of bitter in this house'; 'Harris had two of Scotch cold here in the summer of '88'; 'Harris was chucked from here in December 1886'.

No, there would be too many of them! It would be the houses that he had never entered that would become famous. 'Only house in South London that Harris never had a drink in!' The people would flock to it to see what could have been the matter with it.

How poor weak-minded King Edwy must have hated Kyningestun! The coronation feast had been too much for him. Maybe boar's head stuffed with sugar-plums did not agree with him (it wouldn't with me, I know), and he had had enough of sack and mead;[2] so he slipped from the noisy revel to steal a quiet moonlight hour with his beloved Elgiva.

Perhaps from the casement, standing hand-in-hand, they were watching the calm moonlight on the river, while from the distant halls the boisterous revelry floated in broken bursts of faint-heard din and tumult.

Then brutal Odo and St Dunstan force their rude way into the quiet room, and hurl coarse insults at the sweet-faced Queen, and drag poor Edwy back to the loud clamour of the drunken brawl.

Years later, to the crash of battle-music, Saxon kings and Saxon revelry were buried side by side, and Kingston's greatness passed away for a time, to rise once more when Hampton Court became the palace of the Tudors and the Stuarts, and the royal barges strained at their moorings on the river's bank, and bright-cloaked gallants swaggered down the water-steps to cry: 'What Ferry, ho! Gadzooks, gramercy.'

Many of the old houses, round about, speak very plainly of those days when Kingston was a royal borough, and nobles and courtiers lived there, near their King, and the long road to the palace gates was gay all day with clanking steel and prancing palfreys and rustling silks and velvets, and fair faces. The large and spacious houses, with their oriel, latticed windows, their huge fireplaces, and their gabled roofs, breathe of the days of hose and doublet, of pearl-embroidered stomachers, and complicated oaths. They were upraised in the days 'when men knew how to build'. The hard red bricks have only grown more firmly set with time, and their oak stairs do not creak and grunt when you try to go down them quietly.

Speaking of oak staircases reminds me that there is a magnificent carved oak staircase in one of the houses in Kingston. It is a shop now, in the market-place, but it was evidently once the mansion of some great personage. A friend of mine, who lives at Kingston, went in there to buy a hat one day, and, in a thoughtless moment, put his hand in his pocket and paid for it then and there.

The shopman (he knows my friend) was naturally a little staggered at first; but, quickly recovering himself, and feeling that something ought to be done to encourage this sort of thing, asked our hero if he would like to see some fine old carved oak. My friend said he would, and the shopman, thereupon, took him through the shop, and up the staircase of the house. The balusters were a superb piece of workmanship and the wall all the way up was oak-panelled, with carving that would have done credit to a palace.

From the stairs they went into the drawing-room, which was a large, bright room, decorated with a somewhat startling though cheerful paper of a blue ground. There was nothing, however, remarkable about the apartment, and my friend wondered why he had been brought there. The proprietor went up to the paper, and tapped it. It gave forth a wooden sound.

'Oak,' he explained. 'All carved oak, right up to the ceiling, just the same as you saw on the staircase.'

'But, great Caesar! man,' expostulated my friend; 'you don't mean to say you have covered over the carved oak with blue wall-paper?'

'Yes,' was the reply: 'it was expensive work. Had to match-board it all over first, of course. But the room looks cheerful now. It was awful gloomy before.'

I can't say I altogether blame the man (which is doubtless a great relief to his mind). From his point of view, which would be that of the average householder, desiring to take life as lightly as possible, and not that of the old curiosity-shop maniac, there is reason on his side. Carved oak is very pleasant to look at, and to have a little of, but it is no doubt somewhat depressing to live in, for those whose fancy does not lie that way. It would be like living in a church.

No, what was sad in his case was that he, who didn't care for carved oak, should have his drawing-room panelled with it, while people who do care for it have to pay enormous prices to get it. It seems to be the rule of this world. Each person has what he doesn't want, and other people have what he does want.

Married men have wives, and don't seem to want them; and young single fellows cry out that they can't get them. Poor people who can hardly keep themselves have eight hearty children. Rich old couples, with no one to leave their money to, die childless.

Then there are girls with lovers. The girls that have lovers never want them. They say they would rather be without them, that they bother them, and why don't they go and make love to Miss Smith and Miss Brown, who are plain and elderly, and haven't got any lovers? They themselves don't want lovers. They never mean to marry.

It does not do to dwell on these things; it makes one so sad.

There was a boy at our school, we used to call him Sandford and Merton.[3] His real name was Stivvings. He was the most extraordinary lad I ever came across. I believe he really liked study. He used to get into awful rows for sitting up in bed and reading Greek; and as for French irregular verbs, there was simply no keeping him away from them. He was full of weird and unnatural notions about being a credit to his parents and an honour to the school; and he yearned to win prizes, and grow up and be a clever man, and had all those sort of weak-minded ideas. I never knew such a strange creature, yet harmless, mind you, as the babe unborn.

Well, that boy used to get ill about twice a week, so that he couldn't go to school. There never was such a boy to get ill as that Sandford and Merton. If there was any known disease going within ten miles of him, he had it, and had it badly. He would take bronchitis in the dog-days, and have hayfever at Christmas. After a six weeks' period of drought, he would be stricken down with rheumatic fever; and he would go out in a November fog and come home with a sunstroke.

They put him under laughing-gas one year, poor lad, and drew all his teeth, and gave him a false set, because he suffered so terribly with toothache; and then it turned to neuralgia and ear-ache. He was never without a cold, except once for nine weeks while he had scarlet fever; and he always had chilblains. During the great cholera scare of 1871,[4] our neighbourhood was singularly free from it. There was only one reputed case in the whole parish: that case was young Stivvings.

He had to stop in bed when he was ill, and eat chicken and custards and hot-house grapes; and he would lie there and sob, because they wouldn't let him do Latin exercises, and took his German grammar away from him.

And we other boys, who would have sacrificed ten terms of our school life for the sake of being ill for a day, and had no desire whatever to give our parents any excuse for being stuck-up about us, couldn't catch so much as a stiff neck. We fooled about in draughts, and it did us good, and freshened us up; and we took things to make us sick, and they made us fat, and gave us an appetite. Nothing we could think of seemed to make us ill until the holidays began. Then, on the breaking-up day, we caught colds, and whooping cough, and all kinds of disorders, which lasted till the term recommenced; when, in spite of everything we could manoeuvre to the contrary, we would get suddenly well again, and be better than ever.

Such is life; and we are but as grass that is cut down, and put into the oven and baked.

To go back to the carved oak question, they must have had very fair notions of the artistic and the beautiful, our great-great-grandfathers. Why, all our art treasures of today are only the dug-up commonplaces of three or four hundred years ago. I wonder if there is any real intrinsic beauty in the old soup-plates, beer-mugs, and candle-snuffers that we prize so now, or if it is only the halo of age glowing around them that gives them their charms in our eyes. The 'old blue'[5] that we hang about our walls as ornaments were the common every-day household utensils of a few centuries ago; and the pink shepherds and the yellow shepherdesses that we hand round now for all our friends to gush over, and pretend they understand, were the unvalued mantel-ornaments that the mother of the eighteenth century would have given the baby to suck when he cried.

Will it be the same in the future? Will the prized treasures of today always be the cheap trifles of the day before? Will rows of our willow-pattern dinner-plates be ranged above the chimney-pieces of the great in the years 2000 and odd? Will the white cups with the gold rim and the beautiful gold flower inside (species unknown), that our Sarah Janes[6] now break in sheer light-heartedness of spirit, be carefully mended, and stood upon a bracket, and dusted only by the lady of the house?

That china dog that ornaments the bedroom of my furnished lodgings. It is a white dog. Its eyes are blue. Its nose is a delicate red, with black spots. Its head is painfully erect, and its expression is amiability carried to the verge of imbecility. I do not admire it myself. Considered as a work of art, I may say it irritates me. Thoughtless friends jeer at it, and even my landlady herself has no admiration for it, and excuses its presence by the circumstance that her aunt gave it to her.

But in 200 years' time it is more than probable that that dog will be dug up from somewhere or other, minus its legs, and with its tail broken, and will be sold for old china, and put in a glass cabinet. And people will pass it round and admire it. They will be struck by the wonderful depth of the colour on the nose, and speculate as to how beautiful the bit of the tail that is lost no doubt was.

We, in this age, do not see the beauty of that dog. We are too familiar with it. It is like the sunset and the stars: we are not awed by their loveliness because they are common to our eyes. So it is with that china dog. In 2288 people will gush over it. The making of such dogs will have become a lost art. Our descendants will wonder how we did it, and say how clever we were. We shall be referred to lovingly as 'those grand old artists that flourished in the nineteenth century, and produced those china dogs'.

The 'sampler' that the eldest daughter did at school will be spoken of as 'tapestry of the Victorian era', and be almost priceless. The blue-and-white mugs of the present-day road-side inn will be hunted up, all cracked and chipped, and sold for their weight in gold, and rich people will use them for claret cups; and travellers from Japan will buy up the 'Presents from Ramsgate', and 'Souvenirs of Margate', that may have escaped destruction, and take them back to Jedo as ancient English curios.

At this point, Harris threw away the sculls, got up and left his seat, and sat on his back, and stuck his legs in the air. Montmorency howled, and turned a somersault, and the top hamper jumped up, and all the things came out.

I was somewhat surprised, but I did not lose my temper. I said, pleasantly enough:

'Hulloa! what's that for?'

'What's that for? Why –'

No, on second thoughts, I will not repeat what Harris said. I may have been to blame, I admit it; but nothing excuses violence of language and coarseness of expression, especially in a man who has been carefully brought up, as I know Harris has been. I was thinking of other things, and forgot, as anyone might easily understand, that I was steering, and the consequence was that we had got mixed up a good deal with the tow-path. It was difficult to say, for the moment, which was us and which was the Middlesex bank of the river, but we found out after a while, and separated ourselves.

Harris, however, said he had done enough for a bit, and proposed that I should take a turn; so, as we were in, I got out and took the tow-line, and ran the boat on past Hampton Court.[7] What a dear old wall that is that runs along by the river there! I never pass it without feeling better for the sight of it. Such a mellow, bright, sweet old wall; what a charming picture it would make, with the lichen creeping here and the moss growing there, a shy young vine peeping over the top at this spot, to see what is going on upon the busy river, and the sober old ivy clustering a little farther down! There are fifty shades and tints and hues in every ten yards of that old wall. If I could only draw, and knew how to paint, I could make a lovely sketch of that old wall, I'm sure. I've often thought I should like to live at Hampton Court. It looks so peaceful and so quiet, and it is such a dear old place to ramble round in the early morning before many people are about.

But, there, I don't suppose I should really care for it when it came to actual practice. It would be so ghastly dull and depressing in the evening, when your lamp cast uncanny shadows on the panelled walls, and the echo of distant feet rang through the cold stone corridors, and now drew nearer, and now died away, and all was death-like silence, save the beating of one's own heart.

We are creatures of the sun, we men and women. We love light and life. That is why we crowd into the towns and cities, and the country grows more and more deserted every year. In the sunlight – in the daytime, when Nature is alive and busy all around us, we like the open hillsides and the deep woods well enough: but in the night, when our Mother Earth has gone to sleep, and left us waking, oh! the world seems so lonesome, and we get frightened, like children in a silent house. Then we sit and sob, and long for the gas-lit streets, and the sound of human voices, and the answering throb of human life. We feel so helpless and so little in the great stillness, when the dark trees rustle in the night-wind. There are so many ghosts about, and their silent sighs make us feel so sad. Let us gather together in the great cities, and light huge bonfires of a million gas-jets, and shout and ring together and feel brave.

Harris asked me if I'd ever been in the maze[8] at Hampton Court. He said he went in once to show somebody else the way. He had studied it up in a map, and it was so simple that it seemed foolish – hardly worth the twopence charged for admission. Harris said he thought the map must have been got up as a practical joke, because it wasn't a bit like the real thing, and only misleading. It was a country cousin that Harris took in. He said:

'We'll just go in here, so that you can say you've been, but it's very simple. It's absurd to call it a maze. You keep on taking the first turning to the right. We'll just walk round for ten minutes, and then go and get some lunch.'

They met some people soon after they had got inside, who said they had been there for three quarters of an hour, and had had about enough of it. Harris told them they could follow him if they liked; he was just going in, and then should turn round and come out again. They said it was very kind of him, and fell behind, and followed.

They picked up various other people who wanted to get it over, as they went along, until they absorbed all the persons in the maze. People who had given up all hopes of ever getting either in or out, or of ever seeing their home and friends again, plucked up courage at the sight of Harris and his party, and joined the procession, blessing him. Harris said he should judge there must have been twenty people following him, in all; and one woman with a baby, who had been there all the morning, insisted on taking his arm, for fear of losing him.

Harris kept on turning to the right, but it seemed a long way, and his cousin said he supposed it was a very big maze.

'Oh, one of the largest in Europe,' said Harris.

'Yes, it must be,' replied the cousin, 'because we've walked a good two miles already.'

Harris began to think it rather strange himself, but he held on until, at last, they passed the half a penny bun on the ground that Harris's cousin swore he had noticed there seven minutes ago. Harris said: 'Oh, impossible!' but the woman with the baby said, 'Not at all,' as she herself had taken it from the child, and thrown it down there, just before she met Harris. She also added that she wished she never had met Harris, and expressed an opinion that he was an impostor. That made Harris mad, and he produced his map, and explained his theory.

'That map may be all right enough,' said one of the party, 'if you know whereabouts in it we are now.'

Harris didn't know, and suggested that the best thing to do would be to go back to the entrance, and begin again. For the beginning again part of it there was not much enthusiasm; but with regard to the advisability of going back to the entrance there was complete unanimity, and so they turned, and trailed after Harris again, in the opposite direction. About ten minutes more passed, and then they found themselves in the centre.

Harris thought at first of pretending that that was what he had been aiming at; but the crowd looked dangerous, and he decided to treat it as an accident.

Anyhow, they had got something to start from then. They did know where they were, and the map was once more consulted, and the thing seemed simpler than ever, and off they started for the third time.

And three minutes later they were back in the centre again.

After that they simply couldn't get anywhere else. Whatever way they turned brought them back to the middle. It became so regular at length, that some of the people stopped there, and waited for the others to take a walk round, and come back to them. Harris drew out his map again, after a while, but the sight of it only infuriated the mob, and they told him to go and curl his hair with it. Harris said that he couldn't help feeling that, to a certain extent, he had become unpopular.

They all got crazy at last, and sang out for the keeper, and the man came and climbed up the ladder outside, and shouted out directions to them. But all their heads were, by this time, in such a confused whirl that they were incapable of grasping anything, and so the man told them to stop where they were, and he would come to them. They huddled together, and waited; and he climbed down, and came in.

He was a young keeper, as luck would have it, and new to the business; and when he got in, he couldn't get to them, and then *he* got lost. They caught sight of him, every now and then, rushing about the other side of the hedge, and he would see them, and rush to get to them, and they would wait there for about five minutes, and then he would reappear again in exactly the same spot, and ask them where they had been.

They had to wait until one of the old keepers came back from his dinner before they got out.

Harris said he thought it was a very fine maze, so far as he was a judge; and we agreed that we would try to get George to go into it, on our way back.

Chapter 7

*The river in its Sunday garb – Dress on the river – A chance for the men –
Absence of taste in Harris – George's blazer – A day with the fashion-plate
young lady – Mrs Thomas's tomb – The man who loves not graves and
coffins and skulls – Harris mad – His views on George and banks
and lemonade – He performs tricks.*

It was while passing through Moulsey lock[1] that Harris told me about his maze experience. It took us some time to pass through, as we were the only boat, and it is a big lock. I don't think I ever remember to have seen Moulsey lock, before, with only one boat in it. It is, I suppose, Boulter's not even excepted, the busiest lock on the river.

I have stood and watched it sometimes, when you could not see any water at all, but only a brilliant tangle of bright blazers, and gay caps, and saucy hats, and many-coloured parasols, and silken rugs, and cloaks, and streaming ribbons, and dainty whites; when looking down into the lock from the quay, you might fancy it was a huge box into which flowers of every hue and shade had been thrown pell-mell and lay piled up in a rainbow heap that covered every corner.

On a fine Sunday it presents this appearance nearly all day long, while, up the stream, and down the stream, lie, waiting their turn, outside the gates, long lines of still more boats; and boats are drawing near and passing away, so that the sunny river, from the Palace up to Hampton Church, is dotted and decked with yellow, and blue, and orange, and white, and red, and pink. All the inhabitants of Hampton and Moulsey dress themselves up in boating costume, and come and mooch round the lock with their dogs, and flirt, and smoke, and watch the boats, and altogether, what with the caps and jackets of the men, the pretty coloured dresses of the women, the excited dogs, the moving boats, the white sails, the pleasant landscape, and the sparkling water, it is one of the gayest sights I know of near this dull old London town.

The river affords a good opportunity for dress. For once in a way, we men are able to show *our* taste in colours, and I think we come out very natty, if you ask me. I always like a little red in my things – red and black. You know my hair is a sort of golden brown, rather a pretty shade I've been told, and a dark red matches it beautifully; and then I always think a light-blue necktie goes so well with it, and a pair of those Russian-leather shoes and a red silk handkerchief round the waist – a handkerchief looks so much better than a belt.

Harris always keeps to shades or mixtures of orange or yellow, but I don't think he is at all wise in this. His complexion is too dark for yellows. Yellows don't suit him; there can be no question about it. I want him to take to blue as a background, with white or cream for relief; but, there! the less taste a person has in dress, the more obstinate he always seems to be. It is a great pity, because he will never be a success as it is, while there are one or two colours in which he might not really look so bad, with his hat on.

George has bought some new things for this trip, and I'm rather vexed about them. The blazer is loud. I should not like George to know that I thought so, but there really is no other word for it. He brought it home and showed it to us on Thursday evening. We asked him what colour he called it, and he said he didn't know. He didn't think there was a name for the colour. The man had told him it was an Oriental design. George put it on, and asked us what we thought of it. Harris said that, as an object to hang over a flower-bed in early spring to frighten the birds away, he should respect it; but that, considered as an article of dress for a human being, except a Margate nigger,[2] it made him ill. George got quite huffy; but as Harris said, if he didn't want his opinion, why did he ask for it?

What troubles Harris and myself, with regard to it, is that we are afraid it will attract attention to the boat.

Girls, also, don't look half bad in a boat, if prettily dressed. Nothing is more fetching, to my thinking, than a tasteful boating costume. But a 'boating costume', it would be as well if all ladies would understand, ought to be a costume that can be worn in a boat, and not merely under a glass case. It utterly spoils an excursion if you have folk in the boat who are thinking all the time a good deal more of their dress than of the trip. It was my misfortune once to go for a water picnic with two ladies of this kind. We did have a lively time!

They were both beautifully got up – all lace and silky stuff, and flowers, and ribbons, and dainty shoes, and light gloves. But they were dressed for a photographic studio, not for a river picnic. They were the 'boating costumes' of a French fashion plate. It was ridiculous, fooling about in them anywhere near real earth, air, and water.

The first thing was that they thought the boat was not clean. We dusted all the seats for them, and then assured them that it was, but they didn't believe us. One of them rubbed the cushion with the forefinger of her glove, and showed the result to the other, and they both sighed, and sat down, with the air of early Christian martyrs trying to make themselves comfortable up against the stake. You are liable to occasionally splash a little when sculling, and it appeared that a drop of water ruined those costumes. The mark never came out, and a stain was left on the dress for ever.

I was stroke. I did my best. I feathered some two feet high, and I paused at the end of each stroke to let the blades drip before returning them, and I picked out a smooth bit of water to drop them into again each time. (Bow said, after a while, that he did not feel himself a sufficiently accomplished oarsman to pull with me, but that he would sit still, if I would allow him, and study my stroke. He said it interested him.) But notwithstanding all this, and try as I would, I could not help an occasional flicker of water from going over those dresses.

The girls did not complain, but they huddled up close together, and set their lips firm, and every time a drop touched them, they visibly shrank and shuddered. It was a noble sight to see them suffering thus in silence, but it unnerved me altogether. I am too sensitive. I got wild and fitful in my rowing, and splashed more and more, the harder I tried not to.

I gave it up at last; I said I'd row bow. Bow thought the arrangement would be better too, and we changed places. The ladies gave an involuntary sigh of relief when they saw me go, and quite brightened up for a moment. Poor girls! they had better have put up with me. The man they had got now was a jolly, light-hearted, thick-headed sort of chap with about as much sensitiveness in him as there might be in a Newfoundland puppy. You might look daggers at him for an hour and he would not notice it, and it would not trouble him if he did. He set a good, rollicking, dashing stroke that sent the spray playing all over the boat like a fountain, and made the whole crowd sit up straight in no time. When he spread more than a pint of water over one of those dresses, he would give a pleasant little laugh, and say:

'I beg your pardon, I'm sure'; and offer them his handkerchief to wipe it off with.

'Oh, it's of no consequence,' the poor girls would murmur in reply, and covertly draw rugs and coats over themselves, and try and protect themselves with their lace parasols.

At lunch they had a very bad time of it. People wanted them to sit on the grass, and the grass was dusty; and the tree-trunks, against which they were invited to lean, did not appear to have been brushed for weeks; so they spread their handkerchiefs on the ground, and sat on those, bolt upright. Somebody, in walking about with a plate of beef-steak pie, tripped up over a root, and sent the pie flying. None of it went over them, fortunately, but the accident suggested a fresh danger to them, and agitated them; and, whenever anybody moved about, after that, with anything in his hand that could fall and make a mess, they watched that person with growing anxiety until he sat down again.

'Now then, you girls,' said our friend bow to them, cheerily, after it was all over, 'come along, you've got to wash up!'

They didn't understand him at first. When they grasped the idea, they said they feared they did not know how to wash up.

'Oh, I'll soon show you,' he cried; 'it's rare fun! You lie down on your – I mean you lean over the bank, you know, and slush the things about in the water.'

The elder sister said that she was afraid that they hadn't got on dresses suited to the work.

'Oh, they'll be all right,' said he lightheartedly; 'tuck 'em up.'

And he made them do it, too. He told them that that sort of thing was half the fun of a picnic. They said it was very interesting.

Now I come to think it over, was that young man as dense-headed as we thought? or was he – no, impossible! there was such a simple, child-like expression about him!

Harris wanted to get out at Hampton Church, to go and see Mrs Thomas's tomb.

'Who is Mrs Thomas?' I asked.

'How should I know?' replied Harris. 'She's a lady that's got a funny tomb, and I want to see it.'

I objected. I don't know whether it is that I am built wrong, but I never did seem to hanker after tombstones myself. I know that the proper thing to do, when you get to a village or town, is to rush off to the churchyard, and enjoy the graves; but it is a recreation that I always deny myself. I take no interest in creeping round dim and chilly churches behind wheezy old men, and reading epitaphs. Not even the sight of a bit of cracked brass let into a stone affords me what I call real happiness.

I shock respectable sextons by the imperturbability I am able to assume before exciting inscriptions, and by my lack of enthusiasm for the local family history, while my ill-concealed anxiety to get outside wounds their feelings.

One golden morning of a sunny day, I leant against the low stone wall that guarded a little village church, and I smoked, and drank in deep, calm gladness from the sweet, restful scene – the grey old church with its clustering ivy and its quaint carved wooden porch, the white lane winding down the hill between tall rows of elms, the thatched-roof cottages peeping above their trim-kept hedges, the silver river in the hollow, the wooded hills beyond!

It was a lovely landscape. It was idyllic, poetical, and it inspired me. I felt good and noble. I felt I didn't want to be sinful and wicked any more. I would come and live here, and never do any more wrong, and lead a blameless, beautiful life, and have silver hair when I got old, and all that sort of thing.

In that moment I forgave all my friends and relations for their wickedness and cussedness, and I blessed them. They did not know that I blessed them. They went their abandoned way all unconscious of what I, far away in that peaceful village, was doing for them; but I did it, and I wished that I could let them know that I had done it, because I wanted to make them happy. I was going on thinking away all these grand, tender thoughts, when my reverie was broken in upon by a shrill piping voice crying out:

'All right, sur; I'm a-coming, I'm a-coming. It's all right, sur; don't you be in a hurry.'

I looked up, and saw an old bald-headed man hobbling across the churchyard towards me, carrying a huge bunch of keys in his hand that shook and jingled at every step.

I motioned him away with silent dignity, but he still advanced, screeching out the while:

'I'm a-coming, sur, I'm a-coming. I'm a little lame. I ain't as spry as I used to be. This way, sur.'

'Go away, you miserable old man,' I said.

'I've come as soon as I could, sur,' he replied. 'My missis never see you till just this minute. You follow me, sur.'

'Go away,' I repeated; 'leave me before I get over the wall, and slay you.'

He seemed surprised.

'Don't you want to see the tombs?' he said.

'No,' I answered. 'I don't. I want to stop here, leaning up against this gritty old wall. Go away, and don't disturb me. I am chock full of beautiful and noble thoughts, and I want to stop like it, because it feels nice and good. Don't you come fooling about, making me mad, chivvying away all my better feelings with this silly tombstone nonsense of yours. Go away, and get somebody to bury you cheap, and I'll pay half the expense.'

He was bewildered for a moment. He rubbed his eyes, and looked hard at me. I seemed human enough on the outside: he couldn't make it out.

He said:

'Yuise a stranger in these parts? You don't live here?'

'No,' I said. 'I don't. *You* wouldn't if *I* did.'

'Well then,' he said, 'you want to see the tombs – graves – folks been buried, you know – coffins!'

'You are an untruther,' I replied, getting roused; 'I do not want to see tombs – not your tombs. Why should I? We have graves of our own, our family has. Why my Uncle Podger has a tomb in Kensal Green Cemetery,[3] that is the pride of all that countryside; and my grandfather's vault at Bow is capable of accommodating eight visitors, while my great-aunt Susan has a brick grave in Finchley Churchyard, with a headstone with a coffee-pot sort of thing in bas-relief upon it, and a six-inch best white stone coping all the way round, that cost pounds. When I want graves, it is to those places that I go and revel. I do not want other folk's. When you yourself are buried, I will come and see yours. That is all I can do for you.'

He burst into tears. He said that one of the tombs had a bit of stone upon the top of it that had been said by some to be probably part of the remains of the figure of a man, and that another had some words carved upon it that nobody had ever been able to decipher.

I still remained obdurate, and, in broken-hearted tones, he said:

'Well, won't you come and see the memorial window?'

I would not even see that, so he fired his last shot. He drew near, and whispered hoarsely:

'I've got a couple of skulls down in the crypt,' he said; 'come and see those. Oh, do come and see the skulls! You are a young man out for a holiday, and you want to enjoy yourself. Come and see the skulls!'

Then I turned and fled, and as I sped I heard him calling to me:

'Oh, come and see the skulls; come back and see the skulls!'

Harris, however, revels in tombs, and graves, and epitaphs, and monumental inscriptions, and the thought of not seeing Mrs Thomas's grave made him crazy. He said he had looked forward to seeing Mrs Thomas's grave from the first moment that the trip was proposed – said he wouldn't have joined if it hadn't been for the idea of seeing Mrs Thomas's tomb.

I reminded him of George, and how we had to get the boat up to

Shepperton by five o'clock to meet him, and then he went for George. Why was George to fool about all day, and leave us to lug this lumbering old top-heavy barge up and down the river by ourselves to meet him? Why couldn't George come and do some work? Why couldn't he have got the day off, and come down with us? Bank be blowed! What good was he at the bank?

'I never see him doing any work there,' continued Harris, 'whenever I go in. He sits behind a bit of glass all day, trying to look as if he was doing something. What's the good of a man behind a bit of glass? I have to work for my living. Why can't he work? What use is he there, and what's the good of their banks? They take your money, and then, when you draw a cheque, they send it back smeared all over with "No effects", "Refer to drawer". What's the good of that? That's the sort of trick they served me twice last week. I'm not going to stand it much longer. I shall withdraw my account. If he was here we could go and see that tomb. I don't believe he's at the bank at all. He's larking about somewhere, that's what he's doing, leaving us to do all the work. I'm going to get out, and have a drink.'

I pointed out to him that we were miles away from a pub; and then he went on about the river, and what was the good of the river, and was everyone who came on the river to die of thirst?

It is always best to let Harris have his head when he gets like this. Then he pumps himself out, and is quiet afterwards.

I reminded him that there was concentrated lemonade in the hamper, and a gallon jar of water in the nose of the boat, and that the two only wanted mixing to make a cool and refreshing beverage.

Then he flew off about lemonade, and 'such-like Sunday-school slops', as he termed them, ginger-beer, raspberry syrup, etc., etc. He said they all produced dyspepsia, and ruined body and soul alike, and were the cause of half the crime in England.

He said he must drink something, however, and climbed upon the seat, and leant over to get the bottle. It was right at the bottom of the hamper, and seemed difficult to find, and he had to lean over farther and farther, and, in trying to steer at the same time, from a topsy-turvy point of view, he pulled the wrong line, and sent the boat into the bank, and the shock upset him, and he dived down right into the hamper, and stood there on his head, holding on to the sides of the boat like grim death, his legs sticking up into the air. He dared not move for fear of going over, and had to stay there till I could get hold of his legs, and haul him back, and that made him madder than ever.

Chapter 8

Blackmailing – The proper course to pursue – Selfish boorishness of riverside landowner – 'Notice' Boards – Unchristianlike feelings of Harris – How Harris sings a comic song – A high-class party – Shameful conduct of two abandoned young men – Some useless information – George buys a banjo.

We stopped under the willows by Kempton Park,[1] and lunched. It is a pretty little spot there; a pleasant grass plateau, running along by the water's edge, and overhung by willows. We had just commenced the third course – the bread and jam – when a gentleman in shirt sleeves and a short pipe came along, and wanted to know if we knew that we were trespassing. We said we hadn't given the matter sufficient consideration as yet to enable us to arrive at a definite conclusion on that point, but that, if he assured us on his word as a gentleman that we *were* trespassing, we would, without further hesitation, believe it.

He gave us the required assurance, and we thanked him, but he still hung about, and seemed to be dissatisfied, so we asked him if there was anything further that we could do for him; and Harris, who is of a chummy disposition, offered him a bit of bread and jam.

I fancy he must have belonged to some society sworn to abstain from bread and jam; for he declined it quite gruffly, as if he were vexed at being tempted with it, and he added that it was his duty to turn us off.

Harris said that if it was a duty it ought to be done, and asked the man what was his idea with regard to the best means for accomplishing it. Harris is what you would call a well-made man of about number one size, and looks hard and bony, and the man measured him up and down, and said he would go and consult his master, and then come back and chuck us both into the river.

Of course, we never saw him any more, and, of course, all he really wanted was a shilling, There are a certain number of riverside roughs who make quite an income during the summer, by slouching about the banks and blackmailing weak-minded noodles in this way. They represent themselves as sent by the proprietor. The proper course to pursue is to offer your name and address, and leave the owner, if he really has anything to do with the matter, to summon you, and prove what damage you have done to his land by sitting down on a bit of it. But the majority of people are so intensely lazy and timid, that they prefer to encourage the imposition by giving in to it rather than put an end to it by the exertion of a little firmness.

Where it is really the owners that are to blame, they ought to be shown up. The selfishness of the riparian proprietor grows with every year. If these men had their way they would close the River Thames altogether. They actually do this along the minor tributary streams and in the backwaters. They drive posts into the bed of the stream, and draw chains across from bank to bank, and nail huge notice-boards on every tree. The sight of those notice-boards rouses every evil instinct in my nature. I feel I want to tear each one down, and hammer it over the head of the man who put it up, until I have killed him, and then I would bury him, and put the board up over the grave as a tombstone.

I mentioned these feelings of mine to Harris, and he said he had them worse than that. He said he not only felt he wanted to kill the man who caused the board to be put up, but that he should like to slaughter the whole of his family and all his friends and relations, and then burn down his house. This seemed to me to be going too far, and I said so to Harris; but he answered: 'Not a bit of it. Serve 'em all jolly well right, and I'd go and sing comic songs on the ruins.'

I was vexed to hear Harris go on in this bloodthirsty strain. We never ought to allow our instincts of justice to degenerate into mere vindictiveness. It was a long while before I could get Harris to take a more Christian view of the subject, but I succeeded at last, and he promised me that he would spare the friends and relations at all events, and would not sing comic songs on the ruins.

You have never heard Harris sing a comic song, or you would understand the service I had rendered to mankind. It is one of Harris's fixed ideas that he *can* sing a comic song; the fixed idea, on the contrary, among those of Harris's friends who have heard him try, is that he *can't*, and never will be able to, and that he ought not to be allowed to try.

When Harris is at a party, and is asked to sing, he replies: 'Well, I can only sing a *comic* song, you know'; and he says it in a tone that implies that his singing of *that*, however, is a thing that you ought to hear once, and then die.

'Oh, that *is* nice,' says the hostess. 'Do sing one, Mr Harris'; and Harris gets up, and makes for the piano, with the beaming cheeriness of a generous-minded man who is just about to give somebody something.

'Now, silence, please, everybody,' says the hostess, turning round, 'Mr Harris is going to sing a comic song!'

'Oh, how jolly!' they murmur; and they hurry in from the conservatory, and come up from the stairs, and go and fetch each other from all over the house, and crowd into the drawing-room, and sit round, all smirking in anticipation.

Then Harris begins.

Well, you don't look for much of a voice in a comic song. You don't expect correct phrasing or vocalization. You don't mind if a man does find out, when in the middle of a note, that he is too high, and comes down with a jerk. You don't bother about time. You don't mind a man being two bars in front of the accompaniment, and easing up in the middle of a line to argue it out with the pianist, and then starting the verse afresh. But you do expect the words.

You don't expect a man to never remember more than the first three lines of the first verse, and to keep on repeating these until it is time to begin the chorus. You don't expect a man to break off in the middle of a line, and snigger, and say, it's very funny, but he's blest if he can think of the rest of it, and then try and make it up for himself, and, afterwards, suddenly recollect it, when he has got to an entirely different part of the song, and break off without a word of warning, to go back and let you have it then and there. You don't – well, I will just give you an idea of Harris's comic singing, and then you can judge for yourself.

HARRIS (*standing up in front of piano and addressing the expectant mob*): I'm afraid it's a very old thing, you know. I expect you all know it, you know. But it's the only thing I know. It's the Judge's song out of *Pinafore*[2] – no, I don't mean *Pinafore* – I mean – you know what I mean – the other thing, you know. You must all join in the chorus, you know.

Murmurs of delight and anxiety to join in the chorus. Brilliant performance of prelude to the Judge's song in 'Trial by Jury' by nervous pianist. Moment arrives for Harris to join in. Harris takes no notice of it. Nervous pianist commences prelude over again, and Harris, commencing singing at the same time, dashes off the first two lines of the First Lord's song out of 'Pinafore'. Nervous pianist tries to push on with prelude, gives it up, and tries to follow Harris with accompaniment to Judge's song out of 'Trial by Jury', finds that doesn't answer, and tries to recollect what he is doing, and where he is, feels his mind giving way, and stops short.

HARRIS (*with kindly encouragement*): It's all right. You're doing it very well, indeed – go on.

NERVOUS PIANIST: I'm afraid there's a mistake somewhere. What are you singing?

HARRIS (*promptly*): Why the Judge's song out of *Trial by Jury*. Don't you know it?

SOME FRIEND OF HARRIS'S (*from the back of the room*): No, you're not, you chuckle-head, you're singing the Admiral's song from *Pinafore*.

Long argument between Harris and Harris's friend as to what Harris is really singing. Friend finally suggests that it doesn't matter what Harris is singing so long as Harris gets on and sings it, and Harris with an evident sense of injustice rankling inside him, requests pianist to begin again. Pianist, thereupon, starts prelude to the Admiral's song, and Harris, seizing what he considers to be a favourable opening in the music, begins.

HARRIS:

When I was young and called to the Bar.

General roar of laughter, taken by Harris as a compliment. Pianist, thinking of his wife and family, gives up the unequal contest and retires; his place being taken by a stronger-nerved man.

THE NEW PIANIST (*cheerily*): Now then, old man, you start off, and I'll follow. We won't bother about any prelude.

HARRIS (*upon whom the explanation of matters has slowly dawned – laughing*): By Jove! I beg your pardon. Of course – I've been mixing up the two songs. It was Jenkins who confused me, you know. Now then.

Singing; his voice appearing to come from the cellar, and suggesting the first low warnings of an approaching earthquake.

When I was young I served a term
As office-boy to an attorney's firm.

(*Aside to pianist*): It is too low, old man; we'll have that over again, if you don't mind.

Sings first two lines over again, in a high falsetto this time. Great surprise on the part of the audience. Nervous old lady near the fire begins to cry, and has to be led out.

HARRIS (*continuing*):

I swept the windows and I swept the door,
And I –

No – no, I cleaned the windows of the big front door. And I polished up the floor – no, dash it – I beg your pardon – funny thing, I can't think of that line. And I – and I – Oh, well, we'll get on to the chorus, and chance it (*sings*):

And I diddle-diddle-diddle-diddle-diddle-diddle-de,
Till now I am ruler of the Queen's navee.

Now then, chorus – it's the last two lines repeated, you know.

GENERAL CHORUS:

And he diddle-diddle-diddle-diddle-diddle-diddle-dēē'd,
Till now he is ruler of the Queen's navēē.

And Harris never sees what an ass he is making of himself, and how he is annoying a lot of people who never did him any harm. He honestly imagines that he has given them a treat, and says he will sing another comic song after supper.

Speaking of comic songs and parties reminds me of a rather curious incident at which I once assisted; which, as it throws much light upon the inner mental working of human nature in general, ought, I think, to be recorded in these pages.

We were a fashionable and highly cultured party. We had on our best clothes, and we talked pretty, and were very happy – all except two young fellows, students, just returned from Germany, common-place young men, who seemed restless and uncomfortable, as if they found the proceedings slow. The truth was, we were too clever for them. Our brilliant but polished conversation, and our high-class tastes were beyond them. They were out of place, among us. They never ought to have been there at all. Everybody agreed upon that, later on.

We played *morceaux*[3] from the old German masters. We discussed philosophy and ethics. We flirted with graceful dignity. We were even humorous – in a high-class way.

Somebody recited a French poem after supper, and we said it was beautiful; and then a lady sang a sentimental ballad in Spanish, and it made one or two of us weep – it was so pathetic.

And then those two young men got up, and asked us if we had ever heard Herr Slossenn Boschen (who had just arrived, and was then down in the supper-room) sing his great German comic song.

None of us had heard it, that we could remember.

The young man said it was the funniest song that had ever been written, and that, if we liked, they would get Herr Slossenn Boschen, whom they knew very well, to sing it. They said it was so funny that, when Herr Slossenn Boschen had sung it once before the German Emperor, he (the German Emperor) had had to be carried off to bed.

They said nobody could sing it like Herr Slossenn Boschen; he was so intensely serious all through it that you might fancy he was reciting a tragedy, and that, of course, made it all the funnier. They said he never once suggested by his tone or manner that he was singing anything funny – that would spoil it. It was his air of seriousness, almost of pathos, that made it so irresistibly amusing.

We said we yearned to hear it, that we wanted a good laugh; and they went downstairs, and fetched Herr Slossenn Boschen.

He appeared to be quite pleased to sing it, for he came up at once, and sat down to the piano without another word.

'Oh, it will amuse you. You will laugh,' whispered the two young men, as they passed through the room, and took up an unobtrusive position behind the Professor's back.

Herr Slossenn Boschen accompanied himself. The prelude did not suggest a comic song exactly. It was a weird, soulful air. It quite made one's flesh creep; but we murmured to one another that it was the German method, and prepared to enjoy it.

I don't understand German myself. I learned it at school, but forgot every word of it two years after I had left, and have felt much better ever since. Still I did not want the people there to guess my ignorance; so I hit upon what I thought to be rather a good idea. I kept my eye on the two young students, and followed them. When they tittered, I tittered; when they roared, I roared; and I also threw in a little snigger all by myself now and then, as if I had seen a bit of humour that had escaped the others. I considered this particularly artful on my part.

I noticed, as the song progressed, that a good many other people seemed to have their eye fixed on the two young men, as well as myself. These other people also tittered when the young men tittered, and roared when the young men roared; and, as the two young men tittered and roared and exploded with laughter pretty continuously all through the song, it went exceedingly well.

And yet that German professor did not seem happy. At first, when we began to laugh the expression on his face was one of intense surprise, as if laughter were the very last thing he had expected to be greeted with. We thought this very funny: we said his earnest manner was half the humour. The slightest hint on his part that he knew how funny he was would have completely ruined it all. As we continued to laugh, his surprise gave way to an air of annoyance and indignation, and he scowled fiercely round upon us all (except upon the two young men who, being behind him, he could not see).

That sent us into convulsions. We told each other that it would be the death of us, this thing. The words alone, we said, were enough to send us into fits, but added to his mock seriousness – oh, it was too much!

In the last verse, he surpassed himself. He glowered round upon us with a look of such concentrated ferocity that, but for our being forewarned as to the German method of comic singing, we should have been nervous; and he threw such a wailing note of agony into the weird music that, if we had not known it was a funny song, we might have wept.

He finished amid a perfect shriek of laughter. We said it was the funniest thing we had ever heard in all our lives. We said how strange it was that, in the face of things like these, there should be a popular notion that the Germans hadn't any sense of humour. And we asked the Professor why he didn't translate the song into English, so that the common people could understand it, and hear what a real comic song was like.

Then Herr Slossenn Boschen got up, and went on awful. He swore at us in German (which I should judge to be a singularly effective language for that purpose), and he danced, and shook his fists, and called us all the English he knew. He said he had never been so insulted in all his life.

It appeared that the song was not a comic song at all. It was about a young girl who lived in the Hartz Mountains, and who had given up her life to save her lover's soul; and he died, and met her spirit in the air; and then, in the last verse, he jilted her spirit and went off with another spirit – I'm not quite sure of the details, but it was something very sad, I know. Herr Boschen said he had sung it once before the German Emperor, and he (the German Emperor) had sobbed like a little child. He (Herr Boschen) said it was generally acknowledged to be one of the most tragic and pathetic songs in the German language.

It was a trying situation for us – very trying. There seemed to be no answer. We looked round for the two young men who had done this thing, but they had left the house in an unostentatious manner immediately after the end of the song.

That was the end of that party. I never saw a party break up so quietly, and with so little fuss. We never said good night even to one another. We came downstairs one at a time, walking softly, and keeping the shady side. We asked the servant for our hats and coats in whispers, and opened the door for ourselves, and slipped out, and got round the corner quickly, avoiding each other as much as possible.

I have never taken much interest in German songs since then.

We reached Sunbury lock at half past three. The river is sweetly pretty just there before you come to the gates, and the backwater is charming; but don't attempt to row up it.

I tried to do so once. I was sculling, and asked the fellows who were steering if they thought it could be done, and they said, oh, yes, they thought so, if I pulled hard. We were just under the little footbridge that crosses it between two weirs, when they said this, and I bent down over the sculls, and set myself up and pulled.

I pulled splendidly. I got well into a steady rhythmical swing. I put my arms, and my legs, and my back into it. I set myself a good, quick, dashing stroke, and worked in really grand style. My two friends said it was a pleasure to watch me. At the end of five minutes, I thought we ought to be pretty near the weir, and I looked up. We were under the bridge, in exactly the same spot that we were when I began, and there were those two idiots, injuring themselves by violent laughing. I had been grinding away like mad to keep that boat stuck still under that bridge. I let other people pull up backwaters against strong streams now.

We sculled up to Walton, a rather large place for a riverside town. As with all riverside places, only the tiniest corner of it comes down to the water, so that from the boat you might fancy it was a village of some half-dozen houses, all told. Windsor and Abingdon are the only towns between London and Oxford that you can really see anything of from the stream. All the others hide round corners and merely peep at the river down one street; my thanks to them for being so considerate, and leaving the river banks to woods and fields and waterworks.

Even Reading, though it does its best to spoil and sully and make hideous as much of the river as it can reach, is good-natured enough to keep its ugly face a good deal out of sight.

Caesar, of course had a little place at Walton – a camp, or entrenchment, or something of that sort. Caesar was a regular up-river man. Also Queen Elizabeth, she was there, too. You can never get away from that woman, go where you will. Cromwell and Bradshaw[4] (not the guide man,[5] but the King Charles's head man) likewise sojourned here. They must have been quite a pleasant little party, altogether.

There is an iron 'scold's bridle'[6] in Walton Church. They used these things in ancient days for curbing women's tongues. They have given up the attempt now. I suppose iron was getting scarce, and nothing else would be strong enough.

There are also tombs of note in the church, and I was afraid I should never get Harris past them; but he didn't seem to think of them, and we went on. Above the bridge the river winds tremendously. This makes it look picturesque; but it irritates you from a towing or sculling point of view, and causes argument between the man who is pulling and the man who is steering.

You pass Oatlands Park on the right bank here. It is a famous old place. Henry VIII stole it from someone or the other, I forget whom now, and lived in it. There is a grotto in the park which you can see for a fee, and which is supposed to be very wonderful; but I cannot see much in it myself. The late Duchess of York, who lived at Oatlands, was very fond of dogs, and kept an immense number. She had a special graveyard made, in which to bury them when they died, and there they lie, about fifty of them, with a tombstone over each, and an epitaph inscribed thereon.

Well, I dare say they deserve it quite as much as the average Christian does.

At 'Corway Stakes' – the first bend above Walton Bridge – was fought a battle between Caesar and Cassivelaunus.[7] Cassivelaunus had prepared the river for Caesar, by planting it full of stakes (and had, no doubt, put up a notice-board). But Caesar crossed in spite of this. You couldn't choke Caesar off that river. He is the sort of man we want round the backwaters now.

Halliford and Shepperton are both pretty little spots where they touch the river; but there is nothing remarkable about either of them. There is a tomb in Shepperton church-yard, however, with a poem on it, and I was nervous lest Harris should want to get out and fool round it. I saw him fix a longing eye on the landing-stage as we drew near it, so I managed, by an adroit movement, to jerk his cap into the water, and in the excitement of recovering that, and his indignation at my clumsiness, he forgot all about his beloved graves.

At Weybridge, the Wey (a pretty little stream, navigable for small boats up to Guildford, and one which I have always been making up my mind to explore, and never have), the Bourne, and the Basingstoke Canal all enter the Thames together. The lock is just opposite the town, and the first thing that we saw, when we came in view of it, was George's blazer on one of the lock gates, closer inspection showing that George was inside it.

Montmorency set up a furious barking, I shrieked, Harris roared; George waved his hat, and yelled back. The lock-keeper rushed out with a drag, under the impression that somebody had fallen into the lock, and appeared annoyed at finding that no one had.

George had rather a curious oilskin-covered parcel in his hand. It was round and flat at one end, with a long straight handle sticking out of it.

'What's that?' said Harris – 'a frying-pan?'

'No,' said George, with a strange, wild look glittering in his eyes, 'they are all the rage this season; everybody has got them up the river. It's a banjo.'

'I never knew you played the banjo!' cried Harris and I, in one breath.

'Not exactly,' replied George; 'but it's very easy, they tell me; and I've got the instruction book!'

Chapter 9

We made George work, now we had got him. He did not want to
work, of course; that goes without saying. He had had a hard time
in the City, so he explained. Harris, who is callous in his nature, and
not prone to pity, said:

'Ah! and now you are going to have a hard time on the river for
a change; change is good for everyone. Out you get!'

He could not in conscience – not even George's conscience –
object, though he did suggest that, perhaps, it would be better for
him to stop in the boat, and get tea ready, while Harris and I towed,
because getting tea was such a worrying work, and Harris and I
looked tired. The only reply we made to this, however, was to pass
him over the tow-line, and he took it, and stepped out.

There is something very strange and unaccountable about a tow-
line. You roll it up with as much patience and care as you would
take to fold up a new pair of trousers, and five minutes afterwards,
when you pick it up, it is one ghastly, soul-revolting tangle.

I do not wish to be insulting, but I firmly believe that if you took
an average tow-line, and stretched it out straight across the middle
of a field, and then turned your back on it for thirty seconds, that,
when you looked round again, you would find that it had got itself
altogether in a heap in the middle of the field, and had twisted itself
up, and tied itself into knots, and lost its two ends, and become all
loops; and it would take a good half-hour, sitting down there on the
grass and swearing all the while, to disentangle it again.

That is my opinion of tow-lines in general. Of course, there may
be honourable exceptions; I do not say that there are not. There
may be tow-lines that are a credit to their profession – conscientious,

respectable tow-lines – tow-lines that do not imagine they are crotchet-work, and try to knit themselves up into antimacassars the instant they are left to themselves. I say there *may* be such tow-lines; I sincerely hope there are. But I have not met with them.

This tow-line I had taken in myself just before we had got to the lock. I would not let Harris touch it, because he is careless. I had looped it round slowly and cautiously, and tied it up in the middle, and folded it in two, and laid it down gently at the bottom of the boat. Harris had lifted it up scientifically, and had put it into George's hand. George had taken it firmly and held it away from him, and had begun to unravel it as if he were taking the swaddling clothes off a new-born infant; and, before he had unwound a dozen yards, the thing was more like a badly made doormat than anything else.

It is always the same, and the same sort of thing always goes on in connexion with it. The man on the bank, who is trying to disentangle it, thinks all the fault lies with the man who rolled it up; and when a man up the river thinks a thing, he says it.

'What have you been trying to do with it, make a fishing net of it? You've made a nice mess you have; why couldn't you wind it up properly, you silly dummy?' he grunts from time to time as he struggles wildly with it, and lays it out flat on the tow-path, and runs round and round it, trying to find the end.

On the other hand, the man who wound it up thinks the whole cause of the muddle rests with the man who is trying to unwind it.

'It was all right when you took it!' he exclaims indignantly. 'Why don't you think what you are doing? You go about things in such a slap-dash style. You'd get a scaffolding pole entangled, *you* would!'

And they feel so angry with one another that they would like to hang each other with the thing. Ten minutes go by, and the first man gives a yell and goes mad, and dances on the rope, and tries to pull it straight by seizing hold of the first piece that comes to his hand and hauling at it. Of course, this only gets it into a tighter tangle than ever. Then the second man climbs out of the boat and comes to help him, and they get in each other's way, and hinder one another. They both get hold of the same bit of line, and pull at it in opposite directions, and wonder where it is caught. In the end, they do get it clear, and then turn round and find that the boat has drifted off, and is making straight for the weir.

This really happened once to my own knowledge. It was up by Boveney, one rather windy morning. We were pulling down-stream, and, as we came round the bend, we noticed a couple of men on the bank. They were looking at each other with as bewildered and helplessly miserable expressions as I have ever witnessed on any human countenance before or since, and they held a long tow-line between them. It was clear that something had happened, so we eased up and asked them what was the matter.

'Why, our boat's gone off!' they replied in an indignant tone. 'We just got out to disentangle the tow-line, and when we looked round, it was gone!'

And they seemed hurt at what they evidently regarded as a mean and ungrateful act on the part of the boat.

We found the truant for them half a mile further down, held by some rushes, and we brought it back to them. I bet they did not give that boat another chance for a week.

I shall never forget the picture of those two men walking up and down the bank with a tow-line, looking for their boat.

One sees a good many funny incidents up the river in connexion with towing. One of the most common is the sight of a couple of towers, walking briskly along, deep in an animated discussion, while the man in the boat, a hundred yards behind them, is vainly shrieking to them to stop, and making frantic signs of distress with a scull. Something has gone wrong; the rudder has come off, or the boathook has slipped overboard, or his hat has dropped into the water, and is floating rapidly down-stream. He calls to them to stop, quite gently and politely at first.

'Hi! Stop a minute, will you?' he shouts cheerily. 'I've dropped my hat overboard.'

Then: 'Hi! Tom – Dick! Can't you hear?' not quite so affably this time.

Then: 'Hi! Confound you, you dunder-headed idiots! Hi! stop! Oh you –!'

After that he springs up, and dances about, and roars himself red in the face, and curses everything he knows. And the small boys on the bank stop and jeer at him, and pitch stones at him as he is pulled along past them, at the rate of four miles an hour, and can't get out.

Much of this sort of trouble would be saved if those who are towing would keep remembering that they *are* towing, and give a pretty frequent look round to see how their man is getting on. It is best to let one person tow. When two are doing it, they get chattering, and forget, and the boat itself, offering, as it does, but little resistance, is of no real service in reminding them of the fact.

As an example of how utterly oblivious a pair of towers can be to their work, George told us, later on in the evening, when we were discussing the subject after supper, of a very curious instance.

He and three other men, so he said, were sculling a very heavily laden boat up from Maidenhead one evening, and a little above Cookham lock they noticed a fellow and a girl, walking along the tow-path, both deep in an apparently interesting and absorbing conversation. They were carrying a boat-hook between them, and attached to the boat-hook was a tow-line, which trailed behind them, its end in the water. No boat was near, no boat was in sight. There must have been a boat attached to that tow-line at some time or other, that was certain; but what had become of it, what ghastly fate had overtaken it, and those who had been left in it, was buried in mystery. Whatever the accident may have been, however, it had in no way disturbed the young lady and gentleman who were towing. They had the boat-hook, and they had the line, and that seemed to be all that they thought necessary to their work.

George was about to call out and wake them up, but, at that moment, a bright idea flashed across him, and he didn't. He got the hitcher instead and reached over, and drew in the end of the tow-line; and they made a loop in it, and put it over their mast, and then they tidied up the sculls, and went and sat down in the stern, and lit their pipes.

And that young man and young woman towed those four hulking chaps and a heavy boat up to Marlow.

George said he never saw so much thoughtful sadness concentrated into one glance before, as when, at the lock, that young couple grasped the idea that, for the last two miles, they had been towing the wrong boat. George fancied that, if it had not been for the restraining influence of the sweet woman at his side, the young man might have given way to violent language.

The maiden was the first to recover her surprise, and, when she did, she clasped her hands and said, wildly:

'Oh, Henry, then *where* is auntie?'

'Did they ever recover the old lady?' asked Harris.

George replied he did not know.

Another example of the dangerous want of sympathy between tower and towed was witnessed by George and myself once up near Walton. It was where the tow-path shelves gently down into the water, and we were camping on the opposite bank, noticing things in general. By and by a small boat came in sight, towed through the water at a tremendous pace by a powerful barge horse, on which sat a very small boy. Scattered about the boat, in dreamy and reposeful attitudes, lay five fellows, the man who was steering having a particularly restful appearance.

'I should like to see him pull the wrong line,' murmured George, as they passed. And at that precise moment the man did it, and the boat rushed up the bank with a noise like the ripping up of forty thousand linen sheets. Two men, a hamper, and three oars immediately left the boat on the larboard side, and reclined on the bank, and one and a half moments afterwards, two other men disembarked from the starboard, and sat down among boat-hooks and sails and carpet-bags and bottles. The last man went on twenty yards farther, and then got out on his head.

This seemed to sort of lighten the boat, and it went on much easier, the small boy shouting at the top of his voice, and urging his steed into a gallop. The fellows sat up and stared at one another. It was some seconds before they realized what had happened to them, but, when they did, they began to shout lustily for the boy to stop. He, however, was too much occupied with the horse to hear them, and we watched them flying after him, until the distance hid them from view.

I cannot say I was sorry at their mishap. Indeed, I only wish that all the young fools who have their boats towed in this fashion – and plenty do – could meet with similar misfortunes. Besides the risk they run themselves, they become a danger and an annoyance to every other boat they pass. Going at the pace they do, it is impossible for them to get out of anybody else's way, or for anybody else to get out of theirs. Their line gets hitched across your mast and overturns you, or it catches somebody in the boat, and either throws them into the water, or cuts their face open. The best plan is to stand your ground, and be prepared to keep them off with the butt-end of a mast.

Of all experiences in connexion with towing, the most exciting is being towed by girls. It is a sensation that nobody ought to miss. It take three girls to tow always; two hold the rope, and the other one runs round and round and giggles. They generally begin by getting themselves tied up. They get the line round their legs, and have to sit down on the path and undo each other, and then they twist it round their necks, and are nearly strangled. They fix it straight, however, at last, and start off at a run, pulling the boat along at quite a dangerous pace. At the end of a hundred yards they are naturally breathless, and suddenly stop, and all sit down on the grass and laugh, and your boat drifts out to midstream and turns round, before you know what has happened, or can get hold of a scull. Then they stand up, and are surprised.

'Oh, look!' they say; 'he's gone right out into the middle.'

They pull on pretty steadily for a bit, after this, and then it all at once occurs to one of them that she will pin up her frock and they ease up for the purpose, and the boat runs aground.

You jump up and push it off, and you shout to them not to stop.

'Yes. What's the matter?' they shout back.

'Don't stop,' you roar.

'Don't what?'

'Don't stop – go on – go on!'

'Go back, Emily, and see what it is they want,' says one; and Emily comes back, and asks what it is.

'What do you want?' she says; 'anything happened?'

'No,' you reply, 'it's all right; only go on, you know – don't stop.'

'Why not?'

'Why, we can't steer, if you keep stopping. You must keep some way on the boat.'

'Keep some what?'

'Some way – you must keep the boat moving.'

'Oh, all right, I'll tell 'em. Are we doing it all right?'

'Oh, yes, very nicely, indeed, only don't stop.'

'It doesn't seem difficult at all. I thought it was so hard.'

'Oh, no, it's simple enough. You want to keep on steady at it, that's all.'

'I see. Give me out my red shawl, it's under the cushion.'

You find the shawl, and hand it out, and by this time another has come back and thinks she will have hers too, and they take Mary's on chance, and Mary does not want it, so they bring it back and have a pocket-comb instead. It is about twenty minutes before they get off again, and, at the next corner, they see a cow, and you have to leave the boat to chivvy the cow out of their way.

There is never a dull moment in the boat while girls are towing it.

George got the line right after a while, and towed us steadily on to Penton Hook.[1] There we discussed the important question of camping. We had decided to sleep on board that night, and we had either to lay up just about there, or go on past Staines. It seemed early to think about shutting up then, however, with the sun still in the heavens, and we settled to push straight on for Runnymede,[2] three and a half miles farther, a quiet wooded part of the river, and where there is good shelter.

We all wished, however, afterward, that we had stopped at Penton Hook. Three or four miles up-stream is a trifle, early in the morning, but it is a weary pull at the end of a long day. You take no interest in the scenery during these last few miles. You do not chat and laugh. Every half-mile you cover seems like two. You can hardly believe you are only where you are, and you are convinced that the map must be wrong; and, when you have trudged along for what seems to you at least ten miles, and still the lock is not in sight, you begin to seriously fear that somebody must have sneaked it and run off with it.

I remember being terribly upset once up the river (in a figurative sense, I mean). I was out with a young lady – cousin on my mother's side – and we were pulling down to Goring. It was rather late, and we were anxious to get in – at least *she* was anxious to get in. It was half-past six when we reached Benson's lock, and dusk was drawing on, and she began to get excited then. She said she must be in to supper. I said it was a thing I felt I wanted to be in at, too; and I drew out a map I had with me to see exactly how far it was. I saw it was just a mile and a half to the next lock – Wallingford – and five on from there to Cleeve.

'Oh, it's all right!' I said. 'We'll be through the next lock before seven, and then there is only one more'; and I settled down and pulled steadily away.

We passed the bridge, and soon after that I asked if she saw the lock. She said no, she did not see any lock; and I said, 'Oh'! and pulled on. Another five minutes went by, and then I asked her to look again.

'No,' she said; 'I can't see any signs of a lock.'

'You – you are sure you know a lock, when you do see one?' I asked hesitatingly, not wishing to offend her.

The question did not offend her, however, and she suggested that I had better look for myself; so I laid down the sculls, and took a view. The river stretched out straight before us in the twilight for about a mile; not a ghost of a lock was to be seen.

'You don't think we have lost our way, do you?' asked my companion.

I did not see how that was possible; though, as I suggested, we might have somehow got into the weir stream, and be making for the falls.

This idea did not comfort her in the least, and she began to cry. She said we should both be drowned, and that it was a judgement on her for coming out with me.

It seemed an excessive punishment, I thought; but my cousin thought not, and hoped it would all soon be over.

I tried to reassure her, and to make light of the whole affair. I said that the fact evidently was that I was not rowing as fast as I fancied I was, but that we should soon reach the lock now; and I pulled on for another mile.

Then I began to get nervous myself. I looked again at the map. There was Wallingford lock, clearly marked, a mile and a half below Benson's. It was a good, reliable map; and, besides, I recollected the lock myself. I had been through it twice. Where were we? What had happened to us? I began to think it must be all a dream, and that I was really asleep in bed, and should wake up in a minute, and be told it was past ten.

I asked my cousin if she thought it could be a dream, and she replied that she was just about to ask me the same question; and then we both wondered if we were both asleep, and if so, who was the real one that was dreaming, and who was the one that was only a dream; it got quite interesting.

I still went on pulling, however, and still no lock came in sight, and the river grew more and more gloomy and mysterious under the gathering shadows of night, and things seemed to be getting weird and uncanny. I thought of hob-goblins and banshees, and will-o'-the-wisps, and those wicked girls who sit up all night on rocks, and lure people into whirlpools and things; and I wished I had been a better man, and knew more hymns; and in the middle of these reflections I heard the blessed strains of 'He's got 'em on', played badly on a concertina, and knew that we were saved.

I do not admire the tones of a concertina, as a rule; but oh! how beautiful the music seemed to us both then – far, far more beautiful than the voice of Orpheus or the lute of Apollo, or anything of that sort could have sounded. Heavenly melody, in our then state of mind, would only have still further harrowed us. A soul-moving harmony, correctly performed, we should have taken as a spirit-warning, and have given up all hope. But about the strains of 'He's got 'em on', jerked spasmodically, and with involuntary variations, out of a wheezy accordion, there was something singularly human and reassuring.

The sweet sounds drew nearer, and soon the boat from which they were worked came alongside us.

It contained a party of provincial 'Arrys and 'Arriets, out for a moonlight sail. (There was not any moon, but that was not their fault.) I never saw more attractive, lovable people in all my life. I hailed them, and asked if they could tell me the way to Wallingford lock; and I explained that I had been looking for it for the last two hours.

'Wallingford lock!' they answered. 'Lor' love you, sir, that's been done away with for over a year. There ain't no Wallingford lock now, sir. You're close to Cleeve now. Blow me tight if 'ere ain't a gentleman been looking for Wallingford lock, Bill!'

I had never thought of that. I wanted to fall upon all their necks and bless them; but the stream was running too strong just there to allow of this, so I had to content myself with mere cold-sounding words of gratitude.

We thanked them over and over again, and we said it was a lovely night, and we wished them a pleasant trip, and, I think, I invited them all to come and spend a week with me, and my cousin said her mother would be so pleased to see them. And we sang the 'Soldiers' Chorus' out of *Faust*,[3] and got home in time for supper after all.

Chapter 10

Our first night – Under canvas – An appeal for help – Contrariness of tea-kettles, how to overcome – Supper – How to feel virtuous – Wanted, a comfortably-appointed, well-drained desert island, neighbourhood of South Pacific Ocean preferred – Funny thing that happened to George's father – A restless night.

Harris and I began to think that Bell Weir lock must have been done away with after the same manner. George had towed us up to Staines, and we had taken the boat from there, and it seemed that we were dragging fifty tons after us, and were walking forty miles. It was half past seven when we were through, and we all got in, and sculled up close to the left bank, looking out for a spot to haul up in.

We had originally intended to go on to Magna Charta Island, a sweetly pretty part of the river, where it winds through a soft, green valley, and to camp in one of the many picturesque inlets to be found round that tiny shore. But, somehow, we did not feel that we yearned for the picturesque nearly so much now as we had earlier in the day. A bit of water between a coal barge and a gasworks would have quite satisfied us for that night. We did not want scenery. We wanted to have our supper and go to bed. However, we did pull up to the point – 'Picnic Point', it is called – and dropped into a very pleasant nook under a great elm tree, to the spreading roots of which we fastened the boat.

Then we thought we were going to have supper (we had dispensed with tea, so as to save time), but George said no; that we had better get the canvas up first, before it got quite dark, and while we could see what we were doing. Then, he said, all our work would be done, and we could sit down to eat with an easy mind.

That canvas wanted more putting up than I think any of us had bargained for. It looked so simple in the abstract. You took five iron arches, like gigantic croquet hoops, and fitted them up over the boat, and then stretched the canvas over them, and fastened it down; it would take quite ten minutes, we thought.

That was an underestimate.

We took up the hoops, and began to drop them into the sockets placed for them. You would not imagine this to be dangerous work; but, looking back now, the wonder to me is that any of us are alive to tell the tale. They were not hoops, they were demons. First they would not fit into their sockets at all, and we had to jump on them, and kick them, and hammer at them with the boat-hook; and, when they were in, it turned out that they were the wrong hoops for those particular sockets, and they had to come out again.

But they would not come out, until two of us had gone and struggled with them for five minutes, when they would jump up suddenly, and try and throw us into the water and drown us. They had hinges in the middle, and, when we were not looking, they nipped us with these hinges in delicate parts of the body; and, while we were wrestling with one side of the hoop, and endeavouring to persuade it to do its duty, the other side would come behind us in a cowardly manner, and hit us over the head.

We got them fixed at last, and then all that was to be done was to arrange the covering over them. George unrolled it, and fastened one end over the nose of the boat. Harris stood in the middle to take it from George and roll it on to me, and I kept by the stern to receive it. It was a long time coming down to me. George did his part all right, but it was new work to Harris, and he bungled it.

How he managed it I do not know, he could not explain himself; but by some mysterious process or other he succeeded, after ten minutes of superhuman effort, in getting himself completely rolled up in it. He was so firmly wrapped round and tucked in and folded over, that he could not get out. He, of course, made frantic struggles for freedom – the birthright of every Englishman – and in doing so (I learned this afterwards), knocked over George; and then George, swearing at Harris, began to struggle too, and got *himself* entangled and rolled up.

I knew nothing about all this at the time. I did not understand the business at all myself. I had been told to stand where I was, and wait till the canvas came to me, and Montmorency and I stood there and waited both as good as gold. We could see the canvas being violently jerked and tossed about, pretty considerably; but we supposed this was part of the method, and did not interfere.

We also heard much smothered language coming from underneath it, and we guessed that they were finding the job rather troublesome, and concluded that we would wait until things had got a little simpler before we joined in.

We waited some time, but matters seemed to get only more and more involved, until, at last, George's head came wriggling out over the side of the boat, and spoke up.

It said:

'Give us a hand here, can't you, you cuckoo; standing there like a stuffed mummy, when you see we are both being suffocated, you dummy!'

I never could withstand an appeal for help, so I went and undid them; not before it was time, either, for Harris was nearly black in the face.

It took us half an hour's hard labour, after that, before it was properly up, and then we cleared the decks, and got out supper. We put the kettle on to boil, up in the nose of the boat, and went down to the stern and pretended to take no notice of it, but set to work to get the other things out.

That is the only way to get a kettle to boil up the river. If it sees that you are waiting for it and are anxious, it will never even sing. You have to go away and begin your meal, as if you were not going to have any tea at all. You must not even look round at it. Then you will soon hear it sputtering away, mad to be made into tea.

It is a good plan, too, if you are in a great hurry, to talk very loudly to each other about how you don't need any tea, and are not going to have any. You get near the kettle, so that it can overhear you, and then you shout out, 'I don't want any tea; do you, George?' to which George shouts back, 'Oh, no, I don't like tea; we'll have lemonade instead – tea's so indigestible.' Upon which the kettle boils over, and puts the stove out.

We adopted this harmless bit of trickery, and the result was that, by the time everything else was ready, the tea was waiting. Then we lit the lantern and squatted down to supper.

We wanted that supper.

For five-and-thirty minutes not a sound was heard throughout the length and breadth of that boat, save the clank of cutlery and crockery, and the steady grinding of four sets of molars. At the end of five-and-thirty minutes, Harris said, 'Ah!' and took his left leg out from under him and put his right one there instead.

Five minutes afterwards, George said, 'Ah!' too, and threw his plate out on the bank; and, three minutes later than that, Montmorency gave the first sign of contentment he had exhibited since we had started, and rolled over on his side, and spread his legs out; and then I said, 'Ah!' and bent my head back, and bumped it against one of the hoops, but I did not mind it. I did not even swear.

How good one feels when one is full – how satisfied with ourselves and with the world! People who have tried it, tell me that a clear conscience makes you very happy and contented; but a full stomach does the business quite as well, and is cheaper, and more easily obtained. One feels so forgiving and generous after a substantial and well-digested meal – so noble-minded, so kindly-hearted.

It is very strange, this domination of our intellect by our digestive organs. We cannot work, we cannot think, unless our stomach wills so. It dictates to us our emotions, our passions. After eggs and bacon, it says, 'Work!' After beefsteak and porter, it says, 'Sleep!' After a cup of tea (two spoonfuls for each cup, and don't let it stand more than three minutes), it says to the brain, 'Now, rise, and show your strength. Be eloquent, and deep, and tender; see, with a clear eye, into Nature and into life; spread your white wings of quivering thought, and soar, a god-like spirit, over the whirling world beneath you, up through long lanes of flaming stars to the gates of eternity!'

After hot muffins, it says, 'Be dull and soulless, like a beast of the field – a brainless animal with listless eye, unlit by any ray of fancy, or of hope, or fear, or love, or life.' And after brandy, taken in sufficient quantity, it says, 'Now, come, fool, grin and tumble, that your fellow-men may laugh – drivel in folly, and splutter in senseless sounds, and show what a helpless ninny is the poor man whose wit and will are drowned, like kittens, side by side, in half an inch of alcohol.'

We are but the veriest, sorriest slaves of our stomach. Reach not after morality and righteousness, my friends; watch vigilantly your stomach, and diet it with care and judgement. Then virtue and contentment will come and reign within your heart, unsought by any effort of your own; and you will be a good citizen, a loving husband, and a tender father – a noble, pious man.

Before our supper, Harris and George and I were quarrelsome and snappy and ill-tempered; after our supper, we sat and beamed on one another, and we beamed upon the dog, too. We loved each other, we loved everybody. Harris, in moving about, trod on George's corn. Had this happened before supper, George would have expressed wishes and desires concerning Harris's fate in this world and the next that would have made a thoughtful man shudder.

As it was, he said, 'Steady, old man; 'ware wheat.'

And Harris, instead of merely observing, in his most unpleasant tones, that a fellow could hardly help treading on some bit of George's foot, if he had to move about at all within ten yards of where George was sitting, suggesting that George never ought to come into an ordinary sized boat with feet that length, and advising him to hang them over the side, as he would have done before supper, now said: 'Oh, I'm sorry, old chap; I hope I haven't hurt you.'

And George said, 'Not at all'; that it was his fault; and Harris said no, it was his.

It was quite pretty to hear them.

We lit our pipes, and sat, looking out on the quiet night, and talked.

George said why could not we be always like this – away from the world, with its sins and temptation, leading sober, peaceful lives, and doing good. I said it was the sort of thing I had often longed for myself; and we discussed the possibility of our going away, we four, to some handy, well-fitted desert island, and living there in the woods.

Harris said that the danger about desert islands, as far as he had heard, was that they were so damp; but George said no, not if properly drained.

And then we got on to drains, and that put George in mind of a very funny thing that happened to his father once. He said his father was travelling with another fellow through Wales, and, one night, they stopped at a little inn, where there were some other fellows, and they joined the other fellows, and spent the evening with them.

They had a very jolly evening, and sat up late, and, by the time they came to go to bed, they (this was when George's father was a very young man) were slightly jolly, too. They (George's father and George's father's friend) were to sleep in the same room, but in different beds. They took the candle, and went up. The candle lurched up against the wall when they got into the room, and went out, and they had to undress and grope into bed in the dark. This they did; but, instead of getting into separate beds, as they thought they were doing, they both climbed into the same one without knowing it – one getting in with his head at the top, and the other crawling in from the opposite side of the compass, and lying with his feet on the pillow.

There was silence for a moment, and then George's father said:
'Joe!'

'What's the matter, Tom?' replied Joe's voice from the other end
of the bed.

'Why, there's a man in my bed,' said George's father, 'here's his
feet on my pillow.'

'Well, it's an extraordinary thing, Tom,' answered the other; 'but
I'm blest if there isn't a man in my bed, too!'

'What are you going to do?' asked George's father.

'Well, I'm going to chuck him out,' replied Joe.

'So am I,' said George's father, valiantly.

There was a brief struggle, followed by two heavy bumps on the
floor, and then a rather doleful voice said:

'I say, Tom!'

'Yes!'

'How have you got on?'

'Well, to tell you the truth, my man's chucked *me* out.'

'So's mine! I say, I don't think much of this inn, do you?'

'What was the name of that inn?' said Harris.

'The "Pig and Whistle",' said George. 'Why?'

'Ah, no, then it isn't the same,' replied Harris.

'What do you mean?' queried George.

'Why it's so curious,' murmured Harris, 'but precisely that very
same thing happened to *my* father once at a country inn. I've often
heard him tell the tale. I thought it might have been the same inn.'

We turned in at ten that night, and I thought I should sleep well,
being tired; but I didn't. As a rule, I undress and put my head on
the pillow, and then somebody bangs at the door, and says it is half
past eight; but, tonight, everything seemed against me; the novelty
of it all, the hardness of the boat, the cramped position (I was lying
with my feet under one seat, and my head on another), the sound of
the lapping water round the boat, and the wind among the branches,
kept me restless and disturbed.

I did get to sleep for a few hours, and then some part of the boat
which seemed to have grown up in the night – for it certainly was
not there when we started, and it had disappeared by the morning

– kept digging into my spine. I slept through it for a while, dreaming that I had swallowed a sovereign, and that they were cutting a hole in my back with a gimlet, so as to try and get it out. I thought it very unkind of them, and I told them I would owe them the money, and they should have it at the end of the month. But they would not hear of that, and said it would be much better if they had it then, because otherwise the interest would accumulate so. I got quite cross with them after a bit, and told them what I thought of them, and then they gave the gimlet such an excruciating wrench that I woke up.

The boat seemed stuffy, and my head ached; so I thought I would step out into the cool night-air. I slipped on what clothes I could find about – some of my own, and some of George's and Harris's – and crept under the canvas on to the bank.

It was a glorious night. The moon had sunk and left the quiet earth alone with the stars. It seemed as if, in the silence and the hush, while we her children slept, they were talking with her, their sister – conversing of mighty mysteries in voices too vast and deep for childish human ears to catch the sound.

They awe us, these strange stars, so cold, so clear. We are as children whose small feet have strayed into some dim-lit temple of the god they have been taught to worship but know not; and, standing where the echoing dome spans the long vista of the shadowy light, glance up, half hoping, half afraid to see some awful vision hovering there.

And yet it seems so full of comfort and of strength, the night. In its great presence, our small sorrows creep away, ashamed. The day has been so full of fret and care, and our hearts have been so full of evil and of bitter thoughts, and the world has seemed so hard and wrong to us. Then Night, like some great loving mother, gently lays her hand upon our fevered head, and turns our little tear-stained face up to hers, and smiles, and, though she does not speak, we know what she would say, and lay our hot flushed cheek against her bosom, and the pain is gone.

Sometimes, our pain is very deep and real, and we stand before her very silent, because there is no language for our pain, only a moan. Night's heart is full of pity for us: she cannot ease our aching; she takes our hand in hers, and the little world grows very small and very far beneath us, and, borne on her dark wings, we pass for a moment into a mightier Presence than her own, and in the wondrous light of that great Presence, all human life lies like a book before us, and we know that Pain and Sorrow are but the angels of God.

Only those who have worn the crown of suffering can look upon that wondrous light; and they, when they return, may not speak of it or tell the mystery they know.

Once upon a time, through a strange country, there rode some goodly knights, and their path lay by a deep wood, where tangled briers grew very thick and strong, and tore the flesh of them that lost their way therein. And the leaves of the trees that grew in the wood were very dark and thick, so that no ray of light came through the branches to lighten the gloom and sadness.

And, as they passed by that dark wood, one knight of those that rode, missing his comrades, wandered far away, and returned to them no more; and they, sorely grieving, rode on without him, mourning him as one dead.

Now, when they reached the fair castle towards which they had been journeying, they stayed there many days, and made merry; and one night, as they sat in cheerful ease around the logs that burned in the great hall, and drank a loving measure, there came the comrade they had lost, and greeted them. His clothes were ragged, like a beggar's, and many sad wounds were on his sweet flesh, but upon his face there shone a great radiance of deep joy.

And they questioned him, asking him what had befallen him: and he told them how in the dark wood he had lost his way, and had wandered many days and nights, till, torn and bleeding, he had lain him down to die.

Then, when he was nigh unto death, lo! through the savage gloom there came to him a stately maiden, and took him by the hand and led him on through devious paths, unknown to any man, until upon the darkness of the wood there dawned a light such as the light of day was unto but as a little lamp unto the sun; and, in that wondrous light, our wayworn knight saw as in a dream a vision, and so glorious, so fair the vision seemed, that of his bleeding wounds he thought no more, but stood as one entrained, whose joy is deep as in the sea, whereof no man can tell the depth.

And the vision faded, and the knight, kneeling upon the ground, thanked the good saint who into that sad wood had strayed his steps, so he had seen the vision that lay there hid.

And the name of the dark forest was Sorrow; but of the vision that the good knight saw therein we may not speak nor tell.

Chapter 11

How George, once upon a time, got up early in the morning – George, Harris, and Montmorency do not like the look of the cold water – Heroism and determination on the part of J. – George and his shirt: story with a moral – Harris as cook – Historical retrospect, specially inserted for the use of schools.

I woke at six the next morning; and found George awake too. We both turned round, and tried to go to sleep again, but we could not. Had there been any particular reason why we should *not* have gone to sleep again, but have got up and dressed then and there, we should have dropped off while we were looking at our watches, and have slept till ten. As there was no earthly necessity for our getting up under another two hours at the very least, and our getting up at that time was an utter absurdity, it was only in keeping with the natural cussedness of things in general that we should both feel that lying down for five minutes more would be death to us.

George said that the same kind of thing, only worse, had happened to him some eighteen months ago, when he was lodging by himself in the house of a certain Mrs Gippings. He said his watch went wrong one evening, and stopped at a quarter past eight. He did not know this at the time because, for some reason or other, he forgot to wind it up when he went to bed (an unusual occurrence with him), and hung it up over his pillow without ever looking at the thing.

It was in the winter when this happened, very near the shortest day, and a week of fog into the bargain, so the fact that it was still very dark when George woke in the morning was no guide to him as to the time. He reached up, and hauled down his watch. It was a quarter past eight.

'Angels and ministers of grace defend us!' exclaimed George; 'and here have I got to be in the City by nine. Why didn't somebody call me? Oh, this is a shame!' And he flung the watch down, and sprang out of bed, and had a cold bath, and washed himself, and dressed himself, and shaved himself in cold water because there was not time to wait for the hot, and then rushed and had another look at the watch.

Whether the shaking it had received in being thrown down on the bed had started it, or how it was, George could not say, but certain it was that from a quarter past eight it had begun to go, and now pointed to twenty minutes to nine.

George snatched it up, and rushed downstairs. In the sitting-room, all was dark and silent; there was no fire, no breakfast. George said it was a wicked shame of Mrs G., and he made up his mind to tell her what he thought of her when he came home in the evening. Then he dashed on his greatcoat and hat, and, seizing his umbrella, made for the front door. The door was not even unbolted. George anathematized Mrs G. for a lazy old woman, and thought it was very strange that people could not get up at a decent, respectable time, unlocked and unbolted the door, and ran out.

He ran hard for a quarter of a mile, and at the end of that distance it began to be borne in upon him as a strange and curious thing that there were so few people about, and that there were no shops open. It was certainly a very dark and foggy morning, but still it seemed an unusual course to stop all business on that account. *He* had to go to business; why should other people stop in bed merely because it was dark and foggy?

At length he reached Holborn. Not a shutter was down! Not a bus was about! There were three men in sight, one of whom was a policeman; a market-cart full of cabbages, and a dilapidated-looking cab. George pulled out his watch and looked at it; it was five minutes to nine! He stood still and counted his pulse. He stooped down and felt his legs. Then, with his watch still in his hand, he went up to the policeman, and asked him if he knew what time it was.

'What's the time?' said the man, eyeing George up and down with evident suspicion; 'why, if you listen you will hear it strike.'

George listened, and a neighbouring clock immediately obliged.

'But it's only gone three!' said George in an injured tone, when it had finished.

'Well, how many did you want it to go?' replied the constable.

'Why, nine,' said George, showing his watch.

'Do you know where you live?' said the guardian of public order severely.

George thought, and gave the address.

'Oh! That's where it is, is it?' replied the man. 'Well, you take my advice and go there quietly, and take that watch of yours with you; and don't let's have any more of it.'

And George went home again, musing as he walked along, and let himself in.

At first, when he got in, he determined to undress and go to bed again; but when he thought of the re-dressing and re-washing, and the having of another bath, he determined he would not, but would sit up and go to sleep in the easy-chair.

But he could not get to sleep; he never felt more wakeful in his life; so he lit the lamp and got out the chess-board and played himself a game of chess. But even that did not enliven him: it seemed slow somehow; so he gave chess up and tried to read. He did not seem able to take any sort of interest in reading either, so he put on his coat again and went out for a walk.

It was horribly lonesome and dismal, and all the policemen he met regarded him with undisguised suspicion, and turned their lanterns on him and followed him about, and this had such an effect upon him at last that he began to feel as if he really had done something, and he got to slinking down the by-streets and hiding in dark doorways when he heard the regulation flip-flop approaching.

Of course, this conduct made the force only more distrustful of him than ever, and they would come and rout him out and ask him what he was doing there; and when he answered Nothing, he had merely come out for a stroll (it was then four o'clock in the morning), they looked as though they did not believe him, and two plain-clothes constables came home with him to see if he really did live where he had said he did. They saw him go in with his key, and then they took up a position opposite and watched his house.

He thought he would light a fire when he got inside, and make himself some breakfast, just to pass away the time; but he did not seem able to handle anything from a scuttleful of coals to a teaspoon without dropping it or falling over it, and making such a noise that he was in mortal fear that it would wake Mrs G. up, and that she would think it was burglars and open the window and call 'Police!' and then these two detectives would rush in and handcuff him, and march him off to the police-court.

He was in a morbidly nervous state by this time, and he pictured the trial, and his trying to explain the circumstances to the jury, and nobody believing him, and his being sentenced to twenty years' penal servitude, and his mother dying of a broken heart. So he gave up trying to get breakfast, and wrapped himself up in his overcoat, and sat in the easy-chair till Mrs G. came down at half past seven.

He said he had never got up too early since that morning; it had been such a warning to him.

We had been sitting huddled up in our rugs while George had been telling me this true story, and on his finishing it I set to work to wake up Harris with a scull. The third prod did it: and he turned over on the other side, and said he would be down in a minute, and that he would have his lace-up boots. We soon let him know where he was, however, by the aid of the hitcher, and he sat up suddenly, sending Montmorency, who had been sleeping the sleep of the just, right on the middle of his chest, sprawling across the boat.

Then we pulled up the canvas, and all four of us poked our head out over the offside, and looked down at the water and shivered. The idea, overnight, had been that we should get up early in the morning, fling off our rugs and shawls, and, throwing back the canvas, spring into the river with a joyous shout, and revel in a long delicious swim. Somehow, now the morning had come, the notion seemed less tempting. The water looked damp and chilly; the wind felt cold.

'Well, who's going to be first in?' said Harris at last.

There was no rush for precedence. George settled the matter so far as he was concerned by retiring into the boat and pulling on his socks. Montmorency gave vent to an involuntary howl, as if merely thinking of the thing had given him the horrors; and Harris said it would be so difficult to get into the boat again, and went back and sorted out his trousers.

I did not altogether like to give in, though I did not relish the plunge. There might be snags about, or weeds, I thought. I meant to compromise matters by going down to the edge and just throwing the water over myself; so I took a towel and crept out on the bank and wormed my way along on to the branch of a tree that dipped down into the water.

It was bitterly cold. The wind cut like a knife. I thought I would not throw the water over myself after all. I would go back into the boat and dress; and I turned to do so; and, as I turned, the silly branch gave way, and I and the towel went in together with a tremendous splash, and I was out midstream with a gallon of Thames water inside me before I knew what had happened.

'By Jove! old J.'s gone in,' I heard Harris say, as I came blowing to the surface. 'I didn't think he'd have the pluck to do it. Did you?'

'Is it all right?' sang out George.

'Lovely,' I spluttered back. 'You are duffers not to come in. I wouldn't have missed this for worlds. Why don't you try it? It only wants a little determination.'

But I could not persuade them.

Rather an amusing thing happened while dressing that morning. I was very cold when I got back into the boat, and, in my hurry to get my shirt on, I accidentally jerked it into the water. It made me awfully wild, especially as George burst out laughing. I could not see anything to laugh at, and I told George so, and he only laughed the more. I never saw a man laugh so much. I quite lost my temper with him at last, and I pointed out to him what a drivelling maniac of an imbecile idiot he was; but he only roared the louder. And then, just as I was landing the shirt, I noticed that it was not my shirt at all, but George's, which I had mistaken for mine; whereupon the humour of the thing struck me for the first time, and *I* began to laugh. And the more I looked from George's wet shirt to George, roaring with laughter, the more I was amused, and I laughed so much that I had to let the shirt fall back into the water again.

'Ar'n't you – you – going to get it out?' said George between his shrieks.

I could not answer him at all for a while, I was laughing so, but at last, between my peals I managed to jerk out:

'It isn't my shirt – it's *yours*!'

I never saw a man's face change from lively to severe so suddenly in all my life before.

'What!' he yelled, springing up. 'You silly cuckoo! Why can't you be more careful what you're doing? Why the deuce don't you go and dress on the bank? You're not fit to be in a boat, you're not. Gimme the hitcher.'

I tried to make him see the fun of the thing, but he could not. George is very dense at seeing a joke sometimes.

Harris proposed that we should have scrambled eggs for breakfast. He said he would cook them. It seemed, from his account, that he was very good at doing scrambled eggs. He often did them at picnics and when out on yachts. He was quite famous for them. People who had once tasted his scrambled eggs, so we gathered from his conversation, never cared for any other food afterwards, but pined away and died when they could not get them.

It made our mouths water to hear him talk about the things, and we handed him out the stove and the frying-pan and all the eggs that had not smashed and gone over everything in the hamper, and begged him to begin.

He had some trouble in breaking the eggs – or rather not so much trouble in breaking them exactly as in getting them into the frying-pan when broken, and keeping them off his trousers, and preventing them from running up his sleeve; but he fixed some half a dozen into the pan at last, and then squatted down by the side of the stove and chivvied them about with a fork.

It seemed harassing work, so far as George and I could judge. Whenever he went near the pan he burned himself, and then he would drop everything and dance round the stove, flicking his fingers about and cursing the things. Indeed, every time George and I looked round at him he was sure to be performing this feat. We thought at first that it was a necessary part of the culinary arrangements.

We did not know what scrambled eggs were, and we fancied that it must be some Red Indian or Sandwich Islands' sort of dish that required dances and incantations for its proper cooking. Montmorency went and put his nose over it once, and the fat spluttered up and scalded him, and then *he* began dancing and cursing. Altogether it was one of the most interesting and exciting operations I have ever witnessed. George and I were both quite sorry when it was over.

The result was not altogether the success that Harris had anticipated. There seemed so little to show for the business. Six eggs had gone into the frying-pan, and all that came out was a teaspoonful of burnt and unappetizing-looking mess.

Harris said it was the fault of the frying-pan, and thought it would have gone better if we had had a fish-kettle and a gas stove; and we decided not to attempt the dish again until we had those aids to housekeeping by us.

The sun had got more powerful by the time we had finished breakfast, and the wind had dropped, and it was as lovely a morning as one could desire. Little was in sight to remind us of the nineteenth century; and, as we looked out upon the river in the morning sunlight, we could almost fancy that the centuries between us and that ever-to-be-famous June morning of 1215 had been drawn aside, and that we, English yeomen's sons in homespun cloth, with dirk at belt, were waiting there to witness the writing of that stupendous page of history, the meaning whereof was to be translated to the common people some four hundred and odd years later by one Oliver Cromwell, who had deeply studied it.

It is a fine summer morning – sunny, soft, and still. But through the air there runs a thrill of coming stir. King John had slept at

THREE MEN IN A BOAT

Duncroft Hall, and all the day before the little town of Staines has echoed to the clang of armed men, and the clatter of great horses over its rough stones, and the shouts of captains, and the grim oaths and surly jests of bearded bowmen, billmen, pikemen, and strange-speaking foreign spearmen.

Gay-cloaked companies of knights and squires have ridden in, all travel-stained and dusty. And all the evening long the timid townsmen's doors have had to be quick opened to let in rough groups of soldiers, for whom there must be found both board and lodging, and the best of both, or woe betide the house and all within; for the sword is judge and jury, plaintiff and executioner, in these tempestuous times, and pays for what it takes by sparing those from whom it takes it, if it pleases it to do so.

Round the camp-fire in the market-place gather still more of the Barons'[1] troops, and eat and drink deep, and bellow forth roystering drinking songs, and gamble and quarrel as the evening grows and deepens into night. The firelight sheds quaint shadows on their piled-up arms and on their uncouth forms. The children of the town steal round to watch them, wondering; and brawny country wenches, laughing, draw near to bandy ale-house jest and jibe with the swaggering troopers so unlike the village swains, who, now despised, stand apart behind, with vacant grins upon their broad, peering faces. And out from the fields around, glitter the faint lights of more distant camps, as here some great lord's followers lie mustered, and there false John French's mercenaries hover like crouching wolves without the town.

And so, with sentinels in each dark street, and twinkling watch-fires on each height around, the night has worn away, and over this fair valley of old Thames has broken the morning of the great day that is to close so big with the fate of ages yet unborn.

Ever since grey dawn, in the lower of the two islands, just above where we are standing, there has been great clamour, and the sound of many workmen. The great pavilion brought there yester eve is being raised, and carpenters are busy nailing tiers of seats, while 'prentices from London town are there with many-coloured stuffs and silks and cloth of gold and silver.

94

And now, lo! down upon the road that winds along the river's bank from Staines there come towards us, laughing and talking together in deep guttural bass, a half a score of stalwart halbert-men² – Baron's men, these – and halt at a hundred yards or so above us, on the other bank, and lean upon their arms, and wait.

And so, from hour to hour, march up along the road ever fresh groups and bands of armed men, their casques³ and breastplates flashing back along the long low lines of morning sunlight, until, as far as eye can reach, the way seems thick with glittering steel and prancing steeds. And shouting horsemen are galloping from group to group, and little banners are fluttering lazily in the warm breeze, and every now and then there is a deeper stir as the ranks make way on either side, and some great Baron on his war-horse, with his guard of squires around him, passes along to take his station at the head of his serfs and vassals.

And up the slope of Cooper's Hill, just opposite, are gathered the wondering rustics and curious townsfolk, who have run from Staines, and none are quite sure what the bustle is about, but each one has a different version of the great event that they have come to see; and some say that much good to all the people will come from this day's work; but the old men shake their heads, for they have heard such tales before.

And all the river down to Staines is dotted with small craft and boats and tiny coracles – which last are growing out of favour now, and are used only by the poorer folk. Over the rapids, where in after years trim Bell Weir lock will stand, they have been forced or dragged by their sturdy rowers, and now are crowding up as near as they dare come to the great covered barges, which lie in readiness to bear King John to where the fateful Charter waits his signing.

It is noon, and we and all the people have been waiting patient for many an hour, and the rumour has run round that slippery John has again escaped from the Barons' grasp, and has stolen away from Duncroft Hall with his mercenaries at his heels, and will soon be doing other work than signing charters for his people's liberty.

Not so! This time the grip upon him has been one of iron, and he has slid and wriggled in vain. Far down the road a little cloud of dust has risen, and draws nearer and grows larger, and the pattering of many hoofs grows louder, and in and out between the scattered groups of drawn-up men, there pushes on its way a brilliant cavalcade of gay-dressed lords and knights. And front and rear, and either flank, there ride the yeomen of the Barons, and in the midst King John.

He rides to where the barges lie in readiness, and the great Barons step forth from their ranks to meet him. He greets them with a smile and a laugh, and pleasant honeyed words, as though it were some feast in his honour to which he had been invited. But as he rises to dismount, he casts one hurried glance from his own French mercenaries drawn up in the rear to the grim ranks of the Barons' men that hem him in.

Is it too late? One fierce blow at the unsuspecting horseman at his side, one cry to his French troops, one desperate charge upon the unready lines before him, and these rebellious Barons might rue the day they dared to thwart his plans! A bolder hand might have turned the game even at that point. Had it been a Richard there! the cup of liberty might have been dashed from England's lips, and the taste of freedom held back for a hundred years.

But the heart of King John sinks before the stern faces of the English fighting men, and the arm of King John drops back on to his rein, and he dismounts and takes his seat in the foremost barge. And the Barons follow in, with each mailed hand upon the sword-hilt, and the word is given to let go.

Slowly the heavy, bright-decked barges leave the shore of Runny-mede. Slowly against the swift current they work their ponderous way, till, with a low grumble, they grate against the bank of the little island that from this day will bear the name of Magna Charta Island. And King John has stepped upon the shore, and we wait in breathless silence till a great shout cleaves the air and the great cornerstone in England's temple of liberty has, now we know, been firmly laid.

Chapter 12

*Henry VIII and Anne Boleyn – Disadvantages of living in same house with
pair of lovers – A trying time for the English nation – A night search for the
picturesque – Homeless and houseless – Harris prepares to die – An angel
comes along – Effect of sudden joy on Harris – A little supper – Lunch –
High price for mustard – A fearful battle – Maidenhead – Sailing – Three
fishers – We are cursed.*

I was sitting on the bank, conjuring up this scene to myself, when
George remarked that when I was quite rested, perhaps I would not
mind helping to wash up, and, thus recalled from the days of the
glorious past to the prosaic present, with all its misery and sin, I
slid down into the boat and cleaned out the frying-pan with a stick
of wood and a tuft of grass, polishing it up finally with George's wet
shirt.

We went over to Magna Charta Island, and had a look at the
stone which stands in the cottage there and on which the great
Charter is said to have been signed; though, as to whether it really
was signed there, or, as some say, on the other bank at Runnymede,
I decline to commit myself. As far as my own personal opinion goes,
however, I am inclined to give weight to the popular island theory.
Certainly, had I been one of the Barons, at the time, I should have
strongly urged upon my comrades the advisability of our getting
such a slippery customer as King John on to the island, where there
was less chance of surprises and tricks.

There are the ruins of an old priory in the grounds of Ankerwyke
House, which is close to Picnic Point, and it was round about the
grounds of this old priory that Henry VIII is said to have waited
for and met Anne Boleyn.[1] He also used to meet her at Hever Castle,
in Kent, and also somewhere near St Albans. It must have been
difficult for the people of England in those days to have found a spot
where these thoughtless young folk were *not* spooning.

Have you ever been in a house where there are a couple courting?
It is most trying. You think you will go and sit in the drawing-room,

and you march off there. As you open the door, you hear a noise as if somebody had suddenly recollected something, and, when you get in, Emily is over by the window, full of interest in the opposite side of the road, and your friend, John Edward, is at the other end of the room with his whole soul held in thrall by photographs of other people's relatives.

'Oh!' you say, pausing at the door, 'I didn't know anybody was here.'

'Oh! didn't you?' says Emily, coldly, in a tone which implies that she does not believe you.

You hang about for a bit, then you say:

'It's very dark. Why don't you light the gas?'

John Edward says, Oh! he hadn't noticed it; and Emily says that papa does not like the gas lit in the afternoon.

You tell them one or two items of news, and give them your views and opinions on the Irish question;[2] but this does not appear to interest them. All they remark on any subject is, 'Oh!' 'Is it?' 'Did he?' 'Yes', and 'You don't say so!' And, after ten minutes of such style of conversation, you edge up to the door, and slip out, and are surprised to find that the door immediately closes behind you, and shuts itself, without your having touched it.

Half an hour later, you think you will try a pipe in the conservatory. The only chair in the place is occupied by Emily; and John Edward, if the language of clothes can be relied upon, has evidently been sitting on the floor. They do not speak, but they give you a look that says all that can be said in a civilized community; and you back out promptly and shut the door behind you.

You are afraid to poke your nose into any room in the house now; so, after walking up and down the stairs for a while, you go and sit in your own bedroom. This becomes uninteresting, however, after a time, and so you put on your hat and stroll out into the garden. You walk down the path, and as you pass the summer-house you glance in, and there are those two young idiots, huddled up into one corner of it; and they see you, and are evidently under the idea that, for some wicked purpose of your own, you are following them about.

'Why don't they have a special room for this sort of thing, and make people keep to it?' you mutter; and you rush back to the hall and get your umbrella and go out.

It must have been much like this when that foolish boy Henry VIII was courting his little Anne. People in Buckinghamshire would have come upon them unexpectedly when they were mooning round Windsor and Wraysbury, and have exclaimed, 'Oh! you here!' and Henry would have blushed and said, Yes, he'd just come over to see a man; and Anne would have said, 'Oh, I'm so glad to see you! Isn't it funny? I've just met Mr Henry VIII in the lane, and he's going the same way as I am.'

Then those people would have gone away and said to themselves: 'Oh! we'd better get out of here while this billing and cooing is on. We'll go down to Kent.'

And they would go down to Kent, and the first thing they would see in Kent, when they got there, would be Henry and Anne fooling round Hever Castle.

'Oh, drat this!' they would have said. 'Here, let's go away. I can't stand any more of it. Let's go to St Albans – nice quiet place, St Albans.'

And when they reached St Albans, there would be that wretched couple, kissing under the Abbey walls. Then these folks would go and be pirates until the marriage was over.

From Picnic Point to Old Windsor lock is a delightful bit of the river. A shady road, dotted here and there with dainty little cottages, runs by the bank up to the 'Bells of Ouseley', a picturesque inn, as most up-river inns are, and a place where a very good glass of ale may be drunk – so Harris says; and on a matter of this kind you can take Harris's word. Old Windsor is a famous spot in its way. Edward the Confessor[3] had a palace here, and here the great Earl Godwin was proved guilty by the justice of that age of having encompassed the death of the King's brother. Earl Godwin broke a piece of bread and held it in his hand.

'If I am guilty,' said the Earl, 'may this bread choke me when I eat it!'

Then he put the bread into his mouth and swallowed it, and it choked him, and he died.

After you pass Old Windsor, the river is somewhat uninteresting, and does not become itself again until you are nearing Boveney. George and I towed up past the Home Park, which stretches along the right bank from Albert to Victoria Bridge; and as we were passing Datchet, George asked me if I remembered our first trip up the river, and when we landed at Datchet at ten o'clock at night, and wanted to go to bed.

I answered that I did remember it. It will be some time before I forget it.

It was the Saturday before the August Bank Holiday. We were tired and hungry, we same three, and when we got to Datchet we took out the hamper, the two bags, and the rugs and coats, and such like things, and started off to look for diggings. We passed a very pretty little hotel, with clematis and creeper over the porch; but there was no honeysuckle about it, and, for some reason or other, I had got my mind fixed on honeysuckle, and I said:

'Oh, don't let's go in there! Let's go on a bit further, and see if there isn't one with honeysuckle over it.'

So we went on till we came to another hotel. That was a very nice hotel, too, and it had honeysuckle on it, round at the side; but Harris did not like the look of a man who was leaning against the front door. He said he didn't look a nice man at all, and he wore ugly boots: so we went on further. We went a goodish way without coming across any more hotels, and then we met a man, and asked him to direct us to a few.

He said:

'Why, you are coming away from them. You must turn right round and go back, and then you will come to the Stag.'

We said:

'Oh, we had been there, and didn't like it – no honeysuckle over it.'

'Well, then,' he said, 'there's the Manor House, just opposite. Have you tried that?'

Harris replied that we did not want to go there – didn't like the look of a man who was stopping there – Harris did not like the colour of his hair, didn't like his boots, either.

'Well, I don't know what you'll do, I'm sure,' said our informant; 'because they are the only two inns in the place.'

'No other inns!' exclaimed Harris.

'None,' replied the man.

'What on earth are we to do?' cried Harris.

Then George spoke up. He said Harris and I could get an hotel built for us, if we liked, and have some people made to put in. For his part, he was going back to the Stag.

The greatest minds never realize their ideals in any matter; and Harris and I sighed over the hollowness of all earthly desires, and followed George.

We took our traps into the Stag, and laid them down in the hall. The landlord came up and said:

'Good evening, gentlemen.'

'Oh, good evening,' said George; 'we want three beds, please.'

'Very sorry, sir,' said the landlord; 'but I'm afraid we can't manage it.'

'Oh, well, never mind,' said George, 'two will do. Two of us can sleep in one bed, can't we?' he continued, turning to Harris and me.

Harris said, 'Oh, yes', he thought George and I could sleep in one bed very easily.

'Very sorry, sir,' again repeated the landlord; 'but we really haven't got a bed vacant in the whole house. In fact, we are putting two, and even three gentlemen in one bed, as it is.'

This staggered us for a bit.

But Harris, who is an old traveller, rose to the occasion, and, laughing cheerily, said:

'Oh, well, we can't help it. We must rough it. You must give us a shake-down in the billiard-room.'

'Very sorry, sir. Three gentlemen sleeping on the billiard-table already, and two in the coffee-room. Can't possibly take you in tonight.'

We picked up our things, and went over to the Manor House. It was a pretty little place. I said I thought I should like it better than the other house; and Harris said, 'Oh, yes,' it would be all right, and we needn't look at the man with the red hair; besides, the poor fellow couldn't help having red hair.

Harris spoke quite kindly and sensibly about it.

The people at the Manor House did not wait to hear us talk. The landlady met us on the doorstep with the greeting that we were the fourteenth party she had turned away within the last hour and a half. As for our meek suggestions of stables, billiard-room, or coal-cellars, she laughed them all to scorn; all these nooks had been snatched up long ago.

Did she know of any place in the whole village where we could get shelter for the night?

Well, if we didn't mind roughing it – she did not recommend it, mind – but there was a little beershop half a mile down the Eton road –

We waited to hear no more; we caught up the hamper and the bags, and the coats and rugs, and parcels, and ran. The distance seemed more like a mile than half a mile, but we reached the place at last, and rushed, panting, into the bar.

The people at the beershop were rude. They merely laughed at us. There were only three beds in the whole house, and they had seven single gentlemen and two married couples sleeping there already. A kind-hearted bargeman, however, who happened to be in the tap-room thought we might try the grocer's next door to the Stag, and we went back.

The grocer's was full. An old woman we met in the shop then kindly took us along with her for a quarter of a mile to a lady friend of hers who occasionally let rooms to gentlemen.

This old woman walked very slowly, and we were twenty minutes getting to her lady friend's. She enlivened the journey by describing to us, as we trailed along, the various pains she had in her back.

Her lady friend's rooms were let. From there we were recommended to No. 27. No. 27 was full, and sent us to No. 32, and No. 32 was full.

Then we went back into the high road, and Harris sat down on the hamper and said he would go no farther. He said it seemed a quiet spot, and he would like to die there. He requested George and me to kiss his mother for him, and to tell all his relations that he forgave them and died happy.

At that moment an angel came by in the disguise of a small boy (and I cannot think of any more effective disguise an angel could have assumed), with a can of beer in one hand, and in the other something at the end of a string, which he let down on to every flat stone he came across, and then pulled up again, this producing a peculiarly unattractive sound, suggestive of suffering.

We asked this heavenly messenger (as we discovered him afterwards to be) if he knew of any lonely house, whose occupants were few and feeble (old ladies or paralysed gentlemen preferred), who could be easily frightened into giving up their beds for the night to three desperate men; or, if not this, could he recommend us to an empty pigsty, or a disused lime-kiln, or anything of that sort. He did not know of any such place – at least not one handy; but he said that, if we liked to come with him, his mother had a room to spare, and could put us up for the night.

We fell upon his neck there in the moonlight and blessed him, and it would have made a very beautiful picture if the boy himself had not been so overpowered by our emotion as to be unable to sustain himself under it, and sunk to the ground, letting us all down on top of him. Harris was so overcome with joy that he fainted, and had to seize the boy's beer-can and half empty it before he could recover consciousness, and then he started off at a run, and left George and me to bring on the luggage.

It was a little four-roomed cottage where the boy lived, and his mother – good soul! – gave us hot bacon for supper, and we ate it all – five pounds – and a jam tart afterwards, and two pots of tea, and then we went to bed. There were two beds in the room; one was a 2 ft 6 in. truckle bed, and George and I slept in that, and kept in by tying ourselves together with a sheet; and the other was the little boy's bed, and Harris had that all to himself, and we found him in the morning, with two feet of bare leg sticking out at the bottom, and George and I used it to hang the towels on while we bathed.

We were not so uppish about what sort of hotel we would have next time we went to Datchet.

To return to our present trip: nothing exciting happened, and we tugged steadily on to a little below Monkey Island, where we drew up and lunched. We tackled the cold beef for lunch, and then we found that we had forgotten to bring any mustard. I don't think I ever in my life, before or since, felt I wanted mustard as badly as I felt I wanted it then. I don't care for mustard as a rule, and it is very seldom that I take it at all, but I would have given worlds for it then.

I don't know how many worlds there may be in the universe, but anyone who had brought me a spoonful of mustard at that precise moment could have had them all. I grow reckless like that when I want a thing and can't get it.

Harris said he would have given worlds for mustard, too. It would have been a good thing for anybody who had come up to that spot with a can of mustard then; he would have been set up in worlds for the rest of his life.

But there! I dare say both Harris and I would have tried to back out of the bargain after we had got the mustard. One makes these extravagant offers in moments of excitement, but, of course, when one comes to think of it, one sees how absurdly out of proportion they are with the value of the required article. I heard a man, going up a mountain in Switzerland, once say he would give worlds for a glass of beer, and when he came to a little shanty where they kept it, he kicked up a most fearful row because they charged him five francs for a bottle of Bass. He said it was a scandalous imposition, and he wrote to *The Times* about it.

It cast a gloom over the boat, there being no mustard. We ate our beef in silence. Existence seemed hollow and uninteresting. We thought of the happy days of childhood, and sighed. We brightened up a bit, however, over the apple-tart, and, when George drew out a tin of pineapple from the bottom of the hamper, and rolled it into the middle of the boat; we felt that life was worth living after all.

We are very fond of pineapple, all three of us. We looked at the picture on the tin; we thought of the juice. We smiled at one another, and Harris got a spoon ready.

Then we looked for the knife to open the tin with. We turned out everything in the hamper. We turned out the bags. We pulled up the boards at the bottom of the boat. We took everything out on to the bank and shook it. There was no tin-opener to be found.

Then Harris tried to open the tin with a pocket-knife, and broke the knife and cut himself badly; and George tried a pair of scissors, and the scissors flew up, and nearly put his eye out. While they were dressing their wounds, I tried to make a hole in the thing with the spiky end of the hitcher, and the hitcher slipped and jerked me out between the boat and the bank into two feet of muddy water, and the tin rolled over, uninjured, and broke a teacup.

Then we all got mad. We took that tin out on the bank, and Harris went up into a field and got a big sharp stone, and I went back into the boat and brought out the mast, and George held the tin and Harris held the sharp end of his stone against the top of it, and I took the mast and poised it high up in the air, and gathered up all my strength and brought it down.

It was George's straw hat that saved his life that day. He keeps that hat now (what is left of it), and, of a winter's evening, when the pipes are lit and the boys are telling stretchers about the dangers they have passed through, George brings it down and shows it round, and the stirring tale is told anew, with fresh exaggerations every time.

Harris got off with merely a flesh wound.

After that I took the tin off myself, and hammered at it with the mast till I was worn out and sick at heart, whereupon Harris took it in hand.

We beat it out flat; we beat it back square; we battered it into every form known to geometry – but we could not make a hole in it. Then George went at it, and knocked it into a shape, so strange, so weird, so unearthly in its wild hideousness, that he got frightened and threw away the mast. Then we all three sat round it on the grass and looked at it.

There was one great dent across the top that had the appearance of a mocking grin, and it drove us furious, so that Harris rushed at the thing, and caught it up, and flung it far into the middle of the river, and as it sank we hurled our curses at it, and we got into the boat and rowed away from the spot, and never paused till we reached Maidenhead.

Maidenhead itself is too snobby to be pleasant. It is the haunt of

the river swell and his overdressed female companion. It is the town
of showy hotels, patronized chiefly by dudes and ballet girls. It is
the witch's kitchen from which go forth those demons of the river
– steam-launches. The *London Journal*[4] duke always has his 'little
place' at Maidenhead; and the heroine of the three-volume novel[5]
always dines there when she goes out on the spree with somebody
else's husband.

We went through Maidenhead quickly, and then eased up, and
took leisurely that grand reach beyond Boulter's and Cookham locks.
Cliveden Woods still wore their dainty dress of spring, and rose up,
from the water's edge, in one long harmony of blended shades of
fairy green. In its unbroken loveliness this is, perhaps, the sweetest
stretch of all the river, and lingeringly we slowly drew our little
boat away from its deep peace.

We pulled up in the backwater, just below Cookham, and had tea;
and, when we were through the lock, it was evening. A stiffish breeze
had sprung up – in our favour, for a wonder; for, as a rule on the
river, the wind is always dead against you whatever way you go. It
is against you in the morning, when you start for a day's trip, and
you pull a long distance, thinking how easy it will be to come back
with the sail. Then, after tea, the wind veers round, and you have
to pull hard in its teeth all the way home.

When you forget to take the sail at all, then the wind is consistently
in your favour both ways. But there! this world is only a probation,
and man was born to trouble as the sparks fly upward.

This evening, however, they had evidently made a mistake, and
had put the wind round at our back instead of in our face. We kept
very quiet about it, and got the sail up quickly before they found it
out, and then we spread ourselves about the boat in thoughtful
attitudes, and the sail bellied out, and strained, and grumbled at the
mast, and the boat flew.

I steered.

There is no more thrilling sensation I know of than sailing. It
comes as near to flying as man has got to yet – except in dreams.
The wings of the rushing wind seem to be bearing you onward, you
know not where. You are no longer the slow, plodding, puny thing

of clay, creeping tortuously upon the ground; you are a part of Nature! Your heart is throbbing against hers. Her glorious arms are round you, raising you up against her heart! Your spirit is at one with hers; your limbs grow light! The voices of the air are singing to you. The earth seems far away and little; and the clouds so close above your head, are brothers, and you stretch your arms to them.

We had the river to ourselves, except that, far in the distance, we could see a fishing-punt, moored in midstream, on which three fishermen sat; and we skimmed over the water, and passed the wooded banks, and no one spoke.

I was steering.

As we drew nearer, we could see that the three men fishing seemed old and solemn-looking men. They sat on three chairs in the punt, and watched intently their lines. And the red sunset threw a mystic light upon the waters, and tinged with fire the towering woods, and made a golden glory of the piled-up clouds. It was an hour of deep enchantment, of ecstatic hope and longing. The little sail stood out against the purple sky, the gloaming lay around us, wrapping the world in rainbow shadows; and, behind us, crept the night.

We seemed like knights of some old legend, sailing across some mystic lake into the unknown realm of twilight, unto the great land of the sunset.

We did not go into the realm of twilight; we went slap into that punt, where those three old men were fishing. We did not know what had happened at first, because the sail shut out the view, but from the nature of the language that rose up upon the evening air, we gathered that we had come into the neighbourhood of human beings, and that they were vexed and discontented.

Harris let the sail down, and then we saw what had happened. We had knocked those three old gentlemen off their chairs into a general heap at the bottom of the boat, and they were now slowly and painfully sorting themselves out from each other, and picking fish off themselves; and as they worked, they cursed us – not with a common cursory curse, but with long, carefully-thought-out, comprehensive curses, that embraced the whole of our career, and went away into the distant future, and included all our relations, and covered everything connected with us – good, substantial curses.

Harris told them they ought to be grateful for a little excitement, sitting there fishing all day, and he also said that he was shocked and grieved to hear men their age give way to temper so.

But it did not do any good.

George said he would steer, after that. He said a mind like mine ought not to be expected to give itself away in steering boats – better let a mere commonplace human being see after that boat, before we jolly well all got drowned; and he took the lines, and brought us up to Marlow.

And at Marlow we left the boat by the bridge, and went and put up for the night at the 'Crown'.

Chapter 13

Marlow – Bisham Abbey – The Medmenham Monks – Montmorency thinks he will murder an old tom cat – But eventually decides that he will let it live – Shameful conduct of a fox-terrier at the Civil Service Stores – Our departure from Marlow – An imposing procession – The steam-launch, useful recipes for annoying and hindering it – We decline to drink the river – A peaceful dog – Strange disappearance of Harris and a pie.

Marlow[1] is one of the pleasantest river centres I know of. It is a bustling, lively little town; not very picturesque on the whole, it is true, but there are many quaint nooks and corners to be found in it, nevertheless – standing arches in the shattered bridge of Time, over which our fancy travels back to the days when Marlow Manor owned Saxon Algar for its lord, ere conquering William seized it to give to Queen Matilda, ere it passed to the Earls of Warwick or to worldly-wise Lord Paget, the councillor of four successive sovereigns.

There is lovely country round about it, too, if, after boating, you are fond of a walk, while the river itself is at its best here. Down to

Cookham, past the Quarry Woods and the meadows, is a lovely reach. Dear old Quarry Woods! with your narrow, climbing paths, and little winding glades, how scented to this hour you seem with memories of sunny summer days! How haunted are your shadowy vistas with the ghosts of laughing faces! how from your whispering leaves there softly fall the voices of long ago!

From Marlow up to Sonning is even fairer yet. Grand old Bisham Abbey, whose stone walls have rung to the shouts of the Knights Templars,[2] and which, at one time, was the home of Anne of Cleves[3] and at another of Queen Elizabeth, is passed on the right bank just half a mile above Marlow Bridge. Bisham Abbey is rich in melodramatic properties. It contains a tapestry bed-chamber, and a secret room hid high up in the thick walls. The ghost of the Lady Hoby, who beat her little boy to death, still walks there at night, trying to wash its ghostly hands clean in a ghostly basin.

Warwick, the king-maker,[4] rests there, careless now about such trivial things as earthly kings and earthly kingdoms; and Salisbury, who did good service at Poitiers.[5] Just before you come to the abbey, and right on the river's bank, is Bisham Church and, perhaps, if any tombs are worth inspecting, they are the tombs and monuments in Bisham Church. It was while floating in his boat under the Bisham beeches that Shelley, who was then living at Marlow (you can see his house now, in West Street), composed *The Revolt of Islam*.[6]

By Hurley Weir, a little higher up, I have often thought that I could stay a month without having sufficient time to drink in all the beauty of the scene. The village of Hurley, five minutes' walk from the lock, is as old a little spot as there is on the river, dating, as it does, to quote the quaint phraseology of those dim days, 'from the time of King Sebert[7] and King Offa'.[8] Just past the weir (going up) is Danes' Field, where the invading Danes once encamped, during their march to Gloucestershire; and a little farther still, nestling by a sweet corner of the stream, is what is left of Medmenham Abbey.

The famous Medmenham monks, or 'Hell Fire Club',[9] as they were commonly called, and of whom the notorious Wilkes[10] was a member, were a fraternity whose motto was 'Do as you please', and that invitation still stands over the ruined doorway of the abbey.

Many years before this bogus abbey, with its congregation of irreverent jesters, was founded, there stood upon this same spot a monastery of a sterner kind, whose monks were of a somewhat different type to the revellers that were to follow them, five hundred years afterwards.

The Cistercian monks, whose abbey stood there in the thirteenth century, wore no clothes but rough tunics and cowls, and ate no flesh, nor fish, nor eggs. They lay upon straw, and they rose at midnight to mass. They spent the day in labour, reading, and prayer; and over all their lives there fell a silence, as of death, for no one spoke.

A grim fraternity, passing grim lives in that sweet spot, that God had made so bright! Strange that Nature's voices all around them – the soft singing of the waters, the whisperings of the river grass, the music of the rushing wind – should not have taught them a truer meaning of life than this. They listened there, through the long days, in silence, waiting for a voice from heaven; and all day long and through the solemn night it spoke to them in myriad tones, and they heard it not.

From Medmenham to sweet Hambledon Lock the river is full of peaceful beauty, but, after it passes Greenlands, the rather uninteresting-looking river residence of my newsagent – a quiet unassuming old gentleman, who may often be met with about these regions, during the summer months, sculling himself along in easy vigorous style, or chatting genially to some old lock-keeper, as he passes through – until well the other side of Henley, it is somewhat bare and dull.

We got up tolerably early on the Monday morning at Marlow, and went for a bathe before breakfast; and, coming back, Montmorency made an awful ass of himself. The only subject on which Montmorency and I have any serious difference of opinion is cats. I like cats; Montmorency does not.

When I meet a cat, I say, 'Poor Pussy!' and stoop down and tickle the side of its head; and the cat sticks up its tail in a rigid, cast-iron manner, arches its back, and wipes its nose up against my trousers; and all is gentleness and peace. When Montmorency meets a cat, the whole street knows about it; and there is enough bad language wasted in ten seconds to last an ordinary respectable man all his life, with care.

I do not blame the dog (contenting myself, as a rule, with merely clouting his head or throwing stones at him), because I take it that it is his nature. Fox-terriers are born with about four times as much original sin in them as other dogs are, and it will take years and years of patient effort on the part of us Christians to bring about any appreciable reformation in the rowdiness of the fox-terrier nature.

I remember being in the lobby of the Haymarket Stores one day, and all round about me were dogs, waiting for the return of their owners, who were shopping inside. There were a mastiff, and one or two collies, and a St Bernard, a few retrievers and Newfoundlands, a boar-hound, a French poodle, with plenty of hair round its head, but mangy about the middle; a bulldog, a few Lowther Arcade[11] sort of animals, about the size of rats, and a couple of Yorkshire tykes.

There they sat, patient, good, and thoughtful. A solemn peacefulness seemed to reign in that lobby. An air of calmness and resignation – of gentle sadness pervaded the room.

Then a sweet young lady entered, leading a meek-looking little fox-terrier, and left him, chained up there, between the bulldog and the poodle. He sat and looked about him for a minute. Then he cast up his eyes to the ceiling, and seemed, judging from his expression, to be thinking of his mother. Then he yawned. Then he looked round at the other dogs, all silent, grave, and dignified.

He looked at the bulldog, sleeping dreamlessly on his right. He looked at the poodle, erect and haughty, on his left. Then, without a word of warning, without the shadow of a provocation, he bit that poodle's near fore-leg, and a yelp of agony rang through the quiet shades of that lobby.

The result of his first experiment seemed highly satisfactory to him, and he determined to go on and make things lively all round. He sprang over the poodle and vigorously attacked a collie, and the collie woke up, and immediately commenced a fierce and noisy contest with the poodle. Then Foxey came back to his own place, and caught the bulldog by the ear, and tried to throw him away; and the bulldog, a curiously impartial animal, went for everything he could reach, including the hall-porter, which gave that dear little terrier the opportunity to enjoy an uninterrupted fight of his own with an equally willing Yorkshire tyke.

Anyone who knows canine nature need hardly be told that, by this time, all the other dogs in the place were fighting as if their hearths and homes depended on the fray. The big dogs fought each other indiscriminately; and the little dogs fought among themselves, and filled up their spare time by biting the legs of the big dogs.

The whole lobby was a perfect pandemonium, and the din was terrific. A crowd assembled outside in the Haymarket, and asked if it was a vestry meeting; or, if not, who was being murdered, and why? Men came with poles and ropes, and tried to separate the dogs, and the police were sent for.

And in the midst of the riot that sweet young lady returned, and snatched up that sweet little dog of hers (he had laid the tyke up for a month, and had on the expression, now, of a new-born lamb) into her arms, and kissed him, and asked him if he was killed, and what those great nasty brutes of dogs had been doing to him; and he nestled up against her, and gazed up into her face with a look that seemed to say: 'Oh, I'm so glad you've come to take me away from this disgraceful scene!'

She said that the people at the Stores had no right to allow great savage things like those other dogs to be put with respectable people's dogs, and that she had a great mind to summon somebody.

Such is the nature of fox-terriers; and, therefore, I do not blame Montmorency for his tendency to row with cats; but he wished he had not given way to it that morning.

We were, as I have said, returning from a dip, and halfway up the High Street a cat darted out from one of the houses in front of us, and began to trot across the road. Montmorency gave a cry of joy – the cry of a stern warrior who sees his enemy given over to his hands – the sort of cry Cromwell might have uttered when the Scots came down the hill – and flew after his prey.

His victim was a large black Tom. I never saw a larger cat, nor a more disreputable-looking cat. It had lost half its tail, one of its ears, and a fairly appreciable proportion of its nose. It was a long, sinewy-looking animal. It had a calm, contented air about it.

Montmorency went for that poor cat at the rate of twenty miles an hour; but the cat did not hurry up – did not seem to have grasped the idea that its life was in danger. It trotted quietly on until its would-be assassin was within a yard of it, and then it turned round and sat down in the middle of the road, and looked at Montmorency with a gentle, inquiring expression, that said:

'Yes! You want me?'

Montmorency does not lack pluck; but there was something about the look of that cat that might have chilled the heart of the boldest dog. He stopped abruptly, and looked back at Tom.

Neither spoke; but the conversation that one could imagine was clearly as follows:

THE CAT: 'Can I do anything for you?'

MONTMORENCY: 'No – no, thanks.'

THE CAT: 'Don't you mind speaking, if you really want anything, you know.'

MONTMORENCY (*backing down the High Street*): 'Oh, no – not at all – certainly – don't trouble. I – I am afraid I've made a mistake. I thought I knew you. Sorry I disturbed you.'

THE CAT: 'Not at all – quite a pleasure. Sure you don't want anything, now?'

MONTMORENCY (*still backing*): 'Not at all, thanks – not at all – very kind of you. Good morning.'

THE CAT: 'Good morning.'

Then the cat rose, and continued his trot; and Montmorency, fitting what he calls his tail carefully into its groove, came back to us, and took up an unimportant position in the rear.

To this day, if you say the word 'Cats!' to Montmorency, he will visibly shrink and look up piteously at you, as if to say:

'Please don't.'

We did our marketing after breakfast, and revictualled the boat for three days. George said we ought to take vegetables – that it was unhealthy not to eat vegetables. He said they were easy enough to cook, and that he would see to that; so we got ten pounds of potatoes, a bushel of peas, and a few cabbages. We got a beefsteak pie, a couple of gooseberry tarts, and a leg of mutton from the hotel; and fruit, and cakes, and bread and butter, and jam, and bacon and eggs, and other things we foraged round about the town for.

Our departure from Marlow I regard as one of our greatest successes. It was dignified and impressive, without being ostentatious. We had insisted at all the shops we had been to that the things should be sent with us then and there. None of your 'Yes, sir, I will send them off at once; the boy will be down there before you are, sir!' and then fooling about on the landing-stage, and going back to the shop twice to have a row about them, for us. We waited while the basket was packed, and took the boy with us.

We went to a good many shops, adopting this principle at each one; and the consequence was that, by the time we had finished, we had as fine a collection of boys with baskets following us around as heart could desire; and our final march down the middle of the High Street, to the river, must have been as imposing a spectacle as Marlow had seen for many a long day.

The order of the procession was as follows:

Montmorency, carrying a stick.
Two disreputable-looking curs, friends of Montmorency's.
George, carrying coats and rugs, and smoking a short pipe.
Harris, trying to walk with easy grace, while carrying a
bulged-out Gladstone bag in one hand and a bottle of
lime-juice in the other.
Greengrocer's boy and baker's boy, with baskets.
Boots from the hotel, carrying hamper.
Confectioner's boy, with basket.
Grocer's boy, with basket.
Long-haired dog.
Cheesemonger's boy, with basket.
Odd man, carrying a bag.
Bosom companion of odd man, with his hands in his pockets,
smoking a short clay.

Fruiterer's boy, with basket.

Myself, carrying three hats and a pair of boots, and trying to
look as if I didn't know it.

Six small boys, and four stray dogs.

When we got down to the landing-stage, the boatman said:

'Let me see, sir; was yours a steam-launch or a houseboat?'

On our informing him it was a double-sculling skiff, he seemed
surprised.

We had a good deal of trouble with steam-launches that morning.
It was just before the Henley week,[12] and they were going up in
large numbers; some by themselves, some towing house-boats. I do
hate steam-launches; I suppose every rowing man does. I never see
a steam-launch but I feel I should like to lure it to a lonely part of
the river, and there, in the silence and the solitude, strangle it.

There is a blatant bumptiousness about a steam-launch, that has
the knack of rousing every evil instinct in my nature, and I yearn
for the good old days, when you could go about and tell people what
you thought of them with a hatchet and a bow and arrows. The
expression on the face of the man who, with his hands in his pockets,
stands by the stern, smoking a cigar, is sufficient to excuse a breach
of the peace by itself; and the lordly whistle for you to get out of
the way would, I am confident, ensure a verdict of 'justifiable homi-
cide', from any jury of river-men.

They used to *have* to whistle for us to get out of their way. If I
may do so, without appearing boastful, I think I can honestly say
that our one small boat, during that week, caused more annoyance
and delay and aggravation to the steam-launches that we came
across than all the other craft on the river put together.

'Steam-launch coming!' one of us would cry out, on sighting the
enemy in the distance; and in an instant, everything was got ready
to receive her. I would take the lines, and Harris and George would
sit down beside me, all of us with our backs to the launch, and the
boat would drift out quietly into midstream.

On would come the launch, whistling, and on we would go,
drifting. At about a hundred yards off, she would start whistling

like mad, and the people would come and lean over the side, and roar at us; but we never heard them! Harris would be telling us an anecdote about his mother, and George and I would not have missed a word of it for worlds.

Then that launch would give one final shriek of a whistle that would nearly burst the boiler, and she would reverse her engines; and blow off steam, and swing round and get aground; everyone on board of it would rush to the bow and yell at us, and the people on the bank would stand and shout at us, and all the other passing boats would stop and join in, till the whole river for miles up and down was in a state of frantic commotion. And then Harris would break off in the most interesting part of his narrative and look up with mild surprise, and say to George:

'Why, George, bless us, if here isn't a steam-launch!'

And George would answer:

'Well, do you know, I *thought* I heard something!'

Upon which we would get nervous and confused, and not know how to get the boat out of the way, and the people in the launch would crowd round and instruct us:

'Pull your right – you, you idiot! Back with your left. No, not *you* – the other one – leave the lines alone, can't you – now, both together. NOT *that* way. Oh, you –!'

Then they would lower a boat and come to our assistance; and, after a quarter of an hour's effort, would get us clean out of their way, so that they could go on; and we would thank them so much, and ask them to give us a tow. But they never would.

Another good way we discovered of irritating the aristocratic type of steam-launch, was to mistake them for a bean-feast,[13] and ask them if they were Messrs Cubit's[14] lot or the Bermondsey Good Templars,[15] and could they lend us a saucepan.

Old ladies, not accustomed to the river, are always intensely nervous of steam-launches. I remember going up once from Staines to Windsor – a stretch of water peculiarly rich in these mechanical monstrosities – with a party containing three ladies of this description. It was very exciting. At the first glimpse of every steam-launch that came in view, they insisted on landing and sitting down on the bank until it was out of sight again. They said they were very sorry, but that they owed it to their families not to be foolhardy.

We found ourselves short of water at Hambledon lock; so we took our jar and went up to the lock-keeper's house to beg for some.

George was our spokesman. He put on a winning smile, and said:

'Oh, please could you spare us a little water?'

'Certainly,' replied the old gentleman; 'take as much as you want, and leave the rest.'

'Thank you so much,' murmured George, looking about him. 'Where – where do you keep it?'

'It's always in the same place, my boy,' was the stolid reply: 'just behind you.'

'I don't see it,' said George, turning round.

'Why, bless us, where's your eyes?' was the man's comment, as he twisted George round and pointed up and down the stream. 'There's enough of it to see, ain't there?'

'Oh!' exclaimed George, grasping the idea; 'but we can't drink the river, you know!'

'No; but you can drink *some* of it,' replied the old fellow. 'It's what *I've* drunk for the last fifteen years.'

George told him that his appearance, after the course, did not seem a sufficiently good advertisement for the brand; and that he would prefer it out of a pump.

We got some from a cottage a little higher up. I dare say *that* was only river water, if we had known. But we did not know, so it was all right. What the eye does not see, the stomach does not get upset over.

We tried river water once, later on in the season, but it was not a success. We were coming down-stream, and had pulled up to have tea in a backwater near Windsor. Our jar was empty, and it was a case of going without our tea or taking water from the river. Harris was for chancing it. He said it must be all right if we boiled the water. He said that the various germs of poison present in the water would be killed by the boiling. So we filled our kettle with Thames backwater, and boiled it; and very careful we were to see that it *did* boil.

We had made the tea, and were just settling down comfortably to drink it, when George, with his cup half-way to his lips, paused and exclaimed:

'What's that?'

'What's what?' asked Harris and I.

'Why that!' said George, looking westward.

Harris and I followed his gaze, and saw, coming down towards us on the sluggish current, a dog. It was one of the quietest and peacefullest dogs I have ever seen. I never met a dog who seemed more contented – more easy in its mind. It was floating dreamily on its back, with its four legs stuck up straight into the air. It was what I should call a full-bodied dog, with a well-developed chest. On he came, serene, dignified, and calm, until he was abreast of our boat, and there, among the rushes, he eased up, and settled down cosily for the evening.

George said he didn't want any tea, and emptied his cup into the water, Harris did not feel thirsty, either, and followed suit. I had drunk half mine, but I wished I had not.

I asked George if he thought I was likely to have typhoid.

He said: Oh no; he thought I had a very good chance indeed of escaping it. Anyhow, I should know in about a fortnight whether I had or had not.

We went up the backwater to Wargrave. It is a short cut, leading out of the right-hand bank about half a mile above Marsh lock, and is well worth taking, being a pretty, shady little piece of stream, besides saving nearly half a mile of distance.

Of course, its entrance is studded with posts and chains, and surrounded with notice-boards, menacing all kinds of torture, imprisonment, and death to everyone who dares set scull upon its waters – I wonder some of those riparian boors don't claim the air of the river and threaten everyone with forty shillings fine who breathes it – but the posts and chains a little skill will easily avoid; and as for the boards, you might, if you have five minutes to spare, and there is nobody about, take one or two of them down and throw them into the river.

Half-way up the backwater we got out and lunched; and it was during this lunch that George and I received rather a trying shock.

Harris received a shock, too; but I do not think Harris's shock could have been anything like so bad as the shock that George and I had over the business.

You see, it was in this way: we were sitting in a meadow, about ten yards from the water's edge, and we had just settled down comfortably to feed. Harris had the beefsteak pie between his knees, and was carving it, and George and I were waiting with our plates ready.

'Have you got a spoon there?' says Harris; 'I want a spoon to help the gravy with.'

The hamper was close behind us, and George and I both turned round to reach one out. We were not five seconds getting it. When we looked round again, Harris and the pie were gone!

It was a wide open field. There was not a tree or a bit of hedge for hundreds of yards. He could not have tumbled into the river, because we were on the water side of him, and he would have had to climb over us to do it.

George and I gazed all about. Then we gazed at each other.

'Has he been snatched up to heaven?' I queried.

'They'd hardly have taken the pie, too,' said George.

There seemed weight in this objection, and we discarded the heavenly theory.

'I suppose the truth of the matter is', suggested George, descending to the commonplace and practicable, 'that there has been an earthquake.'

And then he added, with a touch of sadness in his voice: 'I wish he hadn't been carving that pie.'

With a sigh, we turned our eyes once more towards the spot where Harris and the pie had last been seen on earth; and there, as our blood froze in our veins and our hair stood up on end, we saw Harris's head – and nothing but his head – sticking bolt upright among the tall grass, the face very red, and bearing upon it an expression of great indignation!

George was the first to recover.

'Speak!' he cried, 'and tell us whether you are alive or dead – and where is the rest of you?'

'Oh, don't be a stupid ass!' said Harris's head, 'I believe you did it on purpose.'

'Did what?' exclaimed George and I.

'Why, put me to sit here – darn silly trick! Here, catch hold of the pie.'

And out of the middle of the earth, as it seemed to us, rose the pie – very much mixed up and damaged; and after it scrambled Harris – tumbled, grubby, and wet.

He had been sitting, without knowing it, on the very verge of a small gully, the long grass hiding it from view; and in leaning a little back he had shot over, pie and all.

He said he had never felt so surprised in all his life, as when he first felt himself going, without being able to conjecture in the slightest what had happened. He thought first that the end of the world had come.

Harris believes to this day that George and I planned it all beforehand. Thus does unjust suspicion follow even the most blameless; for, as the poet says, 'Who shall escape calumny?'[16]

Who, indeed!

Chapter 14

Wargrave – Wax-works – Sonning – Our stew – Montmorency is sarcastic – Fight between Montmorency and the tea-kettle – George's banjo studies meet with discouragement – Difficulties in the way of the musical amateur – Learning to play the bagpipes – Harris feels sad after supper – George and I go for a walk – Return hungry and wet – There is a strangeness about Harris – Harris and the swans, a remarkable story – Harris has a troubled night.

We caught a breeze, after lunch, which took us gently up past Wargrave and Shiplake. Mellowed in the drowsy sunlight of a summer's afternoon, Wargrave, nestling where the river bends, makes a sweet old picture as you pass it, and one that lingers upon the retina of memory.

The 'George and Dragon' at Wargrave boasts a sign, painted on the one side by Leslie, R.A., and on the other by Hodgson of that ilk. Leslie has depicted the fight; Hodgson has imagined the scene 'After the Fight' – George, the work done, enjoying his pint of beer.

Day, the author of *Sandford and Merton*, lived and – more credit to the place still – was killed at Wargrave. In the church is a memorial to Mrs Sarah Hill, who bequeathed £1 annually, to be divided at Easter, between two boys and two girls who 'had never been undutiful to their parents; who had never been known to swear or to tell untruths, to steal, or to break windows'. Fancy giving up all that for five shillings a year! It is not worth it.

It is rumoured in the town that once, many years ago, a boy appeared who really never had done these things – or at all events, which was all that was required or could be expected, had never been *known* to do them – and thus won the crown of glory. He was exhibited for three weeks afterwards in the Town Hall, under a glass case.

What has become of the money since no one knows. They say it is always handed over to the nearest wax-works show.

Shiplake is a pretty village, but it cannot be seen from the river, being upon the hill. Tennyson was married in Shiplake Church.

The river up to Sonning winds in and out through many islands and is very placid, hushed, and lonely. Few folk, except, at twilight, a pair or two of rustic lovers, walk along its banks. 'Arry and Lord Fitznoodle[1] have been left behind at Henley, and dismal, dirty Reading is not yet reached. It is a part of the river in which to dream of bygone days, and vanished forms and faces, and things that might have been, but are not, confound them.

We got out at Sonning, and went for a walk round the village. It is the most fairy-like little nook on the whole river. It is more like a stage village than one built of bricks and mortar. Every house is smothered in roses, and now, in early June, they were bursting forth in clouds of dainty splendour. If you stop at Sonning, put up at the 'Bull', behind the church. It is a veritable picture of an old country inn, with green, square courtyard in front, where, on seats beneath the trees, the old men group of an evening to drink their ale and gossip over village politics; with low, quaint rooms and latticed windows, and awkward stairs and winding passages.

We roamed about sweet Sonning for an hour or so, and then, it being too late to push on past Reading, we decided to go back to one of the Shiplake islands, and put up there for the night. It was still early when we got settled, and George said that, as we had plenty of time, it would be a splendid opportunity to try a good slap-up supper. He said he would show us what could be done up the river in the way of cooking, and suggested that, with the vegetables and the remains of the cold beef and general odds and ends, we should make an Irish stew.

It seemed a fascinating idea. George gathered wood and made a fire, and Harris and I started to peel the potatoes. I should never have thought that peeling potatoes was such an undertaking. The job turned out to be the biggest thing of its kind that I had ever been in. We began cheerfully, one might almost say skittishly, but our lightheartedness was gone by the time the first potato was finished. The more we peeled, the more peel there seemed to be left on; by the time we had got all the peel off and all the eyes out, there was no potato left – at least none worth speaking of. George came and had a look at it – it was about the size of a pea-nut. He said:

'Oh, that won't do! You're wasting them. You must scrape them.'

So we scraped them, and that was harder work than peeling. They are such an extraordinary shape, potatoes – all bumps and warts and hollows. We worked steadily for five-and-twenty minutes, and did four potatoes. Then we struck. We said we should require the rest of the evening for scraping ourselves.

I never saw such a thing as potato-scraping for making a fellow in a mess. It seemed difficult to believe that the potato-scrapings in which Harris and I stood half-smothered, could have come off four potatoes. It shows you what can be done with economy and care.

George said it was absurd to have only four potatoes in an Irish stew, so we washed half a dozen or so more, and put them in without peeling. We also put in a cabbage and about half a peck² of peas. George stirred it all up, and then he said that there seemed to be a lot of room to spare, so we over-hauled both the hampers, and picked out all the odds and ends and the remnants, and added them to the stew. There were half a pork pie and a bit of cold boiled bacon left, and we put them in. Then George found half a tin of potted salmon, and he emptied that into the pot.

He said that was the advantage of Irish stew: you got rid of such a lot of things. I fished out a couple of eggs that had got cracked, and we put those in. George said they would thicken the gravy.

I forget the other ingredients, but I know nothing was wasted; and I remember that, towards the end, Montmorency, who had evinced great interest in the proceedings throughout, strolled away with an earnest and thoughtful air, reappearing, a few minutes afterwards, with a dead water-rat in his mouth, which he evidently wished to present as his contribution to the dinner; whether in a sarcastic spirit, or with a genuine desire to assist, I cannot say.

We had a discussion as to whether the rat should go in or not. Harris said that he thought it would be all right, mixed up with the other things, and that every little helped; but George stood up for precedent. He said he had never heard of water-rats in Irish stew, and he would rather be on the safe side, and not try experiments.

Harris said:

'If you never try a new thing, how can you tell what it's like? It's men such as you that hamper the world's progress. Think of the man who first tried German sausage!'

It was a great success, that Irish stew. I don't think I ever enjoyed a meal more. There was something so fresh and piquant about it. One's palate gets so tired of the old hackneyed things: here was a dish with a new flavour, with a taste like nothing else on earth.

And it was nourishing, too. As George said, there was good stuff in it. The peas and potatoes might have been a bit softer, but we all had good teeth, so that did not matter much; and as for the gravy, it was a poem – a little too rich, perhaps, for a weak stomach, but nutritious.

We finished up with tea and cherry tart. Montmorency had a fight with the kettle during tea-time, and came off a poor second.

Throughout the trip he had manifested great curiosity concerning the kettle. He would sit and watch it, as it boiled, with a puzzled expression, and would try and rouse it every now and then by growling at it. When it began to splutter and steam he regarded it as a challenge, and would want to fight it, only, at that precise moment, someone would always dash up and bear off his prey before he could get at it.

Today he determined he would be beforehand. At the first sound the kettle made, he rose, growling, and advanced towards it in a threatening attitude. It was only a little kettle, but it was full of pluck, and it up and spat at him.

'Ah! would ye!' growled Montmorency, showing his teeth; 'I'll teach ye to cheek a hard-working, respectable dog; ye miserable, long-nosed, dirty-looking scoundrel, ye. Come on!'

And he rushed at that poor little kettle, and seized it by the spout.

Then, across the evening stillness, broke a blood-curdling yelp, and Montmorency left the boat, and did a constitutional three times round the island at the rate of thirty-five miles an hour, stopping every now and then to bury his nose in a bit of cool mud.

From that day Montmorency regarded the kettle with a mixture of awe, suspicion, and hate. Whenever he saw it he would growl and back at a rapid rate, with his tail shut down, and the moment it was put upon the stove he would promptly climb out of the boat, and sit on the bank, till the whole tea business was over.

George got out his banjo[3] after supper, and wanted to play it, but Harris objected: he said he had got a headache, and did not feel strong enough to stand it. George thought the music might do him good – said music often soothed the nerves and took away a headache; and he twanged two or three notes, just to show Harris what it was like.

Harris said he would rather have the headache.

George has never learned to play the banjo to this day. He has had too much all-round discouragement to meet. He tried on two or three evenings, while we were up the river, to get a little practice, but it was never a success. Harris's language used to be enough to unnerve any man; added to which, Montmorency would sit and howl steadily, right through the performance. It was not giving the man a fair chance.

'What's he want to howl like that for when I'm playing?' George would exclaim indignantly, while taking aim at him with a boot.

'What do you want to play like that for when he is howling?' Harris would retort, catching the boot. 'You let him alone. He can't help howling. He's got a musical ear, and your playing *makes* him howl.'

So George determined to postpone study of the banjo until he reached home. But he did not get much opportunity even there. Mrs P. used to come up and say she was very sorry — for herself, she liked to hear him — but the lady upstairs was in a very delicate state, and the doctor was afraid it might injure the child.

Then George tried taking it out with him late at night and practising round the square. But the inhabitants complained to the police about it, and a watch was set for him one night, and he was captured. The evidence against him was very clear, and he was bound over to keep the peace for six months.

He seemed to lose heart in the business after that. He did make one or two feeble efforts to take up the work again when the six months had elapsed, but there was always the same coldness — the same want of sympathy on the part of the world to fight against; and, after a while, he despaired altogether, and advertised the instrument for sale at a great sacrifice — 'owner having no further use for same' — and took to learning card tricks instead.

It must be disheartening work learning a musical instrument. You would think that Society, for its own sake, would do all it could to assist a man to acquire the art of playing a musical instrument. But it doesn't!

I knew a young fellow once who was studying to play the bagpipes, and you would be surprised at the amount of opposition he had to contend with. Why, not even from the members of his own family did he receive what you call active encouragement. His father was dead against the business from the beginning, and spoke quite unfeelingly on the subject.

My friend used to get up early in the morning to practise, but he had to give that plan up, because of his sister. She was somewhat religiously inclined, and she said it seemed such an awful thing to begin the day like that.

So he sat up at night instead, and played after the family had gone to bed, but that did not do, as it got the house such a bad name. People, going home late, would stop outside to listen, and then put it about all over the town, the next morning, that a fearful murder had been committed at Mr Jefferson's the night before; and would describe how they had heard the victim's shrieks and the brutal oaths and curses of the murderer, followed by the prayer for mercy, and the last dying gurgle of the corpse.

So they let him practise in the day-time, in the back kitchen with all the doors shut; but his more successful passages could generally be heard in the sitting-room, in spite of these precautions, and would affect his mother almost to tears.

She said it put her in mind of her poor father (he had been swallowed by a shark, poor man, while bathing off the coast of New Guinea – where the connexion came in, she could not explain).

Then they knocked up a little place for him at the bottom of the garden, about a quarter of a mile from the house, and made him take the machine down there when he wanted to work it; and sometimes a visitor would come to the house who knew nothing of the matter, and they would forget to tell him all about it and caution him, and he would go out for a stroll round the garden and suddenly get within earshot of those bagpipes without being prepared for it, or knowing what it was. If he were a man of strong mind, it only gave him fits; but a person of mere average intellect it usually sent mad.

There is, it must be confessed, something very sad about the early efforts of an amateur in bagpipes. I have felt that myself when listening to my young friend. They appear to be a trying instrument to perform upon. You have to get enough breath for the whole tune before you start – at least, so I gathered from watching Jefferson.

He would begin magnificently with a wild, full, come-to-the-battle sort of note, that quite roused you. But he would get more and more piano as he went on, and the last verse generally collapsed in the middle with a splutter and a hiss.

You want to be in good health to play the bagpipes.

Young Jefferson only learnt to play one tune on those bagpipes: but I never heard any complaints about the insufficiency of his repertoire – none whatever. This tune was 'The Campbells are Coming, Hooray – Hooray!' so he said, though his father always held that it was 'The Blue Bells of Scotland'. Nobody seemed quite sure what it was exactly, but they all agreed that it sounded Scotch.

Strangers were allowed three guesses, and most of them guessed a different tune each time.

Harris was disagreeable after supper – I think it must have been the stew that had upset him: he is not used to high living – so George and I left him in the boat, and settled to go for a mooch round Henley. He said he should have a glass of whisky and a pipe, and fix things up for the night. We were to shout when we returned, and he would row over from the island and fetch us.

'Don't go to sleep, old man,' we said as we started.

'Not much fear of that while this stew is on,' he grunted, as he pulled back to the island.

Henley was getting ready for the regatta, and was full of bustle. We met a goodish number of men we knew about the town, and in their pleasant company the time slipped by somewhat quickly; so that it was nearly eleven o'clock before we set off on our four-mile walk home – as we had learned to call our little craft by this time.

It was a dismal night, coldish, with a thin rain falling; and as we trudged through the dark, silent fields, talking low to each other, and wondering if we were going right or not, we thought of the cosy boat, with the bright light streaming through the tight-drawn canvas; of Harris and Montmorency, and the whisky, and wished that we were there.

We conjured up the picture of ourselves inside, tired and a little hungry; of the gloomy river and the shapeless trees; and like a giant glow-worm underneath them, our dear old boat, so snug and warm and cheerful. We could see ourselves at supper there, pecking away at cold meat, and passing each other chunks of bread; we could hear the cheery clatter of our knives, the laughing voices, filling all the space, and over-flowing through the opening out into the night. And we hurried on to realize the vision.

We struck the tow-path at length, and that made us happy; because prior to this we had not been sure whether we were walking towards

the river or away from it, and when you are tired and want to go
to bed, uncertainties like that worry you. We passed Shiplake as the
clock was striking the quarter to twelve; and then George said,
thoughtfully:

'You don't happen to remember which of the islands it was, do
you?'

'No,' I replied, beginning to grow thoughtful too, 'I don't. How
many are there?'

'Only four,' answered George. 'It will be all right, if he's awake.'

'And if not?' I queried; but we dismissed that train of thought.

We shouted when we came opposite the first island, but there was
no response; so we went to the second, and tried there, and obtained
the same result.

'Oh! I remember now,' said George; 'it was the third one.'

And we ran on hopefully to the third one, and hallooed.

No answer!

The case was becoming serious. It was now past midnight. The
hotels at Shiplake and Henley would be crammed; and we could not
go round, knocking up cottagers and householders in the middle of
the night, to know if they let apartments! George suggested walking
back to Henley and assaulting a policeman, and so getting a night's
lodging in the station-house. But then there was the thought, 'Suppose he only hits us back and refuses to lock us up!'

We could not pass the whole night fighting policemen. Besides,
we did not want to overdo the thing and get six months.

We despairingly tried what seemed in the darkness to be the
fourth island, but met with no better success. The rain was coming
down fast now, and evidently meant to last. We were wet to the
skin, and cold and miserable. We began to wonder whether there
were only four islands or more, or whether we were near the islands
at all, or whether we were anywhere within a mile of where we
ought to be, or in the wrong part of the river altogether; everything
looked so strange and different in the darkness. We began to understand the sufferings of the Babes in the Wood.[*]

Just when we had given up all hope – yes, I know that is always
the time that things do happen in novels and tales; but I can't help

it. I resolved when I began to write this book, that I would be strictly truthful in all things; and so I will be, even if I have to employ hackneyed phrases for the purpose.

It *was* just when we had given up all hope, and I must therefore say so. Just when we had given up all hope, then, I suddenly caught sight, a little way below us, of a strange, weird sort of glimmer flickering amongst the trees on the opposite bank. For an instant I thought of ghosts; it was such a shadowy, mysterious light. The next moment it flashed across me that it was our boat, and I sent up such a yell across the water that made the night seem to shake in its bed.

We waited breathless for a minute, and then – oh! divinest of music of the darkness! – we heard the answering bark of Montmorency. We shouted back loud enough to wake the Seven Sleepers[5] – I never could understand myself why it should take more noise to waken seven sleepers than one – and, after what seemed an hour, but what was really, I suppose, about five minutes, we saw the lighted boat creeping slowly over the blackness, and heard Harris's sleepy voice asking where we were.

There was an unaccountable strangeness about Harris. It was something more than mere ordinary tiredness. He pulled the boat against a part of the bank from which it was quite impossible for us to get into it, and immediately went to sleep.

It took us an immense amount of screaming and roaring to wake him up again, and put some sense into him; but we succeeded at last, and got safely on board.

Harris had a sad expression on him, so we noticed, when we got into the boat. He gave you the idea of a man who had been through trouble. We asked him if anything had happened, and he said –

'Swans!'

It seemed we had moored close to a swan's nest, and soon after George and I had gone, the female swan came back and kicked up a row about it. Harris had chivvied her off, and she had gone away, and fetched up her old man. Harris said he had had quite a fight with these two swans; but courage and skill had prevailed in the end, and he had defeated them.

Half an hour afterwards they returned with eighteen other swans! It must have been a fearful battle, so far as we could understand Harris's account of it. The swans had tried to drag him and Montmorency out of the boat and drown them; and he had defended himself like a hero for four hours, and had killed the lot, and they had all paddled away to die.

'How many swans did you say there were?' asked George.

'Thirty-two,' replied Harris, sleepily.

'You said eighteen just now,' said George.

'No, I didn't,' grunted Harris; 'I said twelve. Think I can't count?'

What were the real facts about these swans we never found out. We questioned Harris on the subject in the morning, and he said, 'What swans?' and seemed to think that George and I had been dreaming.

Oh, how delightful it was to be safe in the boat, after our trials and fears! We ate a hearty supper, George and I, and we should have had some toddy after it, if we could have found the whisky, but we could not. We examined Harris as to what he had done with it; but he did not seem to know what we meant by 'whisky', or what we were talking about at all. Montmorency looked as if he knew something, but said nothing.

I slept well that night, and should have slept better if it had not been for Harris. I have a vague recollection of having been woken up at least a dozen times during the night by Harris wandering about the boat with the lantern, looking for his clothes. He seemed to be worrying about his clothes all night.

Twice he routed up George and myself to see if we were lying on his trousers. George got quite wild the second time.

'What the thunder do you want your trousers for, in the middle of the night?' he asked indignantly. 'Why don't you lie down, and go to sleep?'

I found him in trouble the next time I awoke because he could not find his socks; and my last hazy remembrance is of being rolled over on my side, and of hearing Harris muttering something about its being an extraordinary thing where his umbrella could have got to.

Chapter 15

We woke late the next morning, and, at Harris's earnest desire, partook of a plain breakfast, with 'non dainties'. Then we cleaned up, and put everything straight (a continual labour, which was beginning to afford me a pretty clear insight into a question that had often posed me – namely, how a woman with the work of only one house on her hands, manages to pass away her time), and, at about ten, set out on what we had determined should be a good day's journey.

We agreed that we would pull this morning, as a change from towing; and Harris thought the best arrangement would be that George and I should scull, and he steer. I did not chime in with this idea at all; I said I thought Harris would have been showing a more proper spirit if he had suggested that he and George should work, and let me rest a bit. It seemed to me that I was doing more than my fair share of the work on this trip, and I was beginning to feel strongly on the subject.

It always does seem to me that I am doing more work than I should do. It is not that I object to the work, mind you; I like work; it fascinates me, I can sit and look at it for hours. I love to keep it by me; the idea of getting rid of it nearly breaks my heart.

You cannot give me too much work; to accumulate work has almost become a passion with me; my study is so full of it now that there is hardly an inch of room for any more. I shall have to throw out a wing soon.

And I am careful of my work, too. Why, some of the work that I have by me now has been in my possession for years and years, and there isn't a finger-mark on it. I take a great pride in my work; I take it down now and then and dust it. No man keeps his work in a better state of preservation than I do.

But, though I crave for work, I still like to be fair. I do not ask for more than my proper share.

But I get it without asking for it – at least, so it appears to me – and this worries me.

George says he does not think I need trouble myself on the subject. He thinks it is only my over-scrupulous nature that makes me fear I am having more than my due; and that, as a matter of fact, I don't have half as much as I ought. But I expect he only says this to comfort me.

In a boat, I have always noticed that it is the fixed idea of each member of the crew that he is doing everything. Harris's notion was, that it was he alone who had been working, and that both George and I had been imposing upon him. George, on the other hand, ridiculed the idea of Harris's having done anything more than eat and sleep, and had a cast-iron opinion that it was he – George himself – who had done all the labour worth speaking of.

He said he had never been out with such a couple of lazy skulks as Harris and I.

That amused Harris.

'Fancy old George talking about work!' he laughed; 'why about half an hour of it would kill him. Have you ever seen George work?' he added, turning to me.

I agreed with Harris that I never had – most certainly not since we had started on this trip.

'Well, I don't see how *you* can know much about it, one way or the other,' George retorted to Harris; 'for I'm blest if you haven't been asleep half the time. Have you ever seen Harris fully awake, except at meal-times?' asked George, addressing me.

Truth compelled me to support George. Harris had been very little good in the boat, so far as helping was concerned, from the beginning.

'Well, hang it all, I've done more than old J., anyhow,' rejoined Harris.

'Well, you couldn't very well have done less,' added George.

'I suppose J. thinks he is the passenger,' continued Harris.

And that was their gratitude to me for having brought them and their wretched old boat all the way up from Kingston, and for having superintended and managed everything for them, and taken care of them, and slaved for them. It is the way of the world.

We settled the present difficulty by arranging that Harris and George should scull up past Reading, and that I should tow the boat on from there. Pulling a heavy boat against a strong stream has few attractions for me now. There was a time, long ago, when I used to clamour for the hard work: now I like to give the youngsters a chance.

I notice that most of the old river hands are similarly retiring, whenever there is any stiff pulling to be done. You can always tell the old river hand by the way in which he stretches himself out upon the cushions at the bottom of the boat, and encourages the rowers by telling them anecdotes about the marvellous feats he performed last season.

'Call what you're doing hard work?' he drawls, between his contented whiffs, addressing the two perspiring novices, who have been grinding away steadily up-stream for the last hour and a half; 'why, Jim Biffles and Jack and I, last season, pulled up from Marlow to Goring in one afternoon – never stopped once. Do you remember that, Jack?'

Jack, who has made himself a bed, in the prow, of all the rugs and coats he can collect, and who has been lying there asleep for the last two hours, partially wakes up on being thus appealed to, and recollects all about the matter, and also remembers that there was an unusually strong stream against them all the way – likewise a stiff wind.

'About thirty-four miles, I suppose, it must have been,' adds the first speaker, reaching down another cushion to put under his head.

'No – no; don't exaggerate, Tom,' murmurs Jack, reprovingly; 'thirty-three at the outside.'

And Jack and Tom, quite exhausted by this conversational effort, drop off to sleep once more. And the two simple-minded youngsters at the sculls feel quite proud of being allowed to row such wonderful oarsmen as Jack and Tom, and strain away harder than ever.

When I was a young man, I used to listen to these tales from my elders, and take them in, and swallow them, and digest every word of them, and then come up for more; but the new generation do not seem to have the simple faith of the old times. We – George, Harris, and myself – took a 'raw 'un' up with us once last season, and we plied him with the customary stretchers about the wonderful things we had done all the way up.

We gave him all the regular ones – the time-honoured lies that have done duty up the river with every boating-man for years past – and added seven entirely original ones that we had invented for ourselves, including a really quite likely story, founded, to a certain extent, on an all but true episode, which had actually happened in a modified degree some years ago to friends of ours – a story that a mere child could have believed without injuring itself much.

And that young man mocked at them all, and wanted us to repeat the feats then and there, and to bet us ten to one that we didn't.

We got to chatting about our rowing experiences this morning, and to recounting stories of our first efforts in the art of oarsmanship. My own earliest boating recollection is of five of us contributing three-pence each and taking out a curiously constructed craft on the Regent's Park lake, drying ourselves subsequently in the park-keeper's lodge.

After that, having acquired a taste for the water, I did a good deal of rafting in various suburban brickfields[1] – an exercise providing more interest and excitement than might be imagined, especially when you are in the middle of the pond and the proprietor of the materials of which the raft is constructed suddenly appears on the bank, with a big stick in his hand.

Your first sensation on seeing this gentleman is that, somehow or other, you don't feel equal to company and conversation, and that, if you could do so without appearing rude, you would rather avoid meeting him; and your object is, therefore, to get off on the opposite side of the pond to which he is and to go home quietly and quickly, pretending not to see him. He, on the contrary, is yearning to take you by the hand, and talk to you.

It appears that he knows your father, and is intimately acquainted with yourself, but this does not draw you towards him. He says he'll teach you to take his boards and make a raft of them; but, seeing that you know how to do this pretty well already, the offer, though doubtless kindly meant, seems a superfluous one on his part, and you are reluctant to put him to any trouble by accepting it.

His anxiety to meet you, however, is proof against all your coolness, and the energetic manner in which he dodges up and down the pond so as to be on the spot to greet you when you land is really quite flattering.

If he be of a stout, and short-winded build, you can easily avoid his advances; but, when he is of the youthful and long-legged type, a meeting is inevitable. The interview is, however, extremely brief, most of the conversation being on his part, your remarks being mostly of an exclamatory and monosyllabic order, and as soon as you can tear yourself away you do so.

I devoted some three months to rafting, and, being then as proficient as there was any need to be at that branch of the art, I determined to go in for rowing proper, and joined one of the Lea boating clubs.

Being out in a boat on the River Lea,[2] especially on Saturday afternoons, soon makes you smart at handling a craft, and spry at escaping being run down by roughs or swamped by barges; and it also affords plenty of opportunity for acquiring the most prompt and graceful method of lying down flat at the bottom of the boat so as to avoid being chucked out into the river by passing tow-lines.

But it does not give you style. It was not till I came to the Thames that I got style. My style of rowing is very much admired now. People say it is so quaint.

George never went near the water until he was sixteen. Then he and eight other gentlemen of about the same age went down in a body to Kew one Saturday, with the idea of hiring a boat there, and pulling to Richmond and back; one of their number, a shock-headed youth, named Joskins, who had once or twice taken out a boat on the Serpentine, told them it was jolly fun, boating!

The tide was running out pretty rapidly when they reached the landing-stage, and there was a stiff breeze blowing across the river, but this did not trouble them at all, and they proceeded to select their boat.

There was an eight-oared racing outrigger drawn up on the stage; that was the one that took their fancy. They said they'd have that one, please. The boatman was away, and only his boy was in charge. The boy tried to damp their ardour for the outrigger and showed them two or three very comfortable-looking boats of the family-party build, but those would not do at all; the outrigger was the boat they thought they would look best in.

So the boy launched it, and they took off their coats and prepared to take their seats. The boy suggested that George, who, even in those days, was always the heavy man of any party, should be number four. George said he should be happy to be number four, and promptly stepped into bow's place and sat down with his back to the stern. They got him into his proper position at last, and then the others followed.

A particularly nervous boy was appointed cox, and the steering principle explained to him by Joskins. Joskins himself took stroke. He told the others that it was simple enough: all they had to do was to follow him.

They said they were ready, and the boy on the landing stage took a boat-hook and shoved them off.

What then followed George is unable to describe in detail. He has a confused recollection of having, immediately on starting, received a violent blow in the small of the back from the butt-end of number five's scull, at the same time that his own seat seemed to disappear from under him by magic, and leave him sitting on the boards. He also noticed, as a curious circumstance, that number two was at the same instant lying on his back at the bottom of the boat, with his legs in the air, apparently in a fit.

They passed under Kew Bridge, broadside, at the rate of eight miles an hour, Joskins being the only one who was rowing. George, on recovering his seat, tried to help him, but, on dipping his oar into the water, it immediately, to his intense surprise, disappeared under the boat, and nearly took him with it.

And the 'cox' threw both rudder lines overboard and burst into tears.

How they got back George never knew, but it took them just forty minutes. A dense crowd watched the entertainment from Kew Bridge with much interest, and everybody shouted out to them different directions. Three times they managed to get the boat back through the arch, and three times they were carried under it again, and every time 'cox' looked up and saw the bridge above him he broke out into renewed sobs.

George said he little thought that afternoon that he should ever come to really like boating.

Harris is more accustomed to sea rowing than to river work, and says that, as an exercise, he prefers it. I don't. I remember taking a small boat out at Eastbourne last summer: I used to do a good deal of sea rowing years ago, and I thought I should be all right; but I found I had forgotten the art entirely. When one scull was deep down underneath the water, the other would be flourishing wildly about in the air.

To get a grip of the water with both at the same time I had to stand up. The parade was crowded with the nobility and gentry, and I had to pull past them in this ridiculous fashion. I landed half-way down the beach, and secured the services of an old boatman to take me back.

I like to watch an old boatman rowing, especially one who has been hired by the hour. There is something so beautifully calm and restful about his method. It is so free from that fretful haste, that vehement striving, that is every day becoming more and more the bane of the nineteenth-century life. He is not for ever straining himself to pass all the other boats. If another boat overtakes him and passes him it does not annoy him; as a matter of fact, they all do overtake him and pass him – all those that are going his way. This would trouble and irritate some people; the sublime equanimity of the hired boatman under the ordeal affords us a beautiful lesson against ambition and uppishness.

Plain practical rowing of the get-the-boat-along order is not a very difficult art to acquire, but it takes a good deal of practice before a man feels comfortable when rowing past girls. It is the 'time' that worries a youngster. 'It's jolly funny,' he says, as for the twentieth time within five minutes he disentangles his sculls from yours; 'I can get on all right when I'm by myself!'

To see two novices try to keep time with one another is very amusing. Bow finds it impossible to keep pace with stroke, because stroke rows in such an extraordinary fashion. Stroke is intensely indignant at this, and explains that what he has been endeavouring to do for the last ten minutes is to adapt his method to bow's limited capacity. Bow, in turn, then becomes insulted, and requests stroke not to trouble his head about him (bow), but to devote his mind to getting a sensible stroke.

'Oh, shall *I* take stroke?' he adds, with the evident idea that that would at once put the whole matter right.

They splash along for another hundred yards with still moderate success, and then the whole secret of their trouble bursts upon stroke like a flash of inspiration.

'I tell you what it is: you've got my sculls,' he cries, turning to bow; 'pass yours over.'

'Well, do you know, I've been wondering how it was I couldn't get on with these,' answers bow, quite brightening up, and most willingly assisting in the exchange. '*Now* we shall be all right.'

But they are not – not even then. Stroke has to stretch his arms nearly out of their sockets to reach his sculls now; while bow's pair, at each recovery, hit him a violent blow in the chest. So they change back again, and come to the conclusion that the man has given them the wrong set altogether; and over their mutual abuse of this man they become quite friendly and sympathetic.

George said he had often longed to take to punting for a change. Punting is not as easy as it looks. As in rowing, you soon learn how to get along and handle the craft, but it takes long practice before you can do this with dignity and without getting the water all up your sleeve.

One young man I knew had a very sad accident happen to him the first time he went punting. He had been getting on so well that he had grown quite cheeky over the business, and was walking up and down the punt, working his pole with a careless grace that was quite fascinating to watch. Up he would march to the head of the punt, plant his pole, and then run along right to the other end, just like an old punter. Oh! it was grand.

And it would all have gone on being grand if he had not unfortunately, while looking round to enjoy the scenery, taken just one step more than there was any necessity for, and walked off the punt altogether. The pole was firmly fixed in the mud, and he was left clinging to it while the punt drifted away. It was an undignified position for him. A rude boy on the bank immediately yelled out to a lagging chum to 'hurry up and see a real monkey on a stick'.

I could not go to his assistance, because, as ill-luck would have it, we had not taken the proper precaution to bring out a spare pole with us. I could only sit and look at him. His expression as the pole slowly sank with him I shall never forget; there was so much thought in it.

I watched him gently let down into the water, and saw him scramble out, sad and wet. I could not help laughing, he looked such a ridiculous figure. I continued to chuckle to myself about it for some time, and then it was suddenly forced upon me that really I had got very little to laugh at when I came to think of it. Here was I, alone in a punt, without a pole, drifting helplessly down midstream – possibly towards a weir.

I began to feel very indignant with my friend for having stepped overboard and gone off in that way. He might, at all events, have left me the pole.

I drifted on for about a quarter of a mile, and then I came in sight of a fishing-punt moored in midstream, in which sat two old fishermen. They saw me bearing down upon them, and they called out to me to keep out of their way.

'I can't,' I shouted back.

'But you don't try,' they answered.

I explained the matter to them when I got nearer, and they caught me and lent me a pole. The weir was just fifty yards below. I am glad they happened to be there.

The first time I went punting was in company with three other fellows; they were going to show me how to do it. We could not all start together, so I said I would go down first and get out the punt, and then I could potter about and practise a bit until they came.

I could not get a punt out that afternoon, they were all engaged; so I had nothing else to do but to sit down on the bank, watching the river, and waiting for my friends.

I had not been sitting there long before my attention became attracted to a man in a punt who, I noticed with some surprise, wore a jacket and cap exactly like mine. He was evidently a novice at punting, and his performance was most interesting. You never knew what was going to happen when he put the pole in; he evidently did not know himself. Sometimes he shot up-stream and sometimes he shot down-stream, and at other times he simply spun round and came up the other side of the pole. And with every result he seemed equally surprised and annoyed.

The people about the river began to get quite absorbed in him after a while, and to make bets with one another as to what would be the outcome of his next push.

In the course of time my friends arrived on the opposite bank, and they stopped and watched him too. His back was towards them, and they only saw his jacket and cap. From this they immediately jumped to the conclusion that it was I, their beloved companion, who was making an exhibition of himself, and their delight knew no bounds. They commenced to chaff him unmercifully.

I did not grasp their mistake at first, and I thought, 'How rude of them to go on like that, with a perfect stranger, too!' But before I could call out and reprove them, the explanation of the matter occurred to me, and I withdrew behind a tree.

Oh, how they enjoyed themselves ridiculing that young man! For five good minutes they stood there, shouting ribaldry at him, deriding him, mocking him, jeering at him. They peppered him with stale jokes, they even made a few new ones and threw them at him. They hurled at him all the private family jokes belonging to our set, which must have been perfectly unintelligible to him. And then, unable to stand their brutal jibes any longer, he turned round on them, and they saw his face!

I was glad to notice that they had sufficient decency left in them to look very foolish. They explained to him that they had thought he was someone they knew. They said they hoped he would not deem them capable of so insulting anyone except a personal friend of their own.

Of course their having mistaken him for a friend excused it. I remember Harris telling me once of a bathing experience he had at Boulogne. He was swimming about there near the beach, when he felt himself suddenly seized by the neck from behind, and forcibly plunged under water. He struggled violently, but whoever had got hold of him seemed to be a perfect Hercules in strength, and all his efforts to escape were unavailing. He had given up kicking, and was trying to turn his thoughts upon solemn things, when his captor released him.

He regained his feet, and looked round for his would-be murderer. The assassin was standing close by him, laughing heartily, but the moment he caught sight of Harris's face, as it emerged from the water, he started back and seemed quite concerned.

'I really beg your pardon,' he stammered confusedly, 'but I took you for a friend of mine!'

Harris thought it was lucky for him the man had not mistaken him for a relation, or he would probably have been drowned outright.

Sailing is a thing that wants knowledge and practice too – though, as a boy, I did not think so. I had an idea it came natural to a body, like rounders and touch.[3] I knew another boy who held this view likewise, and so, one windy day, we thought we would try the sport. We were stopping down at Yarmouth, and we decided we would go for a trip up the Yare. We hired a sailing boat at the yard by the bridge, and started off.

'It's rather a rough day,' said the man to us, as we put off: 'better take in a reef and luff[*] sharp when you get round the bend.'

We said we would make a point of it, and left him with a cheery 'Good morning', wondering to ourselves how you 'luffed', and where we were to get a 'reef' from, and what we were to do with it when we had got it.

We rowed until we were out of sight of the town, and then, with a wide stretch of water in front of us, and the wind blowing a perfect hurricane across it, we felt that the time had come to commence operations.

Hector – I think that was his name – went on pulling while I unrolled the sail. It seemed a complicated job, but I accomplished it at length, and then came the question, which was the top end?

By a sort of natural instinct, we, of course, eventually decided that the bottom was the top, and set to work to fix it upside-down. But it was a long time before we could get it up, either that way or any other way. The impression on the mind of the sail seemed to be that we were playing at funerals, and that I was the corpse and itself was the winding sheet.

When it found that this was not the idea, it hit me over the head with the boom, and refused to do anything.

'Wet it,' said Hector; 'drop it over and get it wet.'

He said people in ships always wetted the sails before they put them up. So I wetted it; but that only made matters worse than they were before. A dry sail clinging to your legs and wrapping itself round your head is not pleasant, but, when the sail is sopping wet, it becomes quite vexing.

We did get the thing up at last, the two of us together. We fixed it, not exactly upside-down – more sideways like – and we tied it up to the mast with the painter, which we cut off for the purpose.

That the boat did not upset I simply state as a fact. Why it did not upset I am unable to offer any reason. I have often thought about the matter since, but I have never succeeded in arriving at any satisfactory explanation of the phenomenon.

Possibly the result may have been brought about by the natural obstinacy of all things in this world. The boat may possibly have come to the conclusion, judging from a cursory view of our behaviour, that we had come out for a morning's suicide, and had thereupon determined to disappoint us. That is the only suggestion I can offer.

By clinging like grim death to the gunwale, we just managed to keep inside the boat, but it was exhausting work. Hector said that pirates and other seafaring people generally lashed the rudder to something or other, and hauled in the main top-jib, during severe squalls, and thought we ought to try to do something of the kind; but I was for letting her have her head to the wind.

As my advice was by far the easiest to follow, we ended by adopting it, and contrived to embrace the gunwale and give her her head.

The boat travelled up-stream for about a mile at a pace I have never sailed at since, and don't want to again. Then, at a bend, she heeled over till half her sail was under water. Then she righted herself by a miracle and flew for a long low bank of soft mud.

That mud-bank saved us. The boat ploughed its way into the middle of it and then stuck. Finding that we were once more able to move according to our ideas, instead of being pitched and thrown about like peas in a bladder, we crept forward, and cut down the sail.

We had had enough sailing. We did not want to overdo the thing and get a surfeit of it. We had had a sail – a good all-round, exciting, interesting sail – and now we thought we would have a row, just for a change like.

We took the sculls and tried to push the boat off the mud, and, in doing so, we broke one of the sculls. After that we proceeded with great caution, but they were a wretched old pair, and the second one cracked almost easier than the first, and left us helpless.

The mud stretched out for about a hundred yards in front of us, and behind us was the water. The only thing to be done was to sit and wait until someone came by.

It was not the sort of day to attract people out on the river, and it was three hours before a soul came in sight. It was an old fisherman who, with immense difficulty, at last rescued us, and we were towed back in an ignominious fashion to the boatyard.

What between tipping the man who had brought us home, and paying for the broken sculls, and for having been out four hours and a half, it cost us a pretty considerable number of weeks' pocket-money, that sail. But we learned experience, and they say that it is always cheap at any price.

Chapter 16

Reading – We are towed by steam-launch – Irritating behaviour of small boats – How they get in the way of steam-launches – George and Harris again shirk their work – Rather a hackneyed story – Streatley and Goring.

We came in sight of Reading about eleven. The river is dirty and dismal here. One does not linger in the neighbourhood of Reading. The town itself is a famous old place, dating from the dim days of King Ethelred,[1] when the Danes anchored their warships in the Kennet, and started from Reading to ravage all the land of Wessex; and here Ethelred and his brother Alfred fought and defeated them, Ethelred doing the praying and Alfred the fighting.

In later years, Reading seems to have been regarded as a handy place to run down to, when matters were becoming unpleasant in London. Parliament generally rushed off to Reading whenever there was a plague on at Westminster; and in 1625, the Law followed suit, and all the courts were held at Reading. It must have been worth while having a mere ordinary plague now and then in London to get rid of both the lawyers and the Parliament.

During the Parliamentary struggle, Reading was besieged by the Earl of Essex,[2] and, a quarter of a century later, the Prince of Orange[3] routed King James's troops there.

Henry I lies buried at Reading, in the Benedictine abbey founded by him there, the ruins of which may still be seen; and, in this same abbey, great John of Gaunt[4] was married to the Lady Blanche.

At Reading lock we came up with a steam-launch, belonging to some friends of mine, and they towed us up to within about a mile of Streatley. It is very delightful being towed up by a launch. I prefer it myself to rowing. The run would have been more delightful still, if it had not been for a lot of wretched small boats that were continually getting in the way of our launch, and, to avoid running down which, we had to be continually easing and stopping. It is really most annoying, the manner in which these rowing boats get in the way of one's launch up the river; something ought to be done to stop it.

And they are so confoundedly impertinent, too, over it. You can whistle till you nearly burst your boiler before they will trouble themselves to hurry. I would have one or two of them run down now and then, if I had my way, just to teach them all a lesson.

The river becomes very lovely from a little above Reading. The railway rather spoils it near Tilehurst, but from Mapledurham up to Streatley it is glorious. A little above Mapledurham lock you pass Hardwick House, where Charles I played bowls. The neighbourhood of Pangbourne, where the quaint little Swan Inn stands, must be as familiar to the *habitués* of the Art Exhibitions as it is to its own inhabitants.

My friends' launch cast us loose just below the grotto and then Harris wanted to make out that it was my turn to pull. This seemed to me most unreasonable. It had been arranged in the morning that I should bring the boat up to three miles above Reading. Well, here we were, ten miles above Reading! Surely it was now their turn again.

I could not get either George or Harris to see the matter in its proper light, however; so, to save argument, I took the sculls. I had not been pulling for more than a minute or so, when George noticed something black floating on the water, and we drew up to it. George leant over, as we neared it, and laid hold of it. And then he drew back with a cry, and a blanched face.

It was the dead body of a woman. It lay very lightly on the water, and the face was sweet and calm. It was not a beautiful face; it was too prematurely aged-looking, too thin and drawn, to be that; but it was a gentle, lovable face, in spite of its stamp of pinch and poverty, and upon it was that look of restful peace that comes to the faces of the sick sometimes when at last the pain has left them.

Fortunately for us – we having no desire to be kept hanging about coroners' courts – some men on the bank had seen the body too, and now took charge of it from us.

We found out the woman's story afterwards. Of course it was the old, old vulgar tragedy. She had loved and been deceived – or had deceived herself. Anyhow, she had sinned – some of us do now and then – and her family and friends, naturally shocked and indignant, had closed their doors against her.

Left to fight the world alone, with the millstone of her shame around her neck, she had sunk ever lower and lower. For a while she had kept both herself and the child on the twelve shillings a week that twelve hours' drudgery a day procured her, paying six shillings out of it for the child, and keeping her own body and soul together on the remainder.

Six shillings a week does not keep body and soul together very unitedly. They want to get away from each other when there is only such a very slight bond as that between them; and one day, I suppose, the pain and the dull monotony of it all had stood before her eyes plainer than usual, and the mocking spectre had frightened her. She had made one last appeal to friends, but against the chill wall of their respectability, the voice of the erring outcast fell unheeded; and then she had gone to see her child – and held it in her arms and kissed it, in a weary, dull sort of way, and without betraying any particular emotion of any kind, and had left it, after putting into its hand a penny box of chocolate she had bought it, and afterwards, with her last few shillings, had taken a ticket and come down to Goring.

It seemed that the bitterest thoughts of her life must have centred about the wooded reaches and the bright green meadows around Goring; but women strangely hug the knife that stabs them, and, perhaps, amidst the gall, there may have mingled also sunny memories of sweetest hours, spent upon those shadowed deeps over which the great trees bend their branches down so low.

She had wandered about the woods by the river's brink all day, and then, when evening fell and the grey twilight spread its dusky robe upon the waters, she stretched her arms out to the silent river that had known her sorrow and her joy. And the old river had taken her into its gentle arms, and had laid her weary head upon its bosom, and had hushed away the pain.

Thus she had sinned in all things – sinned in living and in dying. God help her! and all other sinners, if any more there be.

Goring on the left bank and Streatley on the right are both or either charming places to stay at for a few days. The reaches down to Pangbourne woo one for a sunny sail or for a moonlight row, and the country round about is full of beauty. We had intended to push on to Wallingford that day, but the sweet smiling face of the river here lured us to linger for a while; and so we left our boat at the bridge, and went up into Streatley, and lunched at the 'Bull'; much to Montmorency's satisfaction.

They say that the hills on each side of the stream here once joined and formed a barrier across what is now the Thames, and that then the river ended there above Goring in one vast lake. I am not in a position either to contradict or affirm this statement, I simply offer it.

It is an ancient place, Streatley, dating back, like most riverside towns and villages, to British and Saxon times. Goring is not nearly so pretty a little spot to stop at as Streatley, if you have your choice; but it is passing fair enough in its way, and is nearer the railway in case you want to slip off without paying your hotel bill.

Chapter 17

Washing day – Fish and fishers – On the art of angling – A conscientious fly-fisher – A fishy story.

We stayed two days at Streatley, and got our clothes washed. We had tried washing them ourselves, in the river, under George's superintendence, and it had been a failure. Indeed, it had been more than a failure, because we were worse off after we had washed our clothes than we were before. Before we had washed them, they had been very, very dirty, it is true; but they were just wearable. *After* we had washed them – well, the river between Reading and Henley was much cleaner, after we had washed our clothes in it, than it was before. All the dirt contained in the river between Reading and Henley we collected, during that wash, and worked it into our clothes.

The washerwoman at Streatley said she felt she owed it to herself to charge us just three times the usual price for that wash. She said it had not been like washing, it had been more in the nature of excavating.

We paid the bill without a murmur.

The neighbourhood of Streatley and Goring is a great fishing centre. There is some excellent fishing to be had here. The river abounds in pike, roach, dace, gudgeon, and eels, just here; and you can sit and fish for them all day.

Some people do. They never catch them. I never knew anybody catch anything up the Thames, except minnows and dead cats, but that has nothing to do, of course, with fishing! The local fisherman's guide doesn't say a word about catching anything. All it says is the place is 'a good station for fishing'; and from what I have seen of the district, I am quite prepared to bear out this statement.

There is no spot in the world where you can get more fishing, or where you can fish for a longer period. Some fishermen come here and fish for a day, and others stop and fish for a month. You can hang on and fish for a year, if you want to: it will be all the same.

The *Angler's Guide to the Thames* says that 'jack and perch are also to be had about here', but there the *Angler's Guide* is wrong. Jack and perch may *be* about there. Indeed, I know for a fact that they are. You can *see* them there in shoals, when you are out for a walk along the banks; they come and stand half out of the water with their mouths open for biscuits. And, if you go for a bathe, they crowd round, and get in your way and irritate you. But they are not to be 'had' by a bit of worm on the end of a hook, nor anything like it – not they!

I am not a good fisherman myself. I devoted a considerable amount of attention to the subject at one time, and was getting on, as I thought, fairly well; but the old hands told me that I should never be any real good at it, and advised me to give it up. They said that I was an extremely neat thrower, and that I seemed to have plenty of gumption for the thing, and quite enough constitutional laziness. But they were sure I should never make anything of a fisherman. I had not got sufficient imagination.

They said that as a poet, or a shilling shocker, or a reporter, or anything of that kind, I might be satisfactory, but that, to gain any position as a Thames angler, would require more play of fancy, more power of invention than I appeared to possess.

Some people are under the impression that all that is required to make a good fisherman is the ability to tell lies easily and without blushing; but this is a mistake. Mere bald fabrication is useless; the veriest tyro can manage that. It is in the circumstantial detail, the embellishing touches of probability, the general air of scrupulous – almost of pedantic – veracity, that the experienced angler is seen.

Anybody can come in and say, 'Oh, I caught fifteen dozen perch yesterday evening'; or 'Last Monday I landed a gudgeon, weighing eighteen pounds, and measuring three feet from the tip of the tail'.

There is no art, no skill, required for that sort of thing. It shows pluck, but that is all.

No; your accomplished angler would scorn to tell a lie, that way. His method is a study in itself.

He comes in quietly with his hat on, appropriates the most comfortable chair, lights his pipe, and commences to puff in silence. He lets the youngsters brag away for a while, and then, during a momentary lull, he removes the pipe from his mouth, and remarks, as he knocks the ashes out against the bars:

'Well, I had a haul on Tuesday evening that it's not much good my telling anybody about.'

'Oh! Why's that?' they ask.

'Because I don't expect anybody would believe me if I did,' replies the old fellow calmly, and without even a tinge of bitterness in his tone, as he refills his pipe, and requests the landlord to bring him three of Scotch, cold.

There is a pause after this, nobody feeling sufficiently sure of himself to contradict the old gentleman. So he has to go on by himself without any encouragement.

'No,' he continues thoughtfully; 'I shouldn't believe it myself if anybody told it to me, but it's a fact, for all that. I had been sitting there all the afternoon and had caught literally nothing – except a few dozen dace and a score of jack; and I was just about giving it up as a bad job when I suddenly felt a rather smart pull at the line. I thought it was another little one, and I went to jerk it up. Hang me, if I could move the rod! It took me half an hour – half an hour, sir! – to land that fish; and every moment I thought the line was going to snap! I reached him at last, and what do you think it was? A sturgeon! a forty-pound sturgeon! taken on a line, sir! Yes, you may well look surprised – I'll have another three of Scotch, landlord, please.'

And then he goes on to tell of the astonishment of everybody who saw it; and what his wife said, when he got home, and of what Joe Buggles thought about it.

I asked the landlord of an inn up the river once, if it did not injure him, sometimes, listening to the tales that the fishermen about there told him; and he said:

'Oh, no; not now, sir. It did used to knock me over a bit at first, but, lor love you! me and the missus we listen to 'em all day now. It's what you're used to, you know. It's what you're used to.'

I knew a young man once, he was a most conscientious fellow and, when he took to fly-fishing, he determined never to exaggerate his hauls by more than twenty-five per cent.

'When I have caught forty fish,' said he, 'then I will tell people that I have caught fifty, and so on. But I will not lie any more than that, because it is sinful to lie.'

But the twenty-five per cent plan did not work well at all. He never was able to use it. The greatest number of fish he ever caught in one day was three, and you can't add twenty-five per cent to three – at least, not in fish.

So he increased his percentage to thirty-three and a third, but that, again, was awkward, when he had only caught one or two; so, to simplify matters, he made up his mind to just double the quantity.

He stuck to this arrangement for a couple of months, and then he grew dissatisfied with it. Nobody believed him when he told them that he only doubled, and he, therefore, gained no credit that way whatever, while his moderation put him at a disadvantage among the other anglers. When he had really caught three small fish, and said he had caught six, it used to make him quite jealous to hear a man, whom he knew for a fact had only caught one, going about telling people he had landed two dozen.

So, eventually he made one final arrangement with himself, which he has religiously held to ever since, and that was to count each fish that he caught as ten, and to assume ten to begin with. For example, if he did not catch any fish at all, then he said he had caught ten fish – you could never catch less than ten fish by his system; that was the foundation of it. Then, if by any chance he really did catch one fish, he called it twenty, while two fish would count thirty, three forty, and so on.

It is a simple and easily worked plan, and there has been some talk lately of its being made use of by the angling fraternity in general. Indeed, the Committee of the Thames Anglers' Association did recommend its adoption about two years ago, but some of the older members opposed it. They said they would consider the idea if the number were doubled, and each fish counted as twenty.

If ever you have an evening to spare, up the river, I should advise you to drop into one of the little village inns, and take a seat in the tap-room. You will be nearly sure to meet one or two old rod-men, sipping their toddy there, and they will tell you enough fishy stories in half an hour to give you indigestion for a month.

George and I – I don't know what had become of Harris; he had gone out and had a shave, early in the afternoon, and had then come back and spent full forty minutes in pipeclaying[1] his shoes, we had not seen him since – George and I, therefore, and the dog, left to ourselves, went for a walk to Wallingford on the second evening, and, coming home, we called in at a little riverside inn, for a rest, and other things.

We went into the parlour and sat down. There was an old fellow there, smoking a long clay pipe, and we naturally began chatting.

He told us that it had been a fine day today and we told him that it had been a fine day yesterday, and then we all told each other that we thought it would be a fine day tomorrow; and George said the crops seemed to be coming up nicely.

After that it came out, somehow or other, that we were strangers in the neighbourhood, and that we were going away the next morning.

Then a pause ensued in the conversation, during which our eyes wandered round the room. They finally rested upon a dusty old glass-case, fixed very high up above the chimney piece, and containing a trout. It rather fascinated me, that trout; it was such a monstrous fish. In fact, at first glance, I thought it was a cod.

'Ah!' said the old gentleman, following the direction of my gaze, 'fine fellow that, ain't he?'

'Quite uncommon,' I murmured; and George asked the old man how much he thought it weighed.

'Eighteen pounds six ounces,' said our friend, rising and taking down his coat. 'Yes,' he continued, 'it wur sixteen year ago, come the third o' next month, that I landed him. I caught him just below the bridge with a minnow. They told me he wur in the river, and I said I'd have him, and so I did. You don't see many fish that size about here now, I'm thinking. Good night, gentlemen, good night.'

And out he went, and left us alone.

We could not take our eyes off the fish after that. It really was a remarkably fine fish. We were still looking at it, when the local carrier, who had just stopped at the inn, came to the door of the room with a pot of beer in his hand, and he also looked at the fish.

'Good-sized trout, that,' said George, turning round to him.

'Ah! you may well say that, sir,' replied the man; and then, after a pull at his beer, he added, 'Maybe you wasn't here, sir, when that fish was caught?'

'No,' we told him. We were strangers in the neighbourhood.

'Ah!' said the carrier, 'then, of course, how should you? It was nearly five years ago that I caught that trout.'

'Oh! Was it you who caught it, then?' said I.

'Yes, sir,' replied the genial old fellow. 'I caught him just below the lock – leastways, what was the lock then – one Friday afternoon; and the remarkable thing about it is that I caught him with a fly. I'd gone out pike fishing, bless you, never thinking of a trout, and when I saw that whopper on the end of my line, blest if it didn't quite take me aback. Well, you see, he weighed twenty-six pound. Good night, gentlemen, good night.'

Five minutes afterwards a third man came in, and described how *he* had caught it early one morning, with bleak; and then he left, and a stolid, solemn-looking, middle-aged individual came in, and sat down over by the window.

None of us spoke for a while; but, at length, George turned to the new-comer, and said:

'I beg your pardon, I hope you will forgive the liberty that we – perfect strangers in the neighbourhood – are taking, but my friend here and myself would be so much obliged if you would tell us how you caught that trout up there.'

'Why, who told you I caught that trout!' was the surprised query.

We said that nobody had told us so, but somehow or other we felt instinctively that it was he who had done it.

'Well, it's a most remarkable thing – most remarkable,' answered the stolid stranger, laughing; 'because, as a matter of fact, you are quite right. I did catch it. But fancy your guessing it like that. Dear me, it's really a most remarkable thing.'

And then he went on, and told us how it had taken him half an hour to land it, and how it had broken his rod. He said he had weighed it carefully when he reached home, and it had turned the scale at thirty-four pounds.

He went in his turn, and when he was gone, the landlord came in to us. We told him the various histories we had heard about his trout, and he was immensely amused, and we all laughed very heartily.

'Fancy Jim Bates and Joe Muggles and Mr Jones and old Billy Maunders all telling you that they had caught it. Ha! ha! ha! Well, that is good,' said the honest old fellow, laughing heartily. 'Yes, they are the sort to give it *me*, to put up in *my* parlour, if *they* had caught it, they are! Ha! ha! ha!'

And then he told us the real history of the fish. It seemed that he had caught it himself, years ago, when he was quite a lad; not by any art or skill, but by that unaccountable luck that appears to always wait upon a boy when he plays the wag from school, and goes out fishing on a sunny afternoon, with a bit of string tied on to the end of a tree.

He said that bringing home that trout had saved him from a whacking, and that even his schoolmaster had said it was worth the rule-of-three and practice put together.

He was called out of the room at this point, and George and I turned our gaze upon the fish.

It really was a most astonishing trout. The more we looked at it, the more we marvelled at it.

It excited George so much that he climbed up on the back of a chair to get a better view of it.

And then the chair slipped, and George clutched wildly at the trout-case to save himself, and down it came with a crash, George and the chair on top of it.

'You haven't injured the fish, have you?' I cried in alarm, rushing up.

'I hope not,' said George, rising cautiously and looking about.

But he had. That trout lay shattered into a thousand fragments – I say a thousand, but they may have only been nine hundred. I did not count them.

We thought it strange and unaccountable that a stuffed trout should break up into little pieces like that.

And so it would have been strange and unaccountable, if it had been a stuffed trout, but it was not.

That trout was plaster of Paris.

Chapter 18

Locks – George and I are photographed – Wallingford – Dorchester – Abingdon – A family-man – A good spot for drowning – A difficult bit of water – Demoralizing effect of river air.

We left Streatley early the next morning, and pulled up to Culham, and slept under the canvas, in the backwater there.

The river is not extraordinarily interesting between Streatley and Wallingford. From Cleeve you get a stretch of six and a half miles without a lock. I believe this is the longest uninterrupted stretch anywhere above Teddington, and the Oxford Club make use of it for their trial eights.

But however satisfactory this absence of locks may be to rowing men, it is to be regretted by the mere pleasure-seeker.

For myself, I am fond of locks. They pleasantly break the monotony of the pull. I like sitting in the boat and slowly rising out of the cool depths up into new reaches and fresh views; or sinking down, as it were, out of the world, and then waiting, while the gloomy gates creak, and the narrow strip of daylight between them widens till the fair smiling river lies full before you, and you push your little boat out from its brief prison on to the welcoming waters once again.

They are picturesque little spots, these locks. The stout old lock-keeper, or his cheerful-looking wife, or bright-eyed daughter, are pleasant folk to have a passing chat with.* You meet other boats there, and river gossip is exchanged. The Thames would not be the fairyland it is without its flower-decked locks.

Talking of locks reminds me of an accident George and I very nearly had one summer's morning at Hampton Court.

It was a glorious day, and the lock was crowded; and, as is a common practice up the river, a speculative photographer was taking a picture of us all as we lay upon the rising waters.

I did not catch what was going on at first, and was, therefore, extremely surprised at noticing George hurriedly smooth out his trousers, ruffle his hair, and stick his cap on in a rakish manner at the back of his head, and then, assuming an expression of mingled affability and sadness, sit down in a graceful attitude, and try to hide his feet.

My first idea was that he had suddenly caught sight of some girl he knew, and I looked about to see who it was. Everybody in the lock seemed to have been suddenly struck wooden. They were all standing or sitting about in the most quaint and curious attitudes I have ever seen off a Japanese fan. All the girls were smiling. Oh, they did look so sweet! And all the fellows were frowning, and looking stern and noble.

And then, at last, the truth flashed across me, and I wondered if

---

* Or rather *were*. The Conservancy[1] of late seems to have constituted itself into a society for the employment of idiots. A good many of the new lock-keepers, especially in the more crowded portions of the river, are excitable, nervous old men quite unfitted for their post.

I should be in time. Ours was the first boat, and it would be unkind of me to spoil the man's picture, I thought.

So I faced round quickly, and took up a position in the prow, where I leant with careless grace upon the hitcher, in an attitude suggestive of agility and strength. I arranged my hair with a curl over the forehead, and threw an air of tender wistfulness into my expression, mingled with a touch of cynicism, which I am told suits me.

As we stood, waiting for the eventful moment, I heard someone behind call out:

'Hi! look at your nose.'

I could not turn round to see what was the matter, and whose nose it was that was to be looked at. I stole a side-glance at George's nose! It was all right – at all events, there was nothing wrong with it that could be altered. I squinted down at my own and that seemed all that could be expected also.

'Look at your nose, you stupid ass!' came the same voice again, louder.

And then another voice cried:

'Push your nose out, can't you, you – you two with the dog!'

Neither George nor I dared to turn round. The man's hand was on the cap and the picture might be taken any moment. Was it us they were calling to? What was the matter with our noses? Why were they to be pushed out!

But now the whole lock started yelling, and a stentorian voice from the back shouted:

'Look at your boat, sir; you in the red and black caps. It's your two corpses that will get taken in that photo, if you ain't quick.'

We looked then, and saw that the nose of our boat had got fixed under the woodwork of the lock, while the in-coming water was rising all around it, and tilting it up. In another moment we should be over. Quick as thought, we each seized an oar, and a vigorous blow against the side of the lock with the butt-ends released the boat, and sent us sprawling on our backs.

We did not come out well in that photograph, George and I. Of course, as was to be expected, our luck ordained it that the man should set his wretched machine in motion at the precise moment that we were both lying on our backs with a wild expression of 'Where am I? and what is it?' on our faces, and our feet waving madly in the air.

Our feet were undoubtedly the leading article in that photograph. Indeed, very little else was to be seen. They filled up the foreground entirely. Behind them, you caught glimpses of the other boats, and bits of the surrounding scenery; but everything and everybody else in the lock looked so utterly insignificant and paltry compared with our feet, that all the other people felt quite ashamed of themselves, and refused to subscribe to the picture.

The owner of one steam-launch, who had bespoke six copies, rescinded the order on seeing the negative. He said he would take them if anybody could show him his launch, but nobody could. It was somewhere behind George's right foot.

There was a good deal of unpleasantness over the business. The photographer thought we ought to take a dozen copies each, seeing that the photo was about nine-tenths us, but we declined. We said we had no objection to being photo'd full-length, but we preferred being taken the right way up.

Wallingford, six miles above Streatley, is a very ancient town, and has been an active centre for the making of English history. It was a rude, mud-built town in the time of the Britons, who squatted there, until the Roman legions evicted them; and replaced their clay-baked walls by mighty fortifications, the trace of which Time has not yet succeeded in sweeping away, so well those old-world masons knew how to build.

But Time, though he halted at Roman walls, soon crumbled Romans to dust; and on the ground, in later years, fought savage Saxons and huge Danes, until the Normans came.

It was a walled and fortified town up to the time of the Parliamentary war, when it suffered a long and bitter siege from Fairfax.[2] It fell at last, and then the walls were razed.

From Wallingford up to Dorchester the neighbourhood of the river grows more hilly, varied, and picturesque. Dorchester stands half a mile from the river. It can be reached by paddling up the

Thames if you have a small boat; but the best way is to leave the river at Day's lock, and take a walk across the fields. Dorchester is a delightfully peaceful old place, nestling in stillness and silence and drowsiness.

Dorchester, like Wallingford, was a city in ancient British times; it was then called Caer Doren, 'the city on the water'. In more recent times the Romans formed a great camp here, the fortifications surrounding which now seem like low, even hills. In Saxon days it was the capital of Wessex. It is very old, and it was very strong and great once. Now it sits aside from the stirring world, and nods and dreams.

Round Clifton Hampden, itself a wonderfully pretty village, old-fashioned, peaceful, and dainty with flowers, the river scenery is rich and beautiful. If you stay the night on land at Clifton, you cannot do better than put up at the 'Barley Mow'. It is, without exception, I should say, the quaintest, most old-world inn up the river. It stands on the right of the bridge, quite away from the village. Its low-pitched gables and thatched roof and latticed windows give it quite a story-book appearance, while inside it is even still more once-upon-a-timeyfied.

It would not be a good place for the heroine of a modern novel to stay at. The heroine of a modern novel is always 'divinely tall', and she is ever 'drawing herself up to her full height'. At the 'Barley Mow' she would bump her head against the ceiling each time she did this.

It would also be a bad house for a drunken man to put up at. There are too many surprises in the way of unexpected steps down into this room and up into that; and as for getting upstairs to his bedroom, or ever finding his bed when he got up, either operation would be an utter impossibility to him.

We were up early the next morning, as we wanted to be in Oxford by the afternoon. It is surprising how early one *can* get up, when camping out. One does not yearn for 'just another five minutes' nearly so much, lying wrapped up in a rug on the boards of a boat, with a Gladstone bag for a pillow, as one does in a feather bed. We had finished breakfast, and were through Clifton lock by half past eight.

From Clifton to Culham the river banks are flat, monotonous, and uninteresting, but, after you get through Culham lock – the coldest and deepest lock on the river – the landscape improves.

At Abingdon, the river passes by the streets. Abingdon is a typical country town of the smaller order – quiet, eminently respectable, clean, and desperately dull. It prides itself on being old, but whether it can compare in this respect with Wallingford and Dorchester seems doubtful. A famous abbey stood here once, and within what is left of its sanctified walls they brew a bitter ale nowadays.

In St Nicholas Church, at Abingdon, there is a monument to John Blackwall and his wife Jane, who both, after leading a happy married life, died on the very same day, August 21, 1625; and in St Helen's Church it is recorded that W. Lee, who died in 1637, 'had in his lifetime issue from his loins two hundred lacking but three'. If you work this out you will find that Mr W. Lee's family numbered one hundred and ninety-seven. Mr W. Lee – five times Mayor of Abingdon – was, no doubt, a benefactor to his generation, but I hope there are not many of his kind about in this overcrowded nineteenth century.

From Abingdon to Nuneham Courtenay is a lovely stretch. Nuneham Park is well worth a visit. It can be viewed on Tuesdays and Thursdays. The house contains a fine collection of pictures and curiosities, and the grounds are very beautiful.

The pool under Sandford lasher,[3] just behind the lock, is a very good place to drown yourself in. The undercurrent is terribly strong, and if you once get down into it you are all right. An obelisk marks the spot where two men have already been drowned, while bathing there; and the steps of the obelisk are generally used as a diving-board by young men now who wish to see if the place really *is* dangerous.

Iffley lock and mill, a mile before you reach Oxford, is a favourite subject with the river-loving brethren of the brush. The real article, however, is rather disappointing, after the pictures. Few things, I have noticed, come quite up to the pictures of them, in this world.

We passed through Iffley lock at about half past twelve, and then, having tidied up the boat and made all ready for landing, we set to work on our last mile.

Between Iffley and Oxford is the most difficult bit of the river I know. You want to be born on that bit of water, to understand it. I have been over it a fairish number of times, but I have never been able to get the hang of it. The man who could row a straight course from Oxford to Iffley ought to be able to live comfortably, under one roof, with his wife, his mother-in-law, his eldest sister, and the old servant who was in the family when he was a baby.

First the current drives you on to the right bank, and then on to the left, then it takes you out into the middle, turns you round three times, and carries you up-stream again, and always ends by trying to smash you up against a college barge.

Of course, as a consequence of this, we got in the way of a good many other boats, during the mile, and they in ours, and, of course, as a consequence of that, a good deal of bad language occurred.

I don't know why it should be, but everybody is always so exceptionally irritable on the river. Little mishaps, that you would hardly notice on dry land, drive you nearly frantic with rage, when they occur on the water. When Harris or George makes an ass of himself on dry land, I smile indulgently; when they behave in a chuckle-head way on the river, I use the most blood-curdling language to them. When another boat gets in my way, I feel I want to take an oar and kill all the people in it.

The mildest-tempered people, when on land, become violent and bloodthirsty when in a boat. I did a little boating once with a young lady. She was naturally of the sweetest and gentlest disposition imaginable, but on the river it was quite awful to hear her.

'Oh, drat the man!' she would exclaim, when some unfortunate sculler would get in her way; 'why don't he look where he's going?'

And, 'Oh, bother the silly old thing!' she would say indignantly, when the sail would not go up properly. And she would catch hold of it, and shake it quite brutally.

Yet, as I have said, when on shore she was kind-hearted and amiable enough.

The air of the river has a demoralizing effect upon one's temper, and this it is, I suppose, which causes even bargemen to be sometimes rude to one another, and to use language which, no doubt, in their calmer moments they regret.

Chapter 19

Oxford – Montmorency's idea of Heaven – The hired up-river boat, its beauties and advantages – 'The Pride of the Thames' – The weather changes – The river under different aspects – Not a cheerful evening – Yearnings for the unattainable – The cheery chat goes round – George performs upon the banjo – A mournful melody – Another wet day – Flight – A little supper and a toast.

We spent two very pleasant days at Oxford. There are plenty of dogs in the town of Oxford. Montmorency had eleven fights on the first day, and fourteen on the second, and evidently thought he had got to Heaven.

Among folk too constitutionally weak, or too constitutionally lazy, whichever it may be, to relish up-stream work, it is a common practice to get a boat at Oxford, and row down. For the energetic, however, the up-stream journey is certainly to be preferred. It does not seem good to be always going with the current. There is more satisfaction in squaring one's back, and fighting against it, and winning one's way forward in spite of it – at least, so I feel, when Harris and George are sculling and I am steering.

To those who do contemplate making Oxford their starting-place, I would say, take your own boat – unless, of course, you can take someone else's without any possible danger of being found out. The boats that, as a rule, are let for hire on the Thames above Marlow, are very good boats. They are fairly water-tight; and so long as they are handled with care, they rarely come to pieces, or sink. There are places in them to sit down on, and they are complete with all the necessary arrangements – or nearly all – to enable you to row them and steer them.

But they are not ornamental. The boat you hire up the river above Marlow is not the sort of boat in which you can flash about and give yourself airs. The hired up-river boat very soon puts a stop to any nonsense of that sort on the part of its occupants. That is its chief – one may say – its only recommendation.

The man in the hired up-river boat is modest and retiring. He likes to keep on the shady side underneath the trees, and to do most of his travelling early in the morning or late at night when there are not many people about on the river to look at him.

When the man in the hired up-river boat sees anyone he knows, he gets out on the bank, and hides behind a tree.

I was one of a party who hired an up-river boat one summer, for a few days' trip. We had none of us ever seen the hired up-river boat before; and we did not know what it was when we did see it.

We had written for a boat – a double sculling skiff; and when we went down with our bags to the yard, and gave our names, the man said:

'Oh, yes; you're the party that wrote for a double sculling skiff. It's all right. Jim, fetch round *The Pride of the Thames*.'

The boy went and reappeared five minutes afterwards, struggling with an antediluvian chunk of wood, that looked as though it had been recently dug out of somewhere and dug out carelessly, so as to have been unnecessarily damaged in the process.

My own idea, on first catching sight of the object, was that it was a Roman relic of some sort, – relic of *what* I do not know, possibly of a coffin.

The neighbourhood of the upper Thames is rich in Roman relics, and my surmise seemed to me a very probable one; but our serious young man, who is a bit of a geologist, pooh-poohed my Roman relic theory, and said it was clear to the meanest intellect (in which category he seemed to be grieved that he could not conscientiously include mine) that the thing the boy had found was the fossil of a whale; and he pointed out to us various evidences proving that it must have belonged to the pre-glacial period.

To settle the dispute, we appealed to the boy. We told him not to be afraid, but to speak the plain truth: Was it the fossil of a pre-Adamite whale, or was it an early Roman coffin?

The boy said it was *The Pride of the Thames.*

We thought this a very humorous answer on the part of the boy at first, and somebody gave him twopence as a reward for his ready wit; but when he persisted in keeping up the joke, as we thought, too long, we got vexed with him.

'Come, come, my lad!' said our captain sharply, 'don't let us have any nonsense. You take your mother's washing-tub home again, and bring us a boat.'

The boat-builder himself came up then, and assured us, on his word as a practical man, that the thing really was a boat – was, in fact, *the* boat, the 'double sculling skiff' selected to take us on our trip down the river.

We grumbled a good deal. We thought he might, at least, have had it whitewashed or tarred – had *something* done to it to distinguish it from a bit of a wreck; but he could not see any fault in it.

He even seemed offended at our remarks. He said he had picked us out the best boat in all his stock, and he thought we might have been more grateful.

He said it, *The Pride of the Thames*, had been in use, just as it now stood (or rather as it now hung together), for the last forty years, to *his* knowledge, and nobody had complained of it before, and he did not see why we should be the first to begin.

We argued no more.

We fastened the so-called boat together with some pieces of string, got a bit of wall-paper and pasted over the shabbier places, said our prayers, and stepped on board.

They charged us thirty-five shillings for the loan of the remnant for six days; and we could have bought the thing out-and-out for four-and-sixpence at any sale of driftwood round the coast.

The weather changed on the third day – Oh! I am talking about our present trip now – and we started from Oxford upon our homeward journey in the midst of a steady drizzle.

The river – with the sunlight flashing from its dancing wavelets, gilding gold the grey-green beech-trunks, glinting through the dark, cool wood paths, chasing shadows o'er the shallows, flinging diamonds from the mill-wheels, throwing kisses to the lilies, wantoning with the weirs' white waters, silvering moss-grown walls and bridges, brightening every tiny townlet, making sweet each lane and meadow, lying tangled in the rushes, peeping, laughing, from each inlet, gleaming gay on many a far sail, making soft the air with glory – is a golden fairy stream.

But the river – chill and weary, with the ceaseless raindrops falling on its brown and sluggish waters, with the sound as of a woman, weeping low in some dark chamber, while the woods, all dark and silent, shrouded in their mists of vapour, stand like ghosts upon the margin; silent ghosts with eyes reproachful, like the ghosts of evil actions, like the ghosts of friends neglected – is a spirit-haunted water through the land of vain regrets.

Sunlight is the life-blood of Nature. Mother Earth looks at us with such dull, soulless eyes, when the sunlight has died away from out of her. It makes us sad to be with her then; she does not seem to know us or to care for us. She is as a widow who has lost the husband she loved, and her children touch her hand, and look up into her eyes, but gain no smile from her.

We rowed on all that day through the rain, and very melancholy work it was. We pretended, at first, that we enjoyed it. We said it was a change, and that we liked to see the river under all its different aspects. We said we could not expect to have it all sunshine, nor should we wish it. We told each other that Nature was beautiful, even in her tears.

Indeed, Harris and I were quite enthusiastic about the business, for the first few hours. And we sang a song about a gipsy's life, and how delightful a gipsy's existence was! – free to storm and sunshine, and to every wind that blew! – and how he enjoyed the rain, and what a lot of good it did him; and how he laughed at people who didn't like it.

George took the fun more soberly, and stuck to the umbrella.

We hoisted the cover before we had lunch, and kept it up all the afternoon, just leaving a little space in the bow, from which one of us could paddle and keep a look-out. In this way we made nine miles, and pulled up for the night a little below Day's lock.

I cannot honestly say that we had a merry evening. The rain poured down with quiet persistency. Everything in the boat was damp and clammy. Supper was not a success. Cold veal pie, when you don't feel hungry, is apt to cloy. I felt I wanted whitebait and a cutlet; Harris babbled of soles and white-sauce, and passed the remains of his pie to Montmorency, who declined it, and, apparently insulted by the offer, went and sat over at the other end of the boat by himself.

George requested that we would not talk about these things, at all events until he had finished his cold boiled beef without mustard.

We played penny nap[1] after supper. We played for about an hour and a half, by the end of which time George had won fourpence – George always is lucky at cards – and Harris and I had lost exactly twopence each.

We thought we would give up gambling then. As Harris said, it breeds an unhealthy excitement when carried too far. George offered to go on and give us our revenge; but Harris and I decided not to battle any further against Fate.

After that, we mixed ourselves some toddy, and sat round and talked. George told us about a man he had known, who had come up the river two years ago, and who had slept out in a damp boat on just such another night as that was, and it had given him rheumatic fever, and nothing was able to save him, and he had died in great agony ten days afterwards. George said he was quite a young man, and was engaged to be married. He said it was one of the saddest things he had ever known.

And that put Harris in mind of a friend of his, who had been in the Volunteers,[2] and who had slept out under canvas one wet night down at Aldershot, 'on just such another night as this', said Harris; and he had woken up in the morning a cripple for life. Harris said he would introduce us both to the man when we got back to town; it would make our hearts bleed to see him.

This naturally led to some pleasant chat about sciatica, fevers, chills, lung diseases, and bronchitis; and Harris said how very awkward it would be if one of us were taken seriously ill in the night, seeing how far away we were from a doctor.

There seemed to be a desire for something frolicsome to follow up this conversation, and in a weak moment I suggested that George should get out his banjo, and see if he could not give us a comic song.

I will say for George that he did not want any pressing. There was no nonsense about having left his music at home, or anything of that sort. He at once fished out his instrument, and commenced to play *Two Lovely Black Eyes*.

I had always regarded *Two Lovely Black Eyes* as rather a commonplace tune until that evening. The rich vein of sadness that George extracted from it quite surprised me.

The desire that grew upon Harris and myself, as the mournful strains progressed, was to fall upon each other's necks and weep; but by great effort we kept back the rising tears, and listened to the wild yearnful melody in silence.

When the chorus came we even made a desperate effort to be merry. We refilled our glasses and joined in; Harris, in a voice trembling with emotion, leading, and George and I following a few words behind:

> Two lovely black eyes
> Oh! what a surprise!
> Only for telling a man he was wrong.
> Two –

There we broke down. The unutterable pathos of George's accompaniment to that 'two' we were, in our then state of depression, unable to bear. Harris sobbed like a little child, and the dog howled till I thought his heart or his jaw must surely break.

George wanted to go on with another verse. He thought that when he had got a little more into the tune, and could throw more 'abandon', as it were, into the rendering, it might not seem so sad. The feeling of the majority, however, was opposed to the experiment.

There being nothing else to do, we went to bed – that is, we undressed ourselves, and tossed about at the bottom of the boat for some three or four hours. After which, we managed to get some fitful slumber until five a.m., when we all got up and had breakfast.

The second day was exactly like the first. The rain continued to pour down, and we sat, wrapped up in our mackintoshes, underneath the canvas, and drifted slowly down.

One of us – I forget which one now, but I rather think it was myself – made a few feeble attempts during the course of the morning to work up the old gipsy foolishness about being children of Nature and enjoying the wet; but it did not go down well at all. That –

I care not for the rain, not I!

was so painfully evident, as expressing the sentiments of each of us, that to sing it seemed unnecessary.

On one point we were all agreed, and that was that, come what might, we would go through with this job to the bitter end. We had come out for a fortnight's enjoyment on the river, and a fortnight's enjoyment on the river we meant to have. If it killed us! – well, that would be a sad thing for our friends and relations, but it could not be helped. We felt that to give in to the weather in a climate such as ours would be a most disastrous precedent.

'It's only two days more,' said Harris, 'and we are young and strong. We may get over it all right, after all.'

At about four o'clock we began to discuss our arrangements for the evening. We were a little past Goring then, and we decided to paddle on to Pangbourne, and put up there for the night.

'Another jolly evening!' murmured George.

We sat and mused on the prospect. We should be in at Pangbourne by five. We should finish our dinner at, say, half past six. After that we could walk about the village in the pouring rain until bedtime; or we could sit in a dimly lit bar-parlour and read the almanac.

'Why, the Alhambra[3] would be almost more lively,' said Harris, venturing his head outside the cover for a moment and taking a survey of the sky.

'With a little supper at the –* to follow,' I added, half unconsciously.

---

* A capital little out-of-the-way restaurant in the neighbourhood of –, where you can get one of the best-cooked and cheapest little French dinners or suppers that I know of, with an excellent bottle of Beaune for three-and-six; and which I am not going to be idiot enough to advertise.

'Yes, it's almost a pity we've made up our minds to stick to this boat,' answered Harris; and then there was silence for a while.

'If we *hadn't* made up our minds to contract our certain deaths in this bally old coffin,' observed George, casting a glance of intense malevolence over the boat, 'it might be worth while to mention that there's a train leaves Pangbourne, I know, soon after five, which would just land us in town in comfortable time to get a chop, and then go on to the place you mentioned afterwards.'

Nobody spoke. We looked at one another, and each one seemed to see his own mean and guilty thoughts reflected in the faces of the others. In silence, we dragged out and overhauled the Gladstone. We looked up the river and down the river; not a soul was in sight!

Twenty minutes later, three figures, followed by a shamed-looking dog, might have been seen creeping stealthily from the boat-house at the 'Swan', towards the railway station, dressed in the following neither neat nor gaudy costume:

Black leather shoes, dirty; suit of boating flannels, very dirty; brown felt hat, much battered; mackintosh, very wet; umbrella.

We had deceived the boatman at Pangbourne. We had not had the face to tell him that we were running away from the rain. We had left the boat, and all it contained, in his charge, with instructions that it was to be ready for us at nine the next morning. If, we said – *if* anything unforeseen should happen, preventing our return, we would write to him.

We reached Paddington at seven, and drove direct to the restaurant I have before described, where we partook of a light meal, left Montmorency, together with suggestions for a supper to be ready at half past ten, and then continued our way to Leicester Square.

We attracted a good deal of attention at the Alhambra. On our presenting ourselves at the pay-box we were gruffly directed to go round to Castle Street, and were informed that we were half an hour behind our time.

We convinced the man, with some difficulty, that we were *not* 'the world-renowned contortionists from the Himalaya Mountains', and he took our money and let us pass.

Inside we were a still greater success. Our fine bronzed counten-
ances and picturesque clothes were followed round the place with
admiring gaze. We were the cynosure of every eye.

It was a proud moment for us all.

We adjourned soon after the first ballet, and wended our way
back to the restaurant, where supper was already awaiting us.

I must confess to enjoying that supper. For about ten days we
seemed to have been living, more or less, on nothing but cold meat,
cake, and bread and jam. It had been a simple, a nutritious diet; but
there had been nothing exciting about it, and the odour of Burgundy,
and the smell of French sauces, and the sight of clean napkins and
long loaves, knocked as a very welcome visitor at the door of our
inner man.

We pegged and quaffed away in silence for a while, until the time
came when, instead of sitting bolt upright, and grasping the knife
and fork firmly, we leant back in our chairs and worked slowly and
carelessly – when we stretched out our legs beneath the table, let
our napkins fall, unheeded, to the floor, and found time to more
critically examine the smoky ceiling than we had hitherto been able
to do – when we rested our glasses at arm's length upon the table,
and felt good, and thoughtful, and forgiving.

Then Harris, who was sitting next to the window, drew aside the
curtain and looked out upon the street.

It glistened darkly in the wet, the dim lamps flickered with each
gust, the rain splashed steadily into the puddles and trickled down
the water-spouts into the running gutters. A few soaked wayfarers
hurried past, crouching beneath their dripping umbrellas, the women
holding up their skirts.

'Well,' said Harris, reaching his hand out for his glass, 'we have
had a pleasant trip, and my hearty thanks for it to old Father Thames
– but I think we did well to chuck it when we did. Here's to Three
Men well out of a Boat!'

And Montmorency, standing on his hind legs, before the window,
peering out into the night, gave a short bark of decided concurrence
with the toast.

Notes

I am very grateful to my daughter Jemima for her help in compiling these notes.

THREE MEN IN A BOAT

Chapter 1

1. (p. 6) *Referee*: weekly sporting paper, first published in 1877.

Chapter 2

1. (p. 10) *patriarchal*: the biblical patriarchs included Abraham, Isaac and Jacob.

Chapter 3

1. (p. 22) *shilling shocker*: short, popular novel, often of a sensational nature. Arrowsmith originally wanted to publish *Three Men in a Boat* at a shilling (5p), but Jerome insisted on its being priced at 3s 6d (17½p), then the alternative 'going rate' for new novels.

Chapter 4

1. (p. 25) *half-a-crown's worth*: a crown was worth five shillings (25p), and there were four crowns to the pound; half-a-crown was worth 12½p.
2. (p. 26) *sovereign*: gold coin of the same value as the pound.
3. (p. 27) *guineas*: a guinea was worth £1.05: smart and expensive items tended to be quoted in guineas.
4. (p. 27) *eight and sixpence*: 42½p.
5. (p. 28) *Gladstone*: defined by the Concise Oxford Dictionary as a 'light portmanteau opening into two equal parts', it was favoured by doctors and named after the Liberal statesman and Prime Minister, W. E. Gladstone (1809–98).

Chapter 5

1. (p. 35) *Boots*: man-servant employed in hotels and inns to clean customers' boots and shoes. The best-known fictional boots is Sam Weller in Dickens's *The Pickwick Papers*.
2. (p. 38) *Great Coram Street murder*: refers to scandalous murder in London on Christmas Day 1872.
3. (p. 38) *Stanley*: the Welsh-born adventurer and explorer H. M. Stanley (1841–1904) is best remembered for greeting David Livingstone with the words 'Dr Livingstone, I presume?' after tracking him down on the shores of Lake Tanganyika in 1871.

Chapter 6

1. (p. 41) *crowned there*: several Anglo-Saxon kings were indeed crowned in Kingston-on-Thames: hence its entitlement to be a royal borough.
2. (p. 41) *sack and mead*: sack was a white wine imported from Spain and the Canary islands; mead an alcoholic brew made from honey: both were traditionally imbibed in the world of Merrie England.
3. (p. 43) *Sandford and Merton*: Thomas Day (1748–89) was a serious-minded educationalist and admirer of Rousseau. In his influential novel *The History of Sandford and Merton* – published in three volumes between 1783 and the year of his death – he tried to show how men can be made good by instruction and appeals to reason. Tommy Merton (rich and disagreeable)

is set against Harry Sandford (kind and decent, and a farmer's son): virtue prevails in the end, and Tommy emerges a better and (no doubt) a duller man.

4. (p. 44) *the great cholera scare of 1871*: given the state of the drains, cholera was one of the hazards of mid-Victorian England. The big cholera scare took place in 1854; during its course, John Snow proved that the disease was water-borne, so leading to improvements in drainage and water supplies.

5. (p. 45) *'old blue' . . . willow-pattern*: both are eighteenth-century china-ware, coloured in blue and white: willow-pattern was introduced in 1780, and incorporates Chinese designs.

6. (p. 45) *Sarah Janes*: maidservants.

7. (p. 47) *Hampton Court*: in 1514 the over-mighty Cardinal Wolsey set out to build himself the largest private house in England on the banks of the Thames. Henry VIII forced him to hand it over to him in 1526, and it became the king's favourite palace. During the reign of Charles II, Christopher Wren added a further quadrangle to the Tudor Palace; all is in red brick.

8. (p. 47) *maze*: during the reign of William and Mary, formal Dutch gardens were laid out in the grounds of Hampton Court, including the famous maze.

Chapter 7

1. (p. 50) *Moulsey Lock*: One of the busiest and most popular locks on the Thames. Boulter's Lock was even busier and more fashionable: 'Boulter's Lock – Sunday Afternoon', by Edward John Gregory RA, gives a good idea of what life was like on the river towards the end of the nineteenth century (Lady Lever Art Gallery, Port Sunlight).

2. (p. 51) *Margate nigger*: Nigger Minstrels originated in the Southern States of America in the 1830s, and were a familiar feature of English piers and music halls by the 1880s. Nigger Minstrels were invariably 'blacked-up' white men; like George, they accompanied themselves on the banjo.

3. (p. 56) *Kensal Green Cemetery*: West London cemetery, opened in 1832; those buried there include W. M. Praed, Sydney Smith, Thomas Hood, Thackeray, Trollope, John Leech, Wilkie Collins and George Cruikshank.

Chapter 8

1. (p. 58) *Kempton Park*: a former seat of royalty, later converted into a race-course.

2. (p. 61) *Pinafore*: HMS *Pinafore* (1878) and *Trial by Jury* (1875) were among the best-known and most popular of the Savoy Operas, the words of which were written by W. S. Gilbert (1836–1911) and the music by Arthur Sullivan (1842–1900). They began their collaboration in 1871, and their joint efforts included *The Pirates of Penzance*, *The Yeomen of the Guard*, *The Mikado* and *Iolanthe*. Gilbert was one of Jerome's clubbish cronies.

3. (p. 63) *morceaux*: bits or scraps.

4. (p. 67) *Bradshaw*: President of the court which condemned Charles I to death in 1649.

5. (p. 67) *the guide man*: the best-known of all railway timetables, *Bradshaw's Railway Guide* was first published in 1839 by George Bradshaw: it appeared every month until 1961.

6. (p. 67) *scold's bridle*: a 'scold' was a nagging wife, the bridle a metal contraption which fitted over the head and prevented her from opening her mouth.

7. (p. 67) *Cassivelaunus*: hot-tempered leader of the Catuvellauni, a tribe of Ancient Britons based on the north bank of the Thames; he led the opposition to Julius Caesar's invasion of Britain in 54 BC.

Chapter 9

1. (p. 75) *Penton Hook*: so named because the Thames nearly doubles back on itself.

2. (p. 75) *Runnymede*: island on the Thames on which, in June 1215, King John is said to have signed the Magna Carta. Victorian historians liked to represent King John as the wickedest and most despotic of English monarchs, and the Magna Carta was the result of his demands for excessive feudal dues and his attacks on Church privileges. Among its clauses were checks against infringements of feudal custom, extortions by officials and the maladministration of justice, and no freeman could be arrested, imprisoned or punished except by the judgement of his peers or by the law of the land. The Magna Carta was rediscovered and reinterpreted by the parliamentary party during the seventeenth century, and came to be regarded as a seminal document in the establishment of personal and political freedoms in the English-speaking world.

3. (p. 78) *Faust*: the opera by Charles Gounod (1818–93) was first performed in London in 1863.

Chapter 11

1. (p. 94) *Barons'*: King John's opponents were collectively referred to as the 'Barons'.

2. (p. 95) *halbert-men*: halberts were combined spears and battleaxes.

3. (p. 95) *casque*: helmet.

Chapter 12

1. (p. 97) *Anne Boleyn*: she became the second wife of Henry VIII after a spell as his mistress. The mother of the future Queen Elizabeth, she was beheaded in 1536, charged with incest and adultery.

2. (p. 98) *Irish question*: Irish independence – or, rather, the degree of self-rule Ireland should be permitted within the framework of the United Kingdom – was a source of incessant debate and agitation. As Prime Minister, Gladstone not only disestablished the Church of Ireland, but sought to introduce Home Rule: his Home Rule Bills of 1886 and 1893 were both defeated.

3. (p. 99) *Edward the Confessor*: other-worldly English king who came to the throne in 1042, but preferred to leave matters in the hands of Earl Godwin and concentrate on religious matters instead. His son, Harold, was slain at the Battle of Hastings in 1066.

4. (p. 106) *London Journal*: a source of fashionable tittle-tattle.

5. (p. 106) *three-volume novel*: see Introduction, p. xiv.

Chapter 13

1. (p. 108) *Marlow*: elegant little riverside town, best known for its graceful suspension bridge – the work of William Tierney Clark, whose other suspension bridges included Hammersmith Bridge and that linking Buda and Pest. Mary Shelley wrote *Frankenstein* in Marlow; on the other side of the river

from the town is The Compleat Angler, one of the best-known riverside pubs.

2. (p. 109) *Knights Templars*: a religious order, founded in 1119, devoted to the recovery of Palestine from the Saracens, active in the Crusades, and suppressed on grounds of heresy in 1307.

3. (p. 109) *Anne of Cleves*: the fourth wife of Henry VIII: she was German and very plain, and the marriage was dissolved.

4. (p. 109) *Warwick, the king-maker*: Machiavellian earl, who fought on both sides during the Wars of the Roses.

5. (p. 109) *Poitiers*: battle during the Hundred Years War between England and France, at which the Black Prince defeated King John of France (1356).

6. (p. 109) *The Revolt of Islam*: epic poem by Percy Bysshe Shelley (1792–1822).

7. (p. 109) *King Sebert*: first Christian king of the East Saxons: died *c.* 616.

8. (p. 109) *King Offa*: Anglo-Saxon King of Mercia: established Mercian supremacy over all of England south of the Humber, and died in 796.

9. (p. 109) *Hell Fire Club*: During the eighteenth century, the rakish baronet Sir Francis Dashwood held orgies at his house in West Wycombe. The orgiasts called themselves the Hell Fire Club, and sometimes dressed up as the 'Franciscans of Medmenham'.

10. (p. 109) *Wilkes*: John Wilkes (1727–97) was the best kind of English radical. Outlawed for his attacks on Lord Bute in his paper *The North Briton* and subsequently imprisoned, he was four times elected MP for Middlesex, but each time the House of Commons refused to admit him. Cross-eyed and hideously ugly, he boasted that he could 'talk away his face in half an hour'.

11. (p. 111) *Lowther Arcade*: shopping arcade off the Strand, built in 1830 and covered by a series of glass domes. It specialized in children's toys, and was demolished in 1904.

12. (p. 115) *Henley week*: a high point in the oarsman's calendar, and the social Season, the Henley Regatta has taken place every July since 1839. It acquired royal status in 1851.

13. (p. 116) *bean-feast*: annual dinner given by employers for their workers.

14. (p. 116) *Cubit's*: William and Thomas Cubitt prospered as builders and property developers in London in the 1840s and 1850s: their white stucco style is well represented in Belgravia and Pimlico.

15. (p. 116) *Bermondsey Good Templars*: a working-men's charitable club.

16. (p. 120) *Who shall escape calumny?*: the poet in question was Shakespeare (*Hamlet*, III. i. 143).

Chapter 14

1. (p. 121) *Lord Fitznoodle*: useful shorthand for the goofier kind of peer.
W. M. Thackeray (1811–63) used the pseudonym George Savage Fitz-
Boodle when publishing the early chapters of *Barry Lyndon* in *Frasers
Magazine*, 1842–3.

2. (p. 122) *half a peck*: a measurement used for dry goods; an imperial peck
was equivalent to two gallons.

3. (p. 124) *banjo*: first associated with slaves in the Southern States of
America, the banjo had crossed the Atlantic, and was much favoured by
Nigger Minstrels and by fashionable young men eager to impress.

4. (p. 128) *Babes in the Wood*: old ballad about a wicked uncle who hires
two villains to murder his nephew and niece. A robin covers their bodies
with leaves; one of the villains repents and kills the other, and the wicked
uncle dies miserably.

5. (p. 129) *Seven Sleepers*: legend of seven noble Christian youths from
Ephesus who, in order to escape persecution during the third century AD,
walled themselves up in a cave and slept for 187 years.

Chapter 15

1. (p. 134) *brickfields*: large ponds were created where clay had been extracted
for the making of bricks.

2. (p. 135) *River Lea*: joins the Thames at Poplar in the East End, where
Jerome spent so much of his youth.

3. (p. 141) *rounders and touch*: children's games.

4. (p. 141) *reef and luff*: sailing terms. Taking in a reef reduces the amount
of sail exposed to the wind; to 'luff' is to bring the boat's head closer in to
the wind.

Chapter 16

1. (p. 144) *King Ethelred*: the King of the West Saxons, he suffered a series
of defeats at the hands of the marauding Danes. He was succeeded as king
in 871 by his younger brother Alfred, who had earlier defeated the Danes
at Ashdown. Known as 'the Great', Alfred went on to become one of the
most celebrated of English kings.

2. (p. 144) *Earl of Essex*: a leader of the parliamentary forces during the English Civil War (1642–8).

3. (p. 144) *Prince of Orange*: William of Orange invaded England in 1688 and, with his wife Mary, was crowned (as William III) in 1689. He finally defeated the previous monarch, James II, at the Battle of the Boyne in 1690.

4. (p. 144) *John of Gaunt*: (1340–99): fourth son of Edward III.

Chapter 17

1. (p. 151) *pipeclaying*: white shoes, canvas belts, etc. were smartened up by applying a mixture of white clay and water.

Chapter 18

1. (p. 155) *Conservancy*: The Thames Conservancy Board was established in 1857, and its powers were extended to cover the river from Staines to Cricklade in 1866.

2. (p. 157 f.n.) *Fairfax*: Thomas Fairfax (1611–72) commanded the parliamentary army during the Civil War: he founded the New Model Army, and defeated Charles I at Naseby (1645).

3. (p. 159) *Sandford lasher*: a 'lasher' comprises both the water rushing over a weir, and the pool below into which it falls. Sandford Lock has one of the deepest falls on the Thames.

Chapter 19

1. (p. 165) *penny nap*: a card game.

2. (p. 165) *Volunteers*: the Victorian equivalent to the Territorial Army, established in 1859.

3. (p. 167) *Alhambra*: the most famous of all Victorian music halls, sited on the north-east corner of Leicester Square. Moorish in style, it started life as an exhibition centre, but was converted into a music hall in 1860. Among those who appeared there were Blondin, the tightrope-walker, and Leotard, 'the daring young man on the flying trapeze'.

PENGUIN ⬤ CLASSICS

The Classics Publisher

'Penguin Classics, one of the world's greatest series' JOHN KEEGAN

'I have never been disappointed with the Penguin Classics. All I have read is a model of academic seriousness and provides the essential information to fully enjoy the master works that appear in its catalogue' MARIO VARGAS LLOSA

'Penguin and Classics are words that go together like horse and carriage or Mercedes and Benz. When I was a university teacher I always prescribed Penguin editions of classic novels for my courses: they have the best introductions, the most reliable notes, and the most carefully edited texts' DAVID LODGE

'Growing up in Bombay, expensive hardback books were beyond my means, but I could indulge my passion for reading at the roadside bookstalls that were well stocked with all the Penguin paperbacks ... Sometimes I would choose a book just because I was attracted by the cover, but so reliable was the Penguin imprimatur that I was never once disappointed by the contents.

   Such access certainly broadened the scope of my reading, and perhaps it's no coincidence that so many Merchant Ivory films have been adapted from great novels, or that those novels are published by Penguin' ISMAIL MERCHANT

'You can't write, read, or live fully in the present without knowing the literature of the past. Penguin Classics opens the door to a treasure house of pure pleasure, books that have never been bettered, which are read again and again with increased delight' JOHN MORTIMER

CLICK ON A CLASSIC
www.penguinclassics.com
The world's greatest literature at your fingertips

Constantly updated information on over 1600 titles, from Icelandic sagas to ancient Indian epics, Russian drama to Italian romance, American greats to African masterpieces

•

The latest news on recent additions to the list, updated editions and specially commissioned translations

•

Original scholarly essays by leading writers: Elaine Showalter on Zola, Laurie R. King on Arthur Conan Doyle, Frank Kermode on Shakespeare, Lisa Appignanesi on Tolstoy

•

A wealth of background material, including biographies of every classic author from Aristotle to Zamyatin, plot synopses, readers' and teachers' guides, useful web links

•

Online desk and examination copy assistance for academics

•

Trivia quizzes, competitions, giveaways, news on forthcoming screen adaptations

•

eBooks available to download

READ MORE IN PENGUIN

In every corner of the world, on every subject under the sun, Penguin represents quality and variety – the very best in publishing today.

For complete information about books available from Penguin – including Puffins and Penguin Classics – and how to order them, write to us at the appropriate address below. Please note that for copyright reasons the selection of books varies from country to country.

In the United Kingdom: *Please write to* Dept EP, Penguin Books Ltd, Bath Road, Harmondsworth, West Drayton, Middlesex UB7 0DA

In the United States: *Please write to* Consumer Services, Penguin Putnam Inc., 405 Murray Hill Parkway, East Rutherford, New Jersey 07073-2136. *VISA and MasterCard holders call 1-800-631-8571 to order Penguin titles*

In Canada: *Please write to* Penguin Books Canada Ltd, 10 Alcorn Avenue, Suite 300, Toronto, Ontario M4V 3B2

In Australia: *Please write to* Penguin Books Australia Ltd, 487 Maroondah Highway, Ringwood, Victoria 3134

In New Zealand: *Please write to* Penguin Books (NZ) Ltd, Private Bag 102902, North Shore Mail Centre, Auckland 10

In India: *Please write to* Penguin Books India Pvt Ltd, 11, Community Centre, Panchsheel Park, New Delhi 110017

In the Netherlands: *Please write to* Penguin Books Netherlands bv, Postbus 3507, NL-1001 AH Amsterdam

In Germany: *Please write to* Penguin Books Deutschland GmbH, Metzlerstrasse 26, 60594 Frankfurt am Main

In Spain: *Please write to* Penguin Books S. A., Bravo Murillo 19, 1°B, 28015 Madrid

In Italy: *Please write to* Penguin Italia s.r.l., Via Vittoria Emanuele 451a, 20094 Corsico, Milano

In France: *Please write to* Penguin France, 12, Rue Prosper Ferradou, 31700 Blagnac

In Japan: *Please write to* Penguin Books Japan Ltd, Iidabashi KM-Bldg, 2-23-9 Koraku, Bunkyo-Ku, Tokyo 112-0004

In South Africa: *Please write to* Penguin Books South Africa (Pty) Ltd, P.O. Box 751093, Gardenview, 2047 Johannesburg

E. W. HORNUNG

Raffles: the Amateur Cracksman

'Old Raffles may or may not have been an exceptional criminal, but as a cricketer I dare swear he was unique'

Gentleman thief Raffles is daring, debonair, devilishly hand-some – and a first-class cricketer. In these eight stories the master burglar indulges his passion for cricket and crime: thieving jewels from a country house, outwitting the law, steal-ing from the nouveau riche and, of course, bowling like a demon – all with the assistance of his plucky sidekick Bunny. Encouraged by a suggestion from his brother-in-law Arthur Conan Doyle to write a series about a public-school villain, and influenced by his own days at Uppingham, Ernest Hornung created a unique form of crime story, where, in stealing as in sport, it is playing the game that counts, and there is always honour among thieves.

This edition of Raffles stories is new to Penguin Classics. It contains a fascinating introduction discussing contemporary events that inspired the plots, placing the stories in their literary context and exploring the connection with Sherlock Holmes.

'One of the most remarkable triumphs of the late nineteenth-century Romantic imagination' C. P. SNOW

Edited with an introduction and notes by
RICHARD LANCELYN GREEN

OSCAR WILDE

Complete Short Fiction

*'He saw a most wonderful sight. Through a
little hole in the wall the children had crept in . . .
And the trees were so glad to have the children
back again that they had covered themselves
with blossoms'*

Fairy tales, ghost stories, detective fiction and comedies of manners – the stories collected in this volume made Oscar Wilde's name as a writer of fiction, showing breathtaking dexterity in a wide range of literary styles. Victorian moral justice is comically inverted in 'Lord Arthur Savile's Crime' and 'The Canterville Ghost', and society's materialism comes under sharp, humorous criticism in 'The Model Millionaire', while 'The Happy Prince' and 'The Nightingale and the Rose' are hauntingly melancholic in their magical evocations of selfless love. These small masterpieces convey the brilliance of Wilde's vision, exploring complex moral issues through an elegant juxtaposition of wit and sentiment.

This edition includes the complete texts of Wilde's three volumes of short fiction, together with 'The Portrait of Mr W. H.' Ian Small's introduction discusses Wilde's life, the cultural and literary background to his fiction and the complex ways in which it can be read.

Edited with an introduction by IAN SMALL

WILKIE COLLINS
The Moonstone

'When you looked down into the stone, you looked into a yellow deep that drew your eyes into it so that they saw nothing else'

The Moonstone, a yellow diamond looted from an Indian temple and believed to bring bad luck to its owner, is bequeathed to Rachel Verinder on her eighteenth birthday. That very night the priceless stone is stolen again and when Sergeant Cuff is brought in to investigate the crime, he soon realizes that no one in Rachel's household is above suspicion. Hailed by T. S. Eliot as 'the first, the longest, and the best of modern English detective novels', *The Moonstone* is a marvellously taut and intricate tale of mystery, in which facts and memory can prove treacherous and not everyone is as they first appear.

Sandra Kemp's introduction examines *The Moonstone* as a work of Victorian sensation fiction and an early example of the detective genre, and discusses the technique of multiple narrators, the role of opium, and Collins's sources and autobiographical references.

'Enthralling and believable ... evokes in vivid language the spirit of a place' P. D. JAMES, *Sunday Times*

Edited with an introduction and notes by SANDRA KEMP

CHARLES DICKENS
A Tale of Two Cities

*'Liberty, equality, fraternity, or death; – the last,
much the easiest to bestow, O Guillotine!'*

After eighteen years as a political prisoner in the Bastille, the
ageing Doctor Manette is finally released and reunited with
his daughter in England. There the lives of two very different
men, Charles Darnay, an exiled French aristocrat, and Sydney
Carton, a disreputable but brilliant English lawyer, become
enmeshed through their love for Lucie Manette. From the tran-
quil roads of London, they are drawn against their will to the
vengeful, bloodstained streets of Paris at the height of the Reign
of Terror, and they soon fall under the lethal shadow of La
Guillotine.

This edition uses the text as it appeared in its first serial publication in 1859 to convey the full scope of Dickens's vision, and
includes the original illustrations by H. K. Browne ('Phiz').
Richard Maxwell's introduction discusses the intricate inter-
weaving of epic drama with personal tragedy.

Edited with an introduction and notes by
RICHARD MAXWELL

JONATHAN SWIFT
Gulliver's Travels

'I felt something alive moving on my left Leg …
when bending my Eyes downwards as much as I
could, I perceived it to be a human Creature not
six Inches high'

Shipwrecked and cast adrift, Lemuel Gulliver wakes to find himself on Lilliput, an island inhabited by little people, whose height makes their quarrels over fashion and fame seem ridiculous. His subsequent encounters – with the crude giants of Brobdingnag, the philosophical Houyhnhnms and the brutish Yahoos – give Gulliver new, bitter insights into human behaviour. Swift's savage satire views mankind in a distorted hall of mirrors as a diminished, magnified and finally bestial species, presenting us with an uncompromising reflection of ourselves.

This text, based on the first edition of 1726, reproduces all its original illustrations and includes an introduction by Robert Demaria, Jr, which discusses the ways *Gulliver's Travels* has been interpreted since its first publication.

'A masterwork of irony … that contains both a dark and bitter meaning and a joyous, extraordinary creativity of imagination. That is why it has lived for so long' MALCOLM BRADBURY

Edited with an introduction and notes by
ROBERT DEMARIA, JR

DANIEL DEFOE
Robinson Crusoe

*'A raging wave, mountain-like, came rowling
a-stern of us ... we were all swallowed up
in a moment'*

The sole survivor of a shipwreck, Robinson Crusoe is washed up on a desert island. In his journal he chronicles his daily battle to stay alive, as he conquers isolation, fashions shelter and clothes, first encounters another human being and fights off cannibals and mutineers. With *Robinson Crusoe*, Defoe wrote what is regarded as the first English novel, and created one of the most popular and enduring myths in literature. Written in an age of exploration and enterprise, it has been variously interpreted as an embodiment of British imperialist values, as a portrayal of 'natural man' or as a moral fable. But above all it is a brilliant narrative, depicting Crusoe's transformation from terrified survivor to self-sufficient master of his island.

This edition contains a full chronology of Defoe's life and times, explanatory notes, glossary and a critical introduction discussing Robinson Crusoe as a pioneering work of modern psychological realism.

'*Robinson Crusoe* has a universal appeal, a story that goes right to the core of existence' SIMON ARMITAGE

Edited with an introduction and notes by JOHN RICHETTI